MW00885030

The Siren's Daughters

By Rebecca Caden

Prologue

The old captain made his way down the rocky hill to the beach on shaking legs. He was tired and the bitter wind whipped his cheeks, but he had to keep going; soon, he would be unable to make the trip.

He slowly crossed the beach and stepped, barefoot, into the receding tide. He gasped at the shock of the icy water but forced himself to wade forward until the water reached his thin shoulders; then he lowered his head beneath the waves.

Through the green haze of sea water, he saw her swimming to meet him. He reached out for her, and she embraced him, wrapping her long tail around his legs. He lost his balance and struggled instinctively to find the sea floor, but she held him firmly and pulled him out to deeper water.

Once they were far enough from the shore, she placed her lips on his and sent a rush of energy into his body. A brief, intense discomfort crowded his chest, then a ripple of numbness flowed over him, and a strange, fluttery sensation ran along his sides. He tried to inhale, and his nose and mouth filled with water, but he didn't choke. Her eyes shimmered as she released him, and he knew she would be smiling broadly if she were human. She had waited so long for him.

***

As a child, he'd had acres of green grass to race across and call his own, but when he turned seventeen, the endless blue of the sea drew him from home, and he left the luxury of his family's estate to become a sailor.

He grew accustomed to the harsh, demanding life of a seaman. He worked his way up through the ranks and became the captain of a merchant ship, where he led his crew for ten years,

1

until his father's health began to decline and his parents pressed him to return to manage the family estate.

He relinquished his post and returned to life on land, where he applied the skills he'd gained at sea to the challenges of running his family's large estate. To appease his mother, he went out in society, and soon met a pretty young woman who was part of his family's social circle. Within a year, he married her, cementing his commitment to a more conventional life.

He'd been married for two years when he received an urgent message from the fleet owner of his former ship. The captain who had replaced him had died suddenly, and the fleet owner needed someone to lead the ship on a brief tour to the north before the goods on board began to spoil. The route, though short, was tricky, plagued by hidden rocks and squalls, but he knew it well. To his wife's dismay, the captain agreed to take on the task. He promised his wife and family it would be his last trip.

The captain and his crew delivered the cargo as planned, but on the voyage home, a sudden, fierce storm surprised them. They rushed to secure the sails and supplies. The ship listed violently as the captain was running down the narrow stairs from the quarter deck, and he tumbled overboard. He fought to keep his head above the water, but he was at the mercy of the heaving waves breaking roughly over him, submerging him, then hurling him upward again. Disoriented and exhausted, he slipped underwater.

There, *she* caught him in her arms. He felt the pressure of her hands holding onto his body, the smoothness of her face as it pressed against his, and he was confused, but strangely unafraid. Her brilliant, jade-green eyes mesmerized him with a calming tenderness, even as pressure built in his lungs.

She placed her lips against his, and a warm euphoria coursed through him. As she began to pull him deeper into the ocean to perform the ritual that would transform him into one of her kind, thick arms broke through the surface and hauled him upward. Startled, she released him. As they pulled him away from her, he could sense her despair.

2

Icy air rushed into his lungs, penetrating the lull of comfort he'd felt in her arms. He struggled against his rescuers, who were dragging him into the lifeboat, but they overpowered him. He tried to sit up, to move to the side and look for her, but his body shuddered, and he coughed violently. His rescuers managed to get him on board the ship, where he tried to stand. The world seemed to tilt sideways before his eyes, and he collapsed.

When he woke the next day, they were well past the squall, and miles from where he'd fallen from the ship.

In the months that followed, he rode from his estate to the seashore every day and stayed for hours, watching the water, leaving his family to discuss if they should intervene in some way, to help him remember his duty to the estate. When they finally, gently, confronted him, he admitted he was desperate to return to the sea. He broke his promise to his wife and family and returned to his post as ship captain.

On every voyage, he watched the sea, hoping to spot her, but he couldn't find her. He couldn't feel her. As the years passed, he'd almost been able to convince himself he had imagined her, but in the quiet sadness of his heart, he knew she was real.

When he retired from his post, he bought farmland by the sea in the remote north, built a house and moved there with his family. His only son had married a girl from the port-side village they'd lived in after the captain's family had disowned him for abandoning his duty to their estate, and they'd had a son. The captain had little patience for his grandson, a sly, arrogant child, but they all lived in the small seaside house together and learned to farm the land.

The captain went to the beach nearly every day, but never set foot in the water. He felt at peace when he was down on the sand, imagining the sea woman was near, but he wouldn't leave his wife, who had remained a steadfast partner even as he'd up-rooted their lives.

When his wife died, many years after they'd moved to the remote little house, he went down to the beach and considered sacrificing himself to the waves, hoping the sea woman would come for him. He paused at the water's edge, but his daughter-in-law had taken ill with the sickness that had claimed his wife, and he knew his family still needed him.

***

Finally, they were together. She swam ahead, leading him through the cool water. He followed, amazed at his ability to propel himself forward with his long, muscular tail fin. His body no longer ached. He felt young, strong and whole again.

***

He adapted quickly to her way of life. He was fascinated by the culture of her kind. The other males in the shoal swam together and spent long periods away from the women and children. Only he and his beloved seemed to pair off. She told him if he sired a child, he would feel compelled to join the males as they roamed the sea in packs. He assured her he would never want to leave her side. When he was with her, he felt the warm, intoxicating joy he'd felt when he'd met her years ago, and he was grateful to her for the new life she'd given him.

Once, he was able to share something wonderful with her, as well. When the shallow water took on a chill, and he could see snowflakes dissolving on the surface of the ocean, he led her to the waters of the wharf beside a city. They swam between the docked boats and waited in the water under the pier. As night fell, they ventured to the side of the wharf, where they could see the glowing yellow lights of candles above the water. He watched her eyes widen. Then, as he'd hoped they would, the carolers began to sing.

The vibrations of the carolers' voices filtered through the water, and he heard and felt the music in a way he had never experienced on land. The songs sounded even more beautiful than he'd expected. She stared at him in joy and wonder, and he was glad he had finally been able to repay at least a small part of the gift she'd given him.

She gave birth to their daughter a year later. He adored his beautiful child, but, because he'd become one of them, he could not resist thousands of years of instinct. The following season,

4

he left the sea woman and his daughter to swim south to the tropics with the other males. Away from her energy, he began to weaken. In the balmy waters of the southern seas, where giant turtles glided overhead, he felt his true, human age catch up to him. He separated from the pack and drifted to the sea floor, passing peacefully and finally away from the magical realm he had come to love.

Part 1

Chapter 1

Aila Barton rested her embroidery on her lap and scrutinized her half-finished sampler. She'd stopped working on it when her mother had fallen ill two years earlier and had forgotten a surprising amount of technique since then. She was improving, but it was slow going.

Before the illness, she and her mother had worked happily together almost every day, sewing side by side on the pale blue sofa near the fire in the winter afternoons or in the upholstered chairs near the front window when the weather was warmer. They'd chatted through the hours, pausing occasionally so Mrs. Barton could check and praise Aila's progress.

Back then, friends had often visited for lively sewing circles. Quiet and reserved with most people, Mrs. Barton had been enchantingly warm toward those closest to her, and her friends had basked in her exclusive radiance. Aila had always been quietly delighted whenever they'd mention how much she resembled her mother. She loved to imagine that she might someday be as beautiful and captivating a hostess.

The summer after Aila turned fifteen, Mrs. Barton began sleeping most of the day. At first, she'd assured Aila that it was just a reaction to the unusually high temperature that year, but even after the heatwave left their village and the air outside cooled to almost chilly, she remained feverish and too exhausted to leave her bed. Friends stopped calling, but Aila still tried to coax her into the sitting room to sew and chat until her father insisted that she let her rest. From then on, Aila spent her days sitting at her mother's bedside, reading to her.

Aila's father was the local physician, respected by the villagers for his skill and quiet composure. He treated his wife with a steadfast conviction that she would recover, even as she seemed to fade further into her illness, which heartened Aila and the household staff for a while. But, late one night, his anguished scream woke Aila, and she ran into her mother's room to find him sitting on the bed, cradling her mother's motionless body.

In the days after his wife's death, Dr. Barton refused to get out of bed. He was tearfully incoherent when Aila or the house-maids tried to talk to him. Aila put her own heartache aside and tried to help him cope with their loss. She took on her mother's role of managing the household and the modest staff of the two housemaids and a cook, and when he was still bedridden nearly two weeks later, she wrote to a friend and medical colleague of her father's, pleading for help and advice. Dr. Biggs rode to the village, tended to Dr. Barton's patients and treated Dr. Barton, who, mercifully, recovered under his care.

When her father fully recuperated, he returned to his prac-tice, but he tried to be home in time to have dinner with Aila as often as possible. Her governess, who had been released from service temporarily while Mrs. Barton was ill, returned to teach Aila. Routines resumed, and things began to feel more normal to everyone in the household.

Aila picked up her needle again, determined to finish the em-broidery. She worked through the afternoon and, even as she struggled with the stitches, she imagined her mother watching over her, smiling affectionately at her efforts, and she enjoyed the warm sensation of peace.

Late that afternoon, when she saw her father's wagon driving up the short road leading to their house, she started to gather her supplies and put her needlework away, intending to greet him outside, but, instead of pausing to chat with the stable boy, he surprised her by rushing through the front door. She shoved her work aside and hurried to meet him in the foyer. Rather than asking about her day as he normally did, he said a brief hello, distractedly kissed her cheek and moved quickly past her down the hall to his study. After the door to his study closed behind him, she stood in the foyer for a moment, the silence around her heavy like a held breath.

***

That evening, Dr. Barton arrived in the dining room promptly for dinner. He smiled and complimented Aila's dress as the housemaid served their meal. They ate in companionable silence, and, once he'd consumed a generous glass of wine and poured himself a second, he cleared his throat. Aila looked up. His expression was sober, and he seemed curiously ill at ease. Recalling his hasty, preoccupied greeting earlier, her heart felt heavy with worry, but she waited for him to speak.

"Do you recall when I treated Mr. Waters for several months?"

She nodded, thinking of the poor blacksmith whose lungs had been decimated by smoke.

"He passed away two weeks ago."

"Oh," she murmured, not sure how to respond. Her father didn't normally discuss his patients with her and very rarely spoke of those who died.

He rotated the stem of his wine glass and watched the swirling liquid.

"Mr. Waters left behind a widow. No children. In recent months, Mrs. Waters and I have developed a... friendship."

Uneasiness stirred in Aila's chest.

"We worked together to try to help him, first to recover and then, when that was clearly no longer possible, to ensure his comfort. She is a very kind woman."

His eyes met hers.

"The thing of it is, my dear, with your mother gone, a home needs a mistress to run it properly. And a young woman needs a mother, a feminine influence. I think Mrs. Waters would make a fine mother for you. As I've said, she is kind and practical. I've asked her to marry me...and she's agreed."

Aila tried to stay calm. Hadn't she shown him she was a responsible young woman, one who certainly did not require a substitute mother? She had stepped in and taken charge of the house when he fell apart. She was the one who'd found help for him and his patients.

9

"I don't, you know. Need a new mother." She kept her voice steady. "I'm sixteen years old now. I am perfectly capable of running the house. I'm doing well in my studies, and I'm quite content and healthy."

"I see all of that." He gave her a gentle smile. "But you'll be old enough to marry soon, and you'll need guidance on how to be a wife and mother."

She never thought about marriage, not in the way of concrete plans. It had always seemed like something she would do eventually, but not something with an age attached to it or guidance required. Her comfortable circumstances had provided her the luxury of not concerning herself with when, or if, she would find a suitable husband. Her mother had never emphasized a need to worry about marriage but, it seemed her father expected her to marry soon, to leave his house to care for a husband. And then he would be alone. She looked at his face, noticed the light spider web of lines in the hollow beneath his eyes, the streaks of gray in his beard and at his temples. His hopeful expression and her love for him weighed on her.

"Yes, I suppose you're right—and I'm happy for you," she said, and he rewarded her with a grateful smile.

"There's my good girl."

"I'm actually feeling a bit tired, Papa. May I go up to my room?" She wasn't sure how long she could maintain her composure. She wanted to ask questions – When would they be married? Would she meet Mrs. Waters before the wedding? – but she wasn't ready to hear the answers. She wanted to get away from him and this shocking news he was so happy about.

"Of course, go on up and rest." He gestured toward the hall, and Aila sensed his relief.

She climbed the staircase to her bedroom, lay down on her bed, and released the confusion and fear she felt, sobbing as quietly as she could into her pillow.

***

Dr. Barton married Hannah Waters a month later. It was a small, quiet event, almost furtive in its lack of festivity. Though their neighbors understood why a widow and a widower would remarry so soon after the deaths of their spouses, it did not sit well with many. Aila's mother had been a dear friend of the prominent ladies of the village. Dr. Barton's arguably swift replacement of his wife following her death inspired in her friends a shared disapproval. Aware of this, the couple was discreet in their wedding arrangements and sober in demeanor whenever they went out together in public, but Aila could tell it chafed her new step-mother to have to go about in such solemnity.

Hannah Waters Barton was only twenty-six years old, with flaxen hair, a buxom figure and a lightly freckled face, and, Aila realized she'd been right to assume her father had been more concerned about his own future than hers when he chose to remarry.

"Well, we could be sisters!" Hannah had proclaimed when Dr. Barton introduced them to one another a week before the wedding, though the only similarities between them were the youthful styles they wore and their distance from middle age. "I wish we were closer in size, though, I'd so love to borrow that dress!"

Aila had watched her father wince slightly at Hannah's remark and wondered if it was the volume of Hannah's voice or the attention she'd drawn to their closeness in age that bothered him.

To Aila's relief, Hannah was more interested in developing a sisterly relationship with her than trying to take on a motherly role. Aila didn't take offense at her frequent silly behavior or comments, and she was careful to be polite to her stepmother, but she could not bring herself to feel deeply fond of the young woman. Becoming a doctor's wife was an advancement in station for Hannah, and she did a poor job of hiding her excitement and self-satisfaction, which rankled everyone in the small household except Dr. Barton, who was charmed and flattered by his wife's obvious pride in him.

Aila had never seen her father so light-hearted. He was a new person in the presence of his young wife, and Aila realized he, too, had been in awe of her mother, never quite able to believe his own luck in having married such an enchanting creature. In his new marriage, he was clearly enjoying the new and lofty sensation of being the more desirable partner.

When, at Hannah's invitation, she occasionally accompanied them on walks or to excursions to other towns, where they could revel more openly in their newlywed status, Aila tended to fall behind them, and her father, caught up in the delusion that he and Hannah were a young, vibrant couple, never seemed to notice. He had never doted on her, and she was used to him barely acknowledging her among the priorities of his practice, but now, with much of his remaining focus on his young wife, Aila felt herself drifting farther out of his notice.

She found solace in studying with her governess and in visits and walks with her childhood friends. She and her friends didn't share troubles or weighty matters of the heart with one another, but time spent with them was a diversion from the strange new atmosphere pervading her home.

***

In early spring, the year after Aila's father remarried, a man named Robert Reed rode into their village with a small team of young, strong horses leading his wagon and an open smile on his face for everyone he met. He had dark, wavy hair and friendly blue eyes, and his well-made, fashionable clothes impressed the shopkeepers, who took him for an important young gentleman when they met him walking in the village.

He stayed at an inn in the center of the high street and explained to the innkeeper and his wife that he'd come down from the north to expand his wool trade. His admiration of their establishment and his confident, smiling demeanor charmed the couple, and they decided to introduce him to townspeople who could help him further his interests.

Mr. Reed spent his first days in the village walking its well-kept streets with the innkeeper. He patronized the shops, gained introductions and engaged those he met in pleasant conversation.

Handsome and affable, he quickly befriended many of the townspeople. Over tea or dinner in their homes, he shared that his grandfather had been a well-born sea captain, who retired from the sea and left city society to settle his family on an estate in the north. He told them stories of growing up on the estate overlooking the ocean. His mother had died when he was a child, and he had lived with his father and grandfather until they each died, a few years apart. Now, he disclosed to his new friends, he was looking to grow his business, find a suitable wife, one his family would welcome.

Eager to help the gregarious young man make a good match, Mrs. Davies, the wife of a local politician, told him about Aila. Mrs. Davies always made it her business to know everyone in the village and to remain apprised of all news. When she and her husband met the young newcomer at a dinner party, she quickly acquainted herself with his plans and decided she could help him. She told him as much as she felt was proper about the girls of marriageable age in the village. She confided to him that, in her opinion, Aila was the jewel of them all. She was beautiful, if a bit exotic, with her shining dark hair and dark eyes, and she was also exceedingly well-mannered and even tempered She was the daughter of the local doctor, a well-respected man, who lived in one of the finer houses in the county, aside from those of the local gentry.

**

Mr. Reed had his chance to appraise Aila at a dance held in the village. His new friends had invited him, and she attended with her father and stepmother. He was standing with Mrs. Davies and her friend, Mrs. Burland, when Mrs. Burland mentioned that the doctor was sitting at a table across the room.

"Is she his daughter?" Mr. Reed asked, nodding towards the fair-haired young woman who sat beside the doctor.

Mrs. Burland snorted with laughter.

"Don't say that to *him*, Mr. Reed!" Mrs. Davies teased. "That lady is the doctor's new wife! His daughter is over there, near the window—the young lady in blue."

She gestured to where Aila stood, surrounded by a group of her friends.

When Mr. Davies arrived to join his wife, Mr. Reed asked if he would kindly introduce him to the doctor, and Mrs. Davies and Mrs. Burland watched, with knowing smiles, as the two men crossed the room toward Dr. and Mrs. Barton.

Aila's friend was telling a story about a ribbon that had fallen out of her hair in the street and attached itself to the feet of multiple people as she'd tried to chase and recover it.

"...And I don't know where to find another with such a lovely pattern," she was saying with a rueful laugh. Aila saw the amusement on her friend's face give way to curiosity as she stopped laughing and stared over Aila's shoulder. Aila turned and saw an unfamiliar young man standing there with a smile on his face. He bowed to the girls.

"Excuse me. I'm sorry to interrupt. My name is Robert Reed. Miss Barton, if I may, will you join me in the next dance?"

"Oh! I'm not sure—my father—" Aila worried her father would be angry if she danced with a stranger. How had he known her name?

"Of course. I should have said! Mr. Davies introduced me to your father, and I've asked for his permission to dance with you. He consented and sent me over, but if you'd rather not, I'll leave you be."

He gave her a questioning smile as he offered his arm, and Aila noticed how handsome he was, how much more grown up he looked than the boys she knew.

She smiled politely and took his arm. He led her to the floor and, as they faced each other and began to dance, Aila glanced over Mr. Reed's shoulder at her father, who gave her a quick smile and a nod before turning away to talk with his wife.

"Do you enjoy dancing, Miss Barton?" Mr. Reed asked once their steps had fallen into a steady rhythm.

"Yes, very much."

"It's evident. You're very graceful." He smiled as he spoke, and the compliment felt strangely intimate. She worried the other dancers might have heard, and she was relieved when the dance steps required them to move apart for a moment.

"What brings you to our village, Mr. Reed?" she asked politely when they joined hands again.

"I own an estate up north with some farmland, where we raise sheep and sell wool. I've built up a steady trade, and I'm looking to expand my route and business. And my social circle. It is beautiful where I live, but a bit remote."

"Do you have family near?"

"Not any longer. My father was the last of my family up there, and he passed away almost two years ago. Now I'm alone, rambling about my estate, and sometimes the only sound I'll hear in the evenings is the roar of the sea."

"The sea! Do you live close to it?" Aila thought of her mother, who had spoken of the beauty of the sea during her feverish last weeks, professing a wild-eyed wish to return to it. "I've never seen it, but I think I would love to."

"Yes, I'm sure you would. It's magnificent. My grandfather was a sea captain until he retired, and he had our house built on a hill overlooking the water so he could always see and hear it."

The dance ended and she bowed and began to step away. He touched her hand, startling her.

"Will you dance the next dance with me?"

A second turn around the dance floor with a near-stranger would raise eyebrows. She should have declined, and was surprised he'd had the audacity to ask, but the warm expression in his blue eyes made her feel strangely reckless, and she was curious to see if her father would chastise her.

"Yes."

As they moved around the room for their second dance, Mr. Reed gave her his full attention, and she forgot about her father. It felt like they were alone, separate from the crowd of cheerful, laughing dancers around them.

They parted when the son of the grocer, who Aila had known

since childhood, requested a dance with her, and she was surprised to feel disappointed and worried that Mr. Reed would find better company in his next dance partner.

But he sought her out several dances later, and she was relieved to be back beside him.

"If you will allow it," he said, with a smile that made her feel weightless, "I would like to see you again while I am in town."

***

Mr. Reed courted Aila, with her father's blessing. He sent her flowers the day after the dance, and they walked together in the early evenings, strolling with her father and Hannah. People smiled and greeted them warmly as they passed, delighting in the sight of the handsome young couple. As their chaperones, Hannah and Dr. Barton enjoyed the acceptance of many in the village who had disapproved of their marriage the year before.

Hannah invited Mr. Reed to dine at their home several times, and, during these visits, Aila noted the respect in her father's eyes when he described the manor and land he'd inherited. Ladies of the town whispered to her stepmother—who promptly shared the information with Aila and Dr. Barton—that the young man came from an esteemed family. When Mr. Reed gently intimated this as well, Aila realized he was trying to impress her father.

***

"He's very handsome, Aila," Hannah remarked teasingly, when the small family convened in the sitting room the morning after one of Mr. Reed's visits. "You make such a lovely couple. Don't you agree, husband?"

"He seems like a well-established young man," her father said, absently, not looking up from his newspaper.

"You both have such dark hair!' Hannah went on. "She doesn't get that from you, does she, dear? Your hair is only a little darker than mine."

Dr. Barton looked up and smiled at his wife, then looked at Aila. She knew he was gazing at her thoughtfully to appease his wife; by now, they both knew that Hannah would continue to

16

try to pull him into a conversation until she felt he'd given it sufficient attention. Aila was surprised to see sadness cloud the amusement in his eyes.

"No, not from me. Her hair color and her beauty came from her mother." He looked quickly down at his paper, but Aila had seen the sudden glisten of tears before he shifted his gaze.

***

One morning, a few weeks after the dance, Aila was walking down the stairs when she heard Mr. Reed's voice coming from the drawing room. By now, she could recognize in an instant his deep, smiling tone. She paused on the steps to listen.

"...and I will make sure she always has all the comforts she's accustomed to, Sir," he was saying, "if you will permit me to ask her to marry me."

She gasped quietly, but quickly tempered her excitement, certain her father would insist the courtship go on much longer before he would allow Aila to marry.

"I've seen the way you watch over my daughter, and I believe you'll take fine care of her. Now, I can't guarantee you she'll say yes," her father said, laughing cheerfully, "but you have my permission to ask her."

Aila rushed back up to her bedroom and sat on her bed. She hadn't expected this, not so soon. She thought she probably did love Mr. Reed. He was kind, good-natured and handsome. He was also intelligent and well-spoken, and seemed like an ambitious man who would provide well for her. But she had only known him for a few weeks. And would living on a large estate far from a town feel lonely and strange? Would the roar of the ocean, which had sounded so exciting when he spoke of it at the dance, keep her awake at night? Would they come back here often enough to visit her father and her friends? She couldn't quite believe her father had agreed to the proposal after so brief a courtship. He wouldn't force her to marry Mr. Reed, but his jovial consent suggested he wanted it to happen. Maybe it answered some of his own concerns. *He wants me gone*, she thought.

When her father sent one of the housemaids to fetch her, Aila walked dutifully down the steps to meet Mr. Reed. Her father was standing beside him in the hall, grinning at her.

"Hello, Miss Barton," Mr. Reed said. "I hope I'm not disturbing you."

He and Dr. Barton shared a conspiratorial glance and a smile.

"No, of course you aren't, Mr. Reed," she said.

"Will you join me for a walk in your garden?"

The excitement in his eyes quelled her anxiousness.

"Yes, I'd like that."

They walked out into the sunshine, and she took his arm. He led her to the old stone bench at the edge of her small garden, where no flowers bloomed yet.

"Shall we sit?" he asked.

She felt the cold of the stone through the fabric of her dress and petticoat.

"Miss Barton." He met her eyes.

The bench was small, and he was close.

"When I came here, I'd hoped to find a place where I could grow my trade, meet some new friends and associates. I didn't expect to fall in love. But I have. I love you. I have to leave soon, and I can't bear the thought of being away from you. I don't presume you could feel for me what I feel for you, but I hope you do. I hope you love me, also."

"I do," she admitted, coaxed by the stormy blue of his eyes and the soft curl of dark hair against his forehead. He took her hand in his and lightly caressed her finger with his thumb, startling, then, entrancing her.

"Will you marry me, Miss Barton?"

"Yes, Mr. Reed."

Chapter 2

During the first few hours of their journey to Aila's new home, she and Robert had talked steadily about their plans and the ride ahead, but they'd lapsed into silence as the afternoon settled around them. Now, after four hours on rutted road surrounded by wide fields, then dense forests, the excitement of their village wedding that morning was wearing off, and Aila was quietly enduring an anxious longing for the place she'd left behind.

Robert had stacked a chest of her clothes, her books and a small box of keepsakes in the wagon, and it had seemed like so little when she saw it tucked in among the supplies and purchases he was bringing home with them, but he'd assured her she wouldn't need to bring much. She imagined his house was stocked with fine furniture, linens, china and the things that made up a home, and she was looking forward to seeing all the things that would be hers when they arrived at the manor. But, as she watched the bobbing heads of the horses pulling them farther away, she felt a strange ache for the curtains her mother had made, the faded spot on the blue sofa and the teacups, with tiny pink and yellow painted roses, they'd used when friends had come to visit.

***

After dusk, they arrived at a coaching inn to stop for the night. Aila followed Robert into their room, and she stood near the door as he crossed to close the drapes over the windows. He turned and smiled at her.

"Aila," he said. Her name, spoken so casually, intimately. That morning, she'd been Miss Barton. He walked over and took her hands.

"Come and sit. You must be tired, my love." He guided her to the bed and sat beside her. She thought of her stepmother's giggling, stilted attempt to prepare her for her first night with her husband. It had been a failed lesson, too uncomfortable for both ladies, and Aila felt nervous and uncertain now.

Robert kissed her cheek softly, his lips pleasantly warm. She felt her body relax a little.

"I am a bit tired," she said. "Are you?"

"I'm exhausted. Not the ideal state for conception, I'm afraid," he said, ruefully, kissing her hand. "Do you mind if we go to sleep?"

"No, of course not," she said, startled by his bluntness. Perhaps, in the north people spoke more frankly. She was relieved that he hadn't pushed for intimacy but also confused to feel a little disappointed.

She changed into her nightclothes behind the dressing screen and climbed into bed beside him. Once they were lying beneath the blankets, he put his arm around her. He fell asleep, and she kissed his hand and listened to him breathe.

***

They left the inn after a dawn breakfast and continued their journey beneath an amber sky. Aila sat close to Robert and pulled her shawl over her shoulders. He smiled at her and told her his grandfather had made a similar journey years before when he drove his family on this same north bound road.

"Why did he build his home so far north?"

"My father told me that, after Grandfather had been disowned by his family, he wanted to live far away from them. And once he stopped sailing, he no longer needed to live near the southern ports."

"Disowned?"

"His parents were very wealthy, and they wanted him to manage their estate. They were furious when he went against their wishes. I only learned about this after my grandfather died. I found some old letters from my great uncle to my grandfather, and I pressed my father to explain. He was reluctant to talk about it – he was as stubborn and proud about the whole situation as my grandfather had been – but I finally persuaded him, and he told me my grandfather was, in fact, from a prosperous family and had left his career at sea once to appease his parents. He married my grandmother, who was from a good family, and they lived on his family's estate for a while. But he went back out to the sea for one last trip, and he fell overboard. He was rescued, of course. But, after that, strangely enough, he became obsessed with sailing."

"He fell overboard? That must have been terrifying! Why do you think he went back?"

"He loved the sea more than anything. He'd stand on the cliff near our house or walk down to the beach every day. He was out there whenever he wasn't working the farm, sleeping or eating. When I was a child, I used to wonder if he was obsessed with besting it somehow. In the end, it bested him."

"What do you mean?"

"He drowned."

"Oh! How awful!"

"Losing him like that was awful for my father and me. My father revered him. But one morning, Grandfather walked down to the water and never returned. Then, articles of his clothing washed up on the beach. That's how we knew he was gone, but we never found—"

He hesitated, as if he suddenly remembered he was speaking to a young lady.

"I mean, we only ever found his clothes."

"I'm so sorry for you!"

He glanced at her, the smile returning to his face. "*I'm* sorry! I shouldn't have gone on about such a dreary topic!"

She shook her head demurely, though she'd found the story fascinating.

"I suppose I can tell you the good news now," he said.

He smiled widely, and she could imagine what he'd looked like as a child.

"My grandfather had two younger brothers. The second son of

the family, my great-uncle, whose letters I found, inherited the family fortune. He married, but none of their children survived past infancy. The youngest brother married also, and his wife had two daughters and one son, but the son never married and recently died. The daughters, my aunts, had only female children. My great-uncle is elderly and unwell, and now there is no male heir, except for me."

"But you said your grandfather was disinherited."

"He was, but I persuaded my great-uncle to see me several months ago, and I made a compelling argument for keeping the estate within the immediate bloodline of the family. He heard me out, and, if I marry—which I have, of course!— and if I can produce a son to offer a male line of succession, he will consider reinstating my right to the inheritance."

Aila marveled at her good fortune. In addition to the manor he owned, her husband was in a position to greatly increase his wealth and property. She knew her father had given a modest dowry to Robert when they'd married, but she'd considered it a customary gesture since he certainly didn't need it. She smiled to herself, imagining Robert had probably tried to politely decline the dowry, but her proud father would have insisted, unaware that in a few years' time his daughter might be the mistress of a *second* grand estate.

***

They reached their home on the afternoon of the seventh day of their journey. Aila was resting, with her eyes closed and her head on Robert's shoulder.

"We're almost home!" Robert said, and Aila opened her eyes. They were heading west now, after riding north for many miles, and the sun was easing its way toward the bottom of the sky. Beyond the sloping green fields along the road, Aila saw a shining expanse of the richest blue she had ever seen. The sea! She stared at the motion and shimmer of it. It seemed to blend right into the sky.

"How beautiful," she whispered.

"And, there is Murrough's Cliff, your new home!" He gestured north at something on the horizon. She could barely see it. She narrowed her eyes, trying to manage a clearer view.

She saw acres of pale grass, several spread-out clusters of large trees and, in the distance, a small dark triangle. As the wagon drew closer, the triangle became a modest stone cottage with a thickly tiled roof. The barn, a long, low building of lighter colored stone, stretched behind the cottage.

Aila stared in confusion. The house was much simpler than what she'd imagined when she'd heard Robert describe it to her father and their neighbors. It looked well and carefully built, with a fieldstone façade, carved wooden shutters on the windows, and a thick stone chimney, but it was much smaller than her father's house. She glanced at Robert, but he was looking toward the house, grinning as if nothing was amiss.

At the front of the house, Robert halted the horses and jumped down from the wagon. He helped Aila to the ground. Her legs felt unstable after the long ride. Robert offered her his arm and led her to the front door. He opened the lock and held the heavy wooden door open for her.

Aila stepped inside and looked around, while Robert went out to the barn to get kindling for the fireplace. The walls were pale plaster and stone, with dark beams supporting the ceiling. Sun-faded woolen rugs lay scattered on the wood floor. A thick wooden table, simple wooden chairs and a large cabinet, built for function rather than decoration, stood in the alcove to the left of the front door. A small kitchen with a stone workspace and a raised hearth for cooking sat beyond the alcove. Beyond the kitchen there appeared to be a storeroom with another door to the outside. She turned her head and saw a sitting room with four cushioned armchairs, a sheepskin rug and a large hearth inlaid with stones. There were two narrow doors at the back of the sitting room.

She crossed the room and opened the first door. Inside, she found a large room with a small fireplace, a rocking chair, a large wooden wardrobe, a plain, wide bed and two windows on the back wall. The walls in the room were unadorned, like the rest of the house. Aila found the second room to be much the same, except it had two beds and featured windows on the back and right-side walls. She stood alone in the second bedroom, while Robert worked to start a fire in the big hearth in the sitting room.

Aila thought of her bedroom in her father's home. She had slept in a bed with a curtained canopy and matching linens. Her walls had been papered in a soft floral pattern, the curtains beside her windows had been lace. She'd had a delicate writing desk and a pretty French chair with a soft, embroidered cushion. Lovely paintings in ornate wooden frames had adorned her bedroom walls.

She hugged herself against the chill that seemed to surround her. Where were all the fine things that had surely belonged to Robert's grandparents, to his grandmother?

"Are you happy, my love?" Robert asked, coming into the room behind her. She nodded because she knew that was what he wanted from her, but she couldn't bring herself to speak. The quiet of the house, the echo of his voice in the stony, sparingly furnished room, unsettled her and filled her with loneliness. Then, a sudden happy thought occurred to her.

"Will your cook and housemaid return tomorrow?" she asked, wondering as she spoke if their quarters were part of the barn or if they lived elsewhere. Having more people in and around the house would surely help remedy this feeling of isolation. Robert's eyes widened, and he smiled, looking as though he wanted to laugh.

"Cook and housemaid? No, my dear, it's just to be us here. Before you came, it was just me. It won't be too much for you to keep up, don't worry, and I don't expect you to make grand meals. My tastes are simple."

She stared at him, nodded in dull comprehension, and turned to walk to the bedroom window as he slipped out of the room to unload the wagon.

She thought of his high-born grandmother arriving here after the luxury of the city and wondered if that lady had found herself at an even greater loss. Perhaps his grandmother had insisted on hiring several girls from the nearest village, wherever that was. Should she insist he hire help? She had vowed to obey him only days before, but did that mean she must accept being brought so low? Her parents had had a silent accord that she'd never bothered to examine, and her father and Hannah seemed to honor a similar coded agreement. Did either of those women negotiate the terms of their marriage or had her father simply been more gracious than Robert? Could a good wife question her husband?

She stared through the back window. Beyond the wild grass waving in the wind, the restless ocean pressed against the grey sky. She closed her eyes and imagined herself arriving at a stately Palladian manor twice the size of her childhood home. Though she could hear the roar of the sea in the distance, the rolling green lawn bordered by well-trimmed hedges assured her of the civility to be found at this place. A footman helped her down from the wagon. Her husband took her arm, as another footman unloaded their belongings. She and Robert entered the grand home, stepping onto a soft carpet of rich reds and golds. A cook, a housekeeper, and several housemaids and footmen stood waiting to greet them. The housekeeper stepped forward and addressed Robert with formal deference, and Robert introduced her to Aila. With a bow, the housekeeper greeted Aila and introduced the rest of the staff. Aila smiled kindly at them all and allowed Robert and the housekeeper to lead her into the drawing room, a lovely, high-ceilinged room, with walls covered in pale blue fabric. A gold clock gleamed from the white marble mantle. A fire blazed in the fireplace. Aila sat in a plush armchair beside the fire, and the housekeeper placed a warm blanket across her lap. Robert sat in the chair beside hers, and the housekeeper assured them that tea would be served presently.

She jumped at the sound of the thick front door slamming shut as Robert re-entered the house. She turned, startled for a moment to see, instead of the soft blue walls of her daydream, the stark stone and timber of her husband's house.

***

Robert had worked long hours on the farm during Aila's first week on the wind-swept hill, and she'd been alone in the little house. At first, she'd tried to think of a way to get back to her father's house or get a letter to him, but, beginning on her third evening in the house, Robert had held her, kissed her softly and had been so gentle and loving that she'd started to miss him whenever he was away from her, even when he was outside in the field or in the barn.

He took her along on a trip to purchase a new cow, and, as they set out for their neighbors' farm, he warned her it was a good distance away, because most people lived further from the sea, where the land was flatter and the weather milder. It took them over two hours to reach the farm. As she began to wonder if they had somehow lost their way, the horses turned into a clearing, and Aila saw a series of long, low buildings in the middle of the field.

As they approached, a man came out to meet them, followed by a woman in a gray wool dress. Aila smiled at them, expecting the sort of warm, neighborly reception she and her parents had enjoyed whenever they'd called upon a neighbor or passed an acquaintance in their village. Her smile faltered when she saw their stern faces.

"Hello, Mr. Jenkins," Robert called out. "I've come to see about purchasing a cow."

"Aye," Mr. Jenkins replied. He had a cloud of white hair, a long white beard and red, wind burned cheeks. His wife's face was thin and deeply lined, and she wore her gray hair in a tight, low bun. She stared impassively at Robert and Aila.

Robert asked Aila to wait in the wagon as he climbed down. He followed Mr. and Mrs. Jenkins into a nearby barn. There were sheep grazing lazily several yards from where Aila sat. She watched them, letting the sun warm her, as she listened to the soft buzz of nature.

When they came out of the barn, Mr. Jenkins was pulling a

26

tethered brown cow behind them. The cow's inky eyes seemed to regard Aila shyly. The farmer and Robert loaded the cow into the wagon, and she moaned in complaint, but soon settled down. As he climbed into the wagon, Robert turned and gestured to Aila.

"This is my wife, Mrs. Reed. Mrs. Reed, meet Mr. and Mrs. Jenkins."

"I'm pleased to meet you," Aila said.

They acknowledged her with efficient smiles.

As they rode off with their new cow, Aila realized she was no longer a doctor's daughter. She was now a farmer's wife. Hopefully, she'd soon be too busy to dwell on what her old friends and former neighbors might think of her situation. She'd spent the past week cooking modest meals. Next week, she'd take on the tasks of milking the cow and tending to their small crop of potatoes and grains.

She glanced back at the farmer's field. In the distance, she saw men working, some riding horses and some farming the land. Maybe some of them were the farmer's grown sons. Maybe they lived here, too, with their wives and children, three generations working together.

Hopefully soon Aila would have infant sons with soft tiny faces and chubby arms to care for. They'd grow into hardy, handsome young men like Robert. She looked at him, and he smiled at her, setting off a little burst of joy in her heart.

She couldn't wait to bear him the sons he wished for. And maybe, after she had several sons, she might have a daughter, too, a little girl to sing to, who would sit and sew beside her as she had done with her mother. She and her lovely daughter would share in the joyful exasperation of living in a home filled with many boisterous men.

Chapter 3

Aila breathed in the heady scent of the dough she was kneading and felt her stomach turn. She stepped away and sat on one of the chairs in the sitting room. It had been nine months since she'd married Robert and had started preparing all their meals, and she was finally used to the work, but lately she'd been tiring so easily, and, now, this horrible nausea. She couldn't understand how she'd gotten ill. She never saw anyone aside from Robert. He'd travelled locally to sell wool, and he might have contracted some illness from one of the townspeople. But he, himself, was healthy, so that seemed unlikely. When he came inside later that morning and found her asleep in a chair by the fire, he woke her gently to see what was wrong, and she told him how she'd been feeling. His grin surprised her.

"Darling, might you be in the family way?"

"I'm not sure." She touched her abdomen, felt hope rising in her heart. He stood.

"I'm going to ride to the nearest village. I'll find a midwife who'll be able to confirm it."

He ran out to the barn. Aila watched him ride off from the window. Instead of finishing her chores, she sat in the old cushioned chair near the fire where she'd dozed off earlier. The waves of heat warmed her hands. She closed her eyes and allowed herself to savor the difference between how she felt now and how she'd felt every other time he'd left her to ride out to the villages. This time she didn't feel alone.

***

Robert returned early that evening with Mrs. Tammery, a woman of fifty-eight, who had helped over sixty infants enter the world. Aila walked outside to meet the wagon, carrying a lit torch to help guide them inside. She watched as Robert offered his hand to the short, portly woman. Mrs. Tammery waved away his outstretched hand, braced herself on the bench and hopped down to the dirt below. She looked up and her eyes met Aila's, and she smiled broadly, bustling past Robert to greet her. Aila led her inside.

Once in the house, Mrs. Tammery stared at Aila's face with an intensity that discomfited her, until the older lady declared, "Yes, I think we'll find you are with child, my dear. You've got the look about you."

Warmed by the confidence in Mrs. Tammery's voice, Aila poured their tea.

***

Aila was grateful when Mrs. Tammery returned to stay with them seven months later. She hadn't been prepared for the changes in her body and her mood, especially in the more recent months. Robert had chastised her for not resting whenever he'd caught her out of bed, but she felt better when she was moving and terrible when she was still for too long. Mrs. Tammery's arrival felt like a sign that her confinement would end soon and she'd feel better.

***

Morgana was born at first light on a spring morning. Her beautiful, serious face enchanted Aila. She could see that Robert was disappointed when Mrs. Tammery announced that they had a daughter, but once the midwife cleaned the baby and handed her into his arms, he looked down at the tiny face.

"She is a marvel, my dear! The next one will surely be a son, but she will be my darling little girl!"

***

Once she recovered, Aila was relieved he wasn't angry. She was delighted with her daughter and didn't want anything to dampen her joy. She stared into the baby's dark, shimmering eyes, and she saw her own mother. Robert hadn't planned on a girl and he had little interest in girls' names, so when Aila suggested they name her after her mother, he agreed. The name was unusual for their part of the country. Robert had never heard it before, but it sounded lovely and regal. As Morgana grew and became more active, her parents shortened her name to Morgan in daily use, and that was the name by which she knew herself.

Chapter 4

When Morgan was six years old, Robert brought home a shaggy, friendly puppy. Though the dog had a job to do and was responsible for herding the sheep, Morgan immediately claimed him as her own and named him Wooly.

Aila had to take care of her second daughter, Hilary, who was just an infant, as well as keep the house and prepare the family's meals, so she was glad that Morgan had the dog's affection. When Robert was travelling, Aila had to take on some of his chores, as well and felt guilty for having so little time to spend with Morgan, so she gave in to Morgan's desperate pleas and allowed Wooly to sleep on the floor of Morgan's bedroom. The little girl and her dog fell asleep each night with her small hand resting in the fur of his back.

"Are you sure that's wise?" Robert had asked her when they climbed into bed one night after he'd learned the dog now slept in their daughter's room. "I don't want him to get lazy."

"I don't have much time for her these days, with the baby. With Wooly around, she doesn't feel lonely."

"My soft-hearted wife. If she'd been a boy, you wouldn't have had to worry about that." He glanced impassively at the baby in the bassinet across the room. "Hopefully, the next one will be."

"Yes, hopefully," Aila agreed, feeling like a traitor to her two daughters. She adored them both and might have said so a year earlier, but lately, Robert seemed quick to lose patience with her. When she spoke about the girls or something he wasn't interested in, instead of feigning curiosity, or even changing the subject, he just stared at her, or stood up and left to do something else.

Morgan's birth, soon after they'd married had been a blessing and a seeming promise of more children to come, and Robert had lavished Aila with affection, bringing her gifts from his trips, reveling in the beauty of their daughter. In the glow of his attention and her own infatuation with him, Aila had forgotten her misgivings about the smallness and simplicity of the house. Instead, it had seemed enchanted to her, like their own private hideaway from the rest of the world, the rustic furniture like something fairies might have made, the unadorned plaster walls a blank canvas excitedly awaiting future needlepoint samplers and paintings by their many future children.

But in the four years after Morgan was born, Aila hadn't been able to conceive again, and Robert had doted on her less and less, reminding her how little she knew him. All of the letters she'd written her father and given to Robert to post had gone unanswered, and, at first, she'd been too besotted with her husband and daughter to be more than annoyed. But as Robert grew increasingly cooler to her, she realized with a pang of grief that several years had passed and her father had fully cast her off.

When she'd been able to announce that she was pregnant again, the charming, loving Robert who'd once professed his love daily seemed to come back to her, only to step away again when Aila gave birth to Hilary, another girl. His second daughter was of little importance to him, though he was still fond of Morgan, his first born

When Robert was home, Morgan and Wooly would follow him around the farm, and he would tell them stories of the villages he visited to trade. Aila felt reassured by the sound of their voices drifting through the window: Robert's deep, exciting baritone, Morgan's high and curious lilt. When Morgan asked to go with Robert on his trips, he always refused her gently, explaining that the ride was a hard one over rough road and Wooly would miss her too much.

Whenever Morgan saw her father's horse and wagon appear in the distance, she ran to meet him, and Aila loved to watch her from the window, racing free through the tall grass, her long, dark hair flying like a flag behind her. Wooly ran beside her. When she reached his wagon, Robert stopped to help her and Wooly climb in so they could all ride home together. Aila always stepped out and waited outside the door of the cottage as they rode up, with Hilary in her arms.

She always smiled when she saw them and made sure to have tea ready and a hearty meal cooking for her husband. Morgan sat by her father's side as he entertained them with tales of his latest journey. Aila told him of any developments on their small farm, and then admired the purchases he'd brought back.

In October of that year, she was able to tell him that she was expecting their third child, and Morgan laughed with delight when he grabbed Aila in his arms and kissed her.

***

"Mama, how does Papa know the baby will be a boy when none of us can see it yet?" Morgan asked Aila. Robert always referred to the baby Aila carried as his son. Aila wanted to explain that he didn't actually know, but she was afraid, almost superstitious, about saying so. She was very close now, and they would find out soon enough, but she hoped he was right.

***

"Is it the wrong baby?" Morgan cried out from her post in the doorway when Mrs. Tammery announced that Aila had given birth to a baby girl. As exhausted as she was, Aila could see by Robert's face that he seemed to share this worry as he stared at the infant when Mrs. Tammery handed her to Aila. Aila held the baby tightly, hoping she couldn't feel her father's disappointment.

***

Robert left them that night. Mrs. Tammery, watched, with her lips pressed together in disapproval, as he stormed out of the house.

She stayed a week longer than she'd planned in order to help where she could and, to Aila's deep embarrassment, had to borrow one of the horses to make her own way home.

Once Mrs. Tammery was gone, Aila had to rely on Morgan to

help her take care of Hilary and prepare their meals as she recovered from childbirth and tended to the newborn infant, who she decided to name Karen. They went to sleep exhausted every night, but Aila knew that Morgan always tried to steal a few minutes each day to run out to the field. She stood, day after day, with Wooly by her side, staring through weary eyes at the road and willing her father to appear. Aila's heart ached as she watched her through the window, but she knew Morgan was doing the only thing she thought she could to bring Robert back to them.

***

When Robert finally did come home a week later, Morgan was asleep. Aila was in the kitchen, preparing breakfast, and she heard hoofbeats coming down their road. She ran to the window and saw him riding up to the house. She stepped away from the window quickly, not ready to face him. He strode into the house, and she worried that he would act as if he'd done nothing wrong, but he rushed up to her.

"Aila, forgive me," he said, taking her hands and dropping to his knees. "My darling, I am so sorry."

"Why did you leave us?" her voice sounded thick as a sob forced its way from her throat and tears sprung to her eyes, the hurt she'd been holding back finally fighting free.

"I don't know. I was angry. I know it isn't your fault, but it has been seven years. And still no male heir. If you could see the house, the life that is waiting for us…"

"I'm not trying *not* to have a son!" she cried.

"I know, I know…shh…I know." He pulled her close and stroked her hair. "I'm back now. I've come home. We'll try again."

Aila allowed herself to lean against him.

A few minutes later, Wooly rushed out of Morgan's room as she opened the door, and he lay by Robert's feet. Morgan watched her parents from the doorway.

"Come here, sweetheart." Robert waved Morgan over to join them. When she reached him, he picked her up and lifted her high above his head and then held her on his hip. She hugged him tightly, and Aila put a steadying hand on her small back, trying to soothe the anxiety in her daughter's tight grip.

Chapter 5

Iｔ took three years for Aila to become pregnant again. In the business of daily chores and taking care of three children, the days had seemed to race by for Aila, and it hardly felt like three years had passed, except for Robert pointedly marking each year without a son, each year further from his grand inheritance.

She noted the way Robert gazed at her growing middle, his expression alternately hopeful and suspicious.

While the family ate breakfast one morning, Robert announced that they couldn't afford to bring Mrs. Tammery to help Aila this time. Aila's heart fell, and she wished he had told her privately when she saw shock, then anger darken Morgan's face. After that, Morgan no longer ran out to meet her father's wagon in the field, and Aila realized her young daughter had been anxiously monitoring her father's mood since the day he'd returned to them. It was too big a burden for such a young person and Aila cursed herself for not noticing sooner, not protecting Morgan from sharing her fears.

***

Aila gave birth late in the evening. The younger girls were asleep, and Morgan and her father worked side by side for hours, caring for Aila. Robert delivered the child and saw that he had another daughter. He handed her quickly to Morgan to swaddle, but Aila caught his furious expression and her heart sank. He left the room without a word, slamming the bedroom door shut behind him.

They could hear him moving around in the house. Aila wanted to call to him, but she had fallen back against her bed cushions and was barely holding onto the baby who was feeding hungrily. Morgan would have to take care of them. Aila allowed herself a small hope that Robert would come back to the room to help her once his temper subsided, as Morgan cleaned the baby and placed her in her basket. She helped Aila wash up and get into a warm, clean shift. As Morgan covered her in layers of blankets, Aila heard the front door shut.

"Go see," she whispered, and Morgan ran to the front room and looked through the window in time to see her father disappear into the night in the faster of their two wagons.

***

Dawn finally arrived, and Aila's daughters were asleep. Emily, now ten days old, was dozing peacefully in her basket. Aila stood slowly, after hours spent hunched and staring out her small window into the darkness.

Between caring for the baby and worrying about their situation, she hadn't slept in days. Once she was able to walk, she'd discovered that Robert had taken the supply of wool and all of their money from the hidden stash in the sitting room. It was only a few weeks before she expected the first snowfall, the time when Robert would normally gather what they had on hand and then ride out and buy them any additional provisions they'd need for the winter. Their store of food and grains was light, and Aila guessed that he'd intended to buy much of what they'd need after his son was born. She and her daughters might be able to make it through the winter, but she knew they wouldn't be able to feed their livestock, and, with no money and no wool or animals to sell, she couldn't see how they'd survive the following year.

Outside, the sky was beginning to lighten from black to violet. Aila's body ached and her eyes were painfully dry. She began to walk with no specific intention, her legs moving as if apart from her control. They carried her outside into the waning darkness and along the dirt lane that led away from the small stone-walled cottage. Bursts of icy wind swirled over the wide fields of frozen grass on either side of her path, biting at her cheeks like ghostly birds of prey. She continued walking toward the edge of the white-faced cliffs which dropped straight down to the ocean below.

She reached the cliff top and stood for a moment, the toes of her worn brown boots close to the edge. She swayed suddenly, nudged forward by a malicious wind. Heart racing, she stepped backward and walked several yards along the cliff until she reached a place where the decline toward the ocean was much more gradual, a long slope of sparse grass and rocky terrain that led down to the beach below. She walked down the hill, gathering up the long skirt of her heavy woolen dress to avoid the grasping branches of the wild thicket along the narrow path.

The beach was a tiny pale crescent beside the massive, black ocean. She absently registered the softness of the sand as she stepped onto the beach. The cliffs loomed like ashen sentries beside her. Her cottage was high above now, out of view. In front of her, a long row of large, black rocks reached out far into the sea, fog nearly obscuring its end. Where the ocean rolled in between this jetty and a jutting section of cliff wall, the water splashed violently, foaming and hissing angrily, as if surprised to find itself trapped there.

She climbed onto the jetty and walked slowly across the uneven surfaces of the rocks, feeling the seawater splash at her dress and the cold mist dampen her hands and face. She continued, despite her discomfort, the jetty like a bridge toward some unknown destination. The fog began to lift, and she saw where the jetty stopped, the endless ocean splashing hungrily up over its edge.

She looked back and was surprised to see how far she had come from the beach. The ocean surrounded her now on three sides. When her eyes travelled up from the little beach to the top of the cliffs, she thought of her daughters, asleep in the house.

She inhaled the salty air. Exhausted, she tried to kneel, folding herself roughly down onto the wet rock. She landed hard on her knees, steadying herself with her hands. She rocked back against the pain, pulled her knees to her chest and began to cry.

Grief and hopelessness seemed to spiral around her on the wind. Her heart ached and she wondered wildly why her body had betrayed her, giving her only daughters when her husband would have stayed for a single son.

Her tears felt hot on her cheeks as they coursed down her face onto the rocks and into the sea. She cried until she felt spent, keening in chorus with the wind, waves crashing like an accompanying percussion. When her tears subsided, she rested, silent and trembling.

As the sun rose behind a raft of clouds, turning the sky pale gray, her anguish turned to anger, and she realized in a rush that it was her husband who had betrayed her.

She thought of Emily's beautiful face and her mind felt clear for the first time since Robert had left. He had never truly loved her. He'd taken her far from her family and the comfort of the only home she'd ever known to this strange, wild place. He'd claimed when she'd met him that he was expanding his business to her father's town, but they journey had taken seven days and, after they'd married, he'd never gone back there. She'd assumed he'd changed his plans because he didn't want to be so far away from her and his children. Now, who knew how far away he'd gone? He'd abandoned them all in this place that resonated with memories of him.

She let her gaze drop to the ocean beside her. There, she saw her blurry reflection. Her eyes looked peculiar. She leaned forward. Beneath the rolling, foamy surface, she saw the face a little more clearly. It was not her own.

Extraordinary green eyes stared into hers. The strange, beautiful face mesmerized Aila. Silvery hair seemed to fan out around it. Meeting the luminous gaze, she felt a melancholy peacefulness wash over her. She felt, rather than heard, the woman beneath the waves ask why she despaired. She shared instinctively, without speaking, the story of Robert's abandonment, of her young daughters, and her fear that, without him, she and her daughters wouldn't have enough money to survive. The beautiful sea woman seemed to share her fears, and it felt as if a physical burden was lifted from Aila's back.

She asked Aila to remain on the rocks until she returned, and she turned and swam off, disappearing beneath the waves. Aila obeyed, spellbound. She waited, despite the chill of the wet wind, soothed by the strange interaction, for close to an hour.

When the sea woman reappeared, she carried a small cloth sack bound by seaweed. She asked Aila to reach into the water. Aila reached down and the sea woman placed the sack in her hands. Aila lifted it out of the water and opened it. Gold coins tumbled onto the rock.

Aila gasped and looked down at the sea woman, who explained that her kind kept the coins they found when ships wrecked because sometimes one of their own would get caught in the net of a ship. The sailors were always amazed and delighted with their catch, intent on bringing her home as a trophy, so the sea woman would call to them and offer them gold to return her sister to the sea. Sometimes they would refuse, and she would tell them their catch would die if kept from the ocean and, when she died, her body would disintegrate into sand. They'd return home, she'd tell them, with a pile of sand, having left behind the riches she was offering them. That usually convinced them.

The sea woman ended her story there. She did not tell her gentle new friend that, if the sailors refused her bargain, her shoal would swarm the bottom of the ship, tearing at the wet wood until the hull was riddled with holes large enough to sink the ship and return the sailors' captive to the safety of her home.

Looking at the gold, Aila's eyes filled with tears of gratitude. She asked the sea woman how she could repay her for her kindness. The sea woman seemed surprised at her offer and considered it. She explained that the sounds of Aila's grief had drawn her because she was suffering as well. A sailing vessel had maimed her own daughter and she could barely swim. Though the sea woman believed her daughter could heal and learn again to swim, the young one, once a proud and adventurous swimmer, had lost the will to live.

The sea woman had once, long ago, heard the land creatures singing. She wondered if her daughter, exposed to such unique and beautiful vibrations, might feel that same joy she had and might feel inspired to try to recover. She asked if Aila would sing for them, once before the water turned warmest and once before the water turned coldest, so her daughter might experience it and then look forward to the next time. Aila agreed, moved by the sea woman's story and eager to help her. They parted, both needing to see to their daughters. Aila watched the sea woman drift out of sight beneath the foamy green water.

She held some of the gold in her hands. Its weight surprised and reassured her. She watched the waves roll rhythmically beneath the dreamy gray sky and put the coins back, preparing to carry them home. She was unable to bind the sack with seaweed again, so she knelt and gathered the front of her skirt to form a makeshift sack, and she pushed the gold coins into it.

Grateful to have her linen underskirt as a barrier against the icy wind, Aila made her way up the hill, careful not to drop a single coin. When she reached the cottage, her daughters were still asleep. She went into her bedroom and placed the gold on the bed. She stared at it, trying to assess its value. If not enough to sustain them forever, it would be more than enough to buy the things they would need to get through the coming winter.

***

Aila heard Emily waking in her basket. She picked her up, and the infant quieted as soon as she was in her mother's arms. Aila held her gently, rocking her tiny body slowly. She fed her, watching the tiny eyelids lower, and feeling the little body shake with deep sighs of contentment, as Emily drifted back to sleep.

Aila placed Emily in her basket and went to the kitchen to retrieve a large pot from the cupboard near the stove. She pushed the coins from the bed into the pot, wincing at the loud noise they made, and then she set the pot beneath a small wooden chair in a corner of her room. She draped a blanket over the chair. She would have to make another blanket for the winter.

Thinking of how she would shear the sheep and spin the wool for her blanket, she decided what else she would do. She would use the gold to buy what they needed to get through the winter. Then, she would teach the girls to help her tend the sheep, shear them, and spin the wool. She would take on her husband's trade, riding out to the nearest villages to sell the wool as he had.

***

Aila decided to travel out to the Jenkins farm to buy feed for the animals, as well as another cow, some pigs and sheep to help get them through the winter. She brought Emily, now a month old, and Hilary, who could help her care for the baby, while Morgan stayed behind with Karen.

As they rode, Hilary held the baby carefully. Aila relied on memory to chart their path. The journey was difficult for all of them, and Aila felt a rush of relief once they arrived in that same clearing she'd entered with Robert many years before. Once the farmer and his wife spotted them on the edge of the pasture, they began walking out to meet the wagon.

"Hello," she said, when she reached them. "I am here to see about purchasing livestock if you have them to sell."

They regarded her with guarded, curious expressions. She looked familiar to them, but neither fully recognized her.

"Who are ye, then?" the farmer asked.

"I'm the wife of Robert Reed," she said. "I came here with him once before, several years ago."

The farmer frowned.

"Mr. Reed usually comes himself to buy from us. Why did he send his wife and bairns?"

Aila felt tired and longed to tell the truth, regardless of the outcome. If they scorned her, so be it, she couldn't bring herself to make up an excuse for his absence.

"He's left us, and I don't think he intends to return," she told them plainly. "I thought it best to get myself and my children sorted before the winter comes."

The farmer's wife gave him a quick look and his expression softened.

"My prices are fair, Mrs. Reed," he said. "But they are what they are."

"Yes, Sir, I understand." She motioned for Hilary to wait in the wagon with the baby, and she climbed down to follow him into the barn. The farmer's wife gave Hilary and Emily a gentle smile.

"I'll take them inside the house for a biscuit, shall I?"

Aila, grateful for this gesture, nodded.

The farmer helped Aila choose a cow, pigs and sheep. She paid him, and he helped her load the animals into the wagon.

As they finished loading the wagon, Mrs. Jenkins brought a fed and satisfied Hilary and a sleeping Emily out to join them. The farmer said a brief farewell and, with a quick glance at his wife, he walked off toward the barn. Mrs. Jenkins lingered beside the wagon, looking uneasy.

"There's something you should know, Mrs. Reed. I don't like to involve myself in other people's concerns but, years ago, your husband was involved in a scandal..." She hesitated.

"Please go on," Aila said, though she wasn't sure she wanted to hear what Mrs. Jenkins had to say.

"He had a dalliance with the daughter of one of the local tenant farmers and she had a child. The girl's father was furious and insisted he marry her, but Mr. Reed refused and offered to pay them instead." She shook her head, recalling the unpleantness.

"But then, he left without making payment. The only way anyone knew he hadn't abandoned his farm and run off forever was because he'd paid one of our sons to come by and see to his livestock. He told our boy he'd be away for a month or two. When he did return, he'd brought you back with him. Word reached the farmer and he was in a rage about it, but soon after he got back, Mr. Reed paid him. The farmer wasn't happy, but he took the money because he needed it."

She paused and sighed wearily, taking in Aila's shocked expression before continuing.

"I wouldn't have seen fit to upset you with this information, Mrs. Reed, and I didn't see how it would benefit you to hear it before, but now that you've told us he's run off, you should know something else we've heard in case you're expecting him to come back someday. The farmer came to us about a month ago, beside himself because his daughter had run off and taken her child with her. Off to a better life, she told him when he came into the house from the fields one morning. He caught her taking some food and saw the bairn sitting in a wagon out front with Robert, waiting for her. She ran out the door, and he chased them down the road, but they didn't stop."

The news felt like a blow to Aila's chest.

"Is the child a boy?" she asked the farmer's wife, not surprised but stung all the same by the woman's quick, confirming nod.

"Yeh—almost a man, I suppose—he must be twelve or thirteen years old by now."

***

They made their way home through the darkening woods. Aila's head felt heavy and thick as she considered this new layer of Robert's deceit. On top of this fresh pain, she felt anxious, as she would with every ride, worried about thieves and treacherous road. She barely heard Hilary's impassioned declarations of concern for the animals, who were bumping around in the back of the wagon, bleating and moaning in complaint.

When they reached the cottage, the animals were settled into the barn, with three little girls fussing happily over them. Then, Aila fed them all dinner and sat by the hearth with Emily in her arms, as the other girls cleaned. She let out a long sigh and closed her eyes, the warmth of the fire like soothing fingers pressing gently on her cheeks and eyelids.

Chapter 6

During the Reeds' first winter as women alone, Aila often sat awake at night listening to the wind howl and press menacingly against the walls of the house. One early evening, the branch of a tree a few yards from the cottage broke beneath the weight of the snow. Her heart leapt at the loud, unexpected sound, and, with a mixture of anger and hope, she rushed to open the door, certain Robert would be standing there, having abandoned, again, the country woman and son who weren't good enough for him years ago.

When she swung the heavy door open, she saw only the icy whiteness of snow covering the meadow, empty of any change besides the newly fallen branch, and she raged silently at the traitorous feeling of disappointment that came over her. She went to her bedroom, assigning Morgan the task of tending to Emily that night. She told Morgan to wake her when Emily needed to be fed.

The girls worked at preparing dinner, and they argued softly about whether they should bring their mother some food. Morgan won, insisting they not disturb her. From her room, Aila could hear them speaking and she was grateful to them all, to the younger ones for wanting to feed her and to Morgan for understanding her need to be left alone.

***

The spring after Robert abandoned them, Aila ventured out for the first time to sell the wool. She didn't know exactly where to go and relied mostly on the horses to remember and lead her.

When she approached the nearest village after an hour on the road, she was relieved, but the horses seemed to want to pass it by. Puzzled and annoyed, she forced them to turn and trot into the center of the tiny town. The buildings were dirty and poorly built, wedged together crookedly. They seemed to be leaning against one another to stay upright. There were a few crudely marked businesses.

She found a millinery and knocked at the door. It swung open, and the shop keeper stood before her. He had long, wiry hair, thin shoulders and a pinched, scowling face.

"What do yeh want?"

"Are you in need of any wool, Sir, for the millinery?" Aila asked nervously.

He looked past her at the wagon, where the two horses stomped and shook their heads impatiently. He gave her an unfriendly sneer.

"Bring a bundle of yer wool into my shop so I can get a look at it."

She brought some to the door for him to inspect, trying to ignore her rising anxiety.

"Travellin' on your own, Miss?" Contempt coated his words.

"I am. My husband was injured and cannot travel yet."

When she mentioned a husband, the man's unpleasant smile faded, but he continued to stare at her in a way that sent a chill across her shoulders. He opened the door to his shop wider.

"Bring it in here."

She looked past him into a dimly lit room, and she could sense suddenly that no one else was in the shop. She would be alone with him if she went in. She stepped back.

"The light is better outside, and I would like you to be able to see it well," she said.

Frowning now, angered by her refusal, he snatched the wool from her hand, shoved her backwards, slammed the door shut and bolted the lock. Her initial shock turned quickly to anger, and she banged on the door.

"You must pay me for that!" she shouted. As she hammered at the door with her fists, a small crowd of people began to shuffle out into the street. A tall man with a red face and a stooped neck rushed toward her, followed by a sour-faced old woman in a worn, brown dress with a filthy, torn hem.

"What're yeh after?" the tall man asked.

"This man stole a bundle of wool from me! He asked to inspect it, and then he took it from me and locked the door!"

The man regarded her coldly, and the woman beside him stared at her through narrowed eyes. The man knocked on the door.

"Jerome," he said. "Open the door."

The door swung open.

"Did yeh take the wool from 'er," he asked, gesturing toward Aila.

"No. Never saw 'er before an I wish she'd stop beatin' on my door!"

The tall man turned to Aila.

"He says he didn't steal yer wool."

"But he did!" Tears burned the corners of her eyes.

The small crowd was growing larger in number, and people were watching with expectant looks on their dirty faces.

"Yeh come to our village, Stranger, and call this man a liar? He's lived 'ere longer than yeh've been alive!" the tall man hollered at her, menace in his voice.

"No," she murmured, backing away from him as if in fear, but moving steadily toward her wagon.

"Tha's a strange mistake!" the old woman cackled, with a gloating, toothless smile. The people in the crowd laughed, too, glancing at one another and murmuring, distracted by their own malignant amusement

Aila took the opportunity to clamber up into the wagon seat. Fortunately, her path was clear, and her horses were able to bolt off, kicking up dirt and dust in the faces of the villagers as they raced out of the village. Shouts and taunts echoed behind her.

***

On the main road, the horses ran in the direction they had originally intended, away from home. Once she was certain no one was pursuing them, shaken and defeated, Aila was ready to turn the horses back toward home. But something in the way they were moving, confidently carrying her forward with calm determination, made her hesitate. If she went back now, she might never be able to summon the courage to go out again. She thought of her children, who had accepted the work of grown adults without complaint, their lives forever changed by circumstances they couldn't control and wouldn't be able to fully understand for years to come. She let the horses carry her forward.

When they reached another village, the horses, evidently familiar with the path, turned onto the high street. Aila saw right away this village was different from the last. This place was larger and alive with people walking the streets, chatting with one another. The buildings were clean and solidly built, and the road was well-tended. Only a few people glanced at her with benign curiosity as she passed. She stopped the horses in front of a millinery and was straightening her bonnet when a man and a woman walked out of the shop and approached her.

"Are you Mr. Reed's wife?" the man asked, with a friendly smile.

"I am."

"We recognized the wagon—and the horses," he explained, as he rubbed the horses' foreheads. "Are you here with our wool?"

"Yes, Sir."

His pleasant tone and his wife's smile reassured her, and she joined them in their shop, where they offered her a cup of tea. They discussed the quantity of wool they needed, and she was delighted to learn they would require the entire supply she'd brought. Neither the man nor his wife asked her why she was delivering it without Robert, and she wondered if they could have heard that he'd left her. If they had, they politely kept it to themselves. After they concluded their transaction, they asked if Aila would continue to deliver their regular order, and she agreed.

When she reached home late that night, she gave the horses treats and stroked their necks as she settled them into their stalls. Then, she went into the house and found her daughters sleeping in their small room. She went into her own room, lay on her bed and slept peacefully for the first time since Robert had left. Tomorrow she would go to the sea and sing for the sea woman and her daughter.

Chapter 7

Manae was dying. She felt the energy draining from her body. She reclined against the rough, uneven floor of the cave and let her gaze wander to the sea beyond. She saw something moving swiftly toward her, too far away to make out clearly, but she could tell, by the familiar way it moved, it was not a predator. As the shape got closer, she saw that it was her mother.

Nai arrived carrying kelp and a small, struggling fish. She pushed them toward her daughter, but Manae shook her head. Her mother's green eyes seemed to bulge in desperation. Manae had never seen her mother so afraid. Even when sharks threatened them, she always remained calm as she repelled them with her scream. Nai's fear unnerved Manae and shook her from her dazed, resigned state.

She had been ready to die. She wanted to. She could no longer swim well. She was only able to move with a jerky motion that would signal her weakened state to any nearby predators.

She could no longer taste her favorite fish. When she had first tried to eat one after her injury, she'd spit it out in shock. She hadn't eaten in days. She would die soon, here on the floor of her cave, the only place where she felt safe.

Nai took Manae's hands and pulled her, trying to drag her out into the open ocean. Despite her weakness, Manae tried to resist. Her mother tugged her hands again, and Manae felt the shakiness of her own will giving way to her mother's strength.

Was her mother going to sacrifice her to a predator? There were ancient codes that governed how their kind lived, foraged and hunted, perhaps how they died, as well. If such customs existed, she knew Nai, as the leader of their shoal, would follow them. Manae sensed it would be better, even if it were slower, to die from hunger in her cave.

Nai wrapped an arm around Manae's midsection to support her and swam for them both, carrying Manae. They were headed toward the shallows, which alarmed Manae even more. One of the rules they all followed was that they must always avoid the shallows. Her mother had warned her never to venture past the area where the ocean floor sloped up steeply and the water was brighter, filled with light from above.

When they glided up to the top of the slope, Nai stopped and held Manae. They rested on the soft ocean floor. Small fish hurried away, panicked by their presence. Manae gazed in wonder at the light streaming down all around her, and she almost reached her hand up to break the surface. She had only swum this close to the surface once before, when the vessel had hit her. The memory made her feel cold and afraid, and she began to struggle instinctively to return to the familiar deep water. The slope was near enough that, if Manae could free herself from her mother's grasp, she could glide down along the sloping sand to deeper water without having to swim. But Nai held her tightly, motioning urgently for her to be still. Manae struggled a moment longer, then gave in, defeated.

Nai gently turned Manae's face toward a formation of rocks lined up in front of them like a wall and stretched out far beyond the slope. Manae could see that the rocks in the shallows broke the surface of the water, but deeper into the ocean, beyond the shallows they sat lower, beneath the water's surface. She was nearly tempted to swim in the narrow space of water between the top of the rocks and the surface of the sea. Not long ago, she would have done so without hesitation. Now, the thought frightened her much more than it tempted her.

Manae felt her mother stir slightly. Nai was alert, listening for something. Then Manae heard it: a series of strange vibrations. The vibrations were undulating over one another through the water. The harmonious sound seemed to travel through her body touching each nerve and sensor. She felt as though the vibrations were lifting her up then dropping her lightly, encircling and filling her body. She turned her face toward it and let the sensation overtake her.

When Manae tried to move closer to the source of the sounds, her mother gently held her back. Manae relented and stayed where she was, surrendering to the wondrous sensation. Mesmerized, she and Nai felt compelled to sing as well, their voices creating a silent, magnetic ambiance that rose above the waves and reached out for miles into the open sea.

When the sunlight began to dim, the sounds stopped and Nai led Manae back down to her cave. Nai left and then returned with a small fish, which Manae accepted, understanding that her mother would take her to the shallows to listen again if she ate. She could not taste the fish, but she felt light and untroubled, the wonder of what she'd heard distracting her from the despair that had plagued her since her injury.

Chapter 8

Aila stood from her cozy armchair and glanced around the sitting room at her daughters. Morgan sat, sewing, in a chair beside the fire, while Karen and Hilary played with Emily on the soft rug Aila had bought a few months earlier. They were settling in for winter, when there would be little chance to go outside and no crops to tend to. Aila was glad to see them resting and enjoying themselves.

In the past two years, since Robert had left them, they had all taken on more work on the farm. As Aila took over Robert's chores, Morgan and Hilary took turns caring for Emily, feeding the animals, shearing the sheep, spinning the wool, and gathering the grain feed for the animals to store for the winter ahead. Aila had always cooked the meals, but Morgan soon began to help her and eventually took on much of the cooking. Their lives were busy, but Aila made sure they had time for learning and for leisure.

In the evenings, she taught them by candlelight. She could see the personalities of her girls in the subjects they liked best. Morgan enjoyed math and learning all about the finances and the business of their farm. Hilary liked grammar and French— she loved to pretend to be outrageous characters when she and Karen played, leveraging exaggerated French phrases or breaking grammatical rules to make her sister laugh. Karen had taken early to reading, following along quietly when Aila taught Morgan and Hilary. Her favorite books featured stories of chivalrous men and virtuous women falling in love and fighting great odds to be together. Emily, at almost four years old, was too young for formal teaching, but she loved to draw pictures of animals and little portraits of her family. She was currently sketching

Karen with arms like twigs, holding a book. Aila smiled.

"I'm going to feed the animals," she said.

"May I help?" Morgan asked.

"No need. I'd like to stretch my legs."

"I'll start dinner soon," Morgan said, and Aila nodded. Morgan needed to feel useful. She had been eager to stay busy since Robert had left, and Aila understood that it helped her cope somehow, but she was often critical of her younger sisters when they played or when they laughed while working, and, for their sakes and hers, Aila wished Morgan could allow herself to relax a bit more once her work for the day was done.

Aila pulled on her boots, wrapped her warm coat around her and lit her lantern and stepped out into the harsh chill of the air, quickly shutting the door behind her to avoid sending a draft in over her daughters. Snow crunched beneath her boots as she walked to the little storage room along the back of the house. She gathered buckets of food and then went into the barn. The animals shuffled and chattered in the darkness beyond her lantern at the sound of her arrival. She hung the lantern on a hook and two others, watching the animals' shapes emerge with the light.

"Settle down," she said soothingly. "I'm here."

She fed the horses first, then the pigs and sheep.

Then, she walked to the storage closet in the back of the barn where they kept large jugs of snow that would melt into water for the animals. The door stuck and she shook it to loosen it. When it flew open, she stumbled back and, then, moved too far forward when catching her balance, accidentally kicking one of the smaller jugs over. She swore under her breath as the water spilled out, and she held her lantern with one hand as she reached down to right it with the other.

The water ran toward the back of the storage bin and she was surprised to see that it didn't stop and pool at the back wall. Worried that mice had chewed through the wood, she stepped in and looked closer. There was a square patch of wall that sat almost imperceptibly higher than the rest of the lower wall. She tapped this area of the wall and heard a hollow reverberation. Crouching to fit into the low closet, she held her lantern closer to the wall. Thin boards had been nailed around the hollow section, in a haphazard frame. Her heart leapt. Could Robert have kept a second stash of money?

Half afraid of finding an animal nesting in the wall, she tried to push the back wall in, but it held fast. She backed out of the bin and grabbed a heavy hoe. She placed the edge of the hoe under the framing and used her foot to push the handle forward until she heard it crack. Once the side frame fell off, the board behind it loosened. She pushed again, but the other three sides of the frame held it in place. She used the hoe to pry them off and the board fell forward. She lifted her lantern and peered cautiously into the gaping hole.

Inside, there were loosely stacked papers, but no money. She reached in, hoping that maybe Robert had left the deed to the land behind. She wasn't sure if she could claim it, but knowing it was here, instead of with him, wherever he was, made it seem to her less likely that he'd be able to return someday and turn them all out.

The deed wasn't among the papers; the stack consisted of old letters, and the paper felt wispy and fragile in her hands.

She sat on the floor of the barn and skimmed the first one. It was a letter from Robert's great-uncle to Robert's grandfather, telling him their father had died and inviting him to come back to the estate with his family. The affection he'd felt for Robert's grandfather was obvious, and she wondered why he'd chosen to stay here. She sifted through the letters to see if the story unfolded further, when a paper with familiar handwriting caught her eye.

She lifted the paper close so she could see it better in the dim lantern light and felt her heart drop. It was a letter from her father, dated three years after her wedding.

"Dear Aila,

I remain troubled and bewildered by your resentment toward your stepmother and myself. When you left us, we had hoped there would be many visits with you in our future, but, for these many years, she and I have written and received no response from you. I'll ask only once more—why, Daughter?

Your husband has written to us in apology and has tried to explain your animosity towards us, but I can tell that he struggles to understand it himself. You are clearly very changed by your new circumstances, and I wish I knew what we have done to offend you, or if perhaps, as your husband has suggested, by way of a possible explanation, there is a charismatic friend among your new social circle who has, for her own selfish reasons, turned your heart against us and convinced you that we are somehow beneath you.

That you would be ashamed of us because you have risen above us in station is hard for me to accept, because that does not sound like the daughter I knew, but I cannot see another explanation for your detachment.

Mr. Reed has communicated your wish that we not write to you again, though he says that we may contact him, but I do not see a reason to prolong the pain or to continue to ask after you if you truly wish to sever all ties with us.

With that, I will withdraw from the effort of trying to reach you, except to express that, should you change your mind, we will forgive you and will always be prepared to receive you. May God bless and guide you, my child

—Your father"

She set the letter down and stood. Her mind raced as she poured water for the animals and tried to make sense of what he'd written. *Risen in station. New social circle.* She shook her head. What lies Robert must have told her father in his letters! Her heart ached with regret for doubting her father.

In the first year after Robert had left, taking on his work had been a punishing mission. On days when it felt like Aila's back would break and her daughters were falling asleep, exhausted, at their evening meal, she had considered using the gold from the sea woman to hire a coach to take them back to her father's home, but because she'd thought he'd never written to her, she didn't think he would welcome her and her daughters, especially in the wake of a failed marriage.

But he hadn't really turned away from her, despite Robert's efforts to deceive them both, and she wondered if she should take the girls to her father's house.

Once they'd become used to life without Robert, Aila had been able to create routines for them here. She did sometimes have to leave them to go to the villages, and leaving them alone always filled her with anxiety, but, by now, she knew the fastest routes to the closest safe villages, and she was always back by nightfall. Over the past summer and autumn, she had bought bookshelves, new chairs, linens, mattresses and other decorations for the house to make it more comfortable for them all, and she liked the contrast of the plain exterior to the relatively opulent, cozy interior—it was like a secret only she and her daughters shared. While the cottage was not as well-appointed as her father's house, and he did have more rooms, her daughters wouldn't be free there to feel that the house was theirs. They would always be something akin to guests.

And, even if he would have them all come and live with them, even if he and Hannah surprised Aila by giving them the run of the house, she imagined his discomfort at having to explain her return to the many curious villagers. Though she had known many of them for most of her life, they would judge her no less harshly for losing her husband than they would a stranger. Robert's abandonment was worse, in the eyes of society, than if she had been widowed, and even widows faced their share of derision for their accidental independence.

The thought of her daughters growing up amid whispers and snickers helped her decide. She would write to her father, but she and her daughters would stay here, on this windswept hill, far from other people, where they had access to well water and their own small crops, and she would raise them to be strong and free.

She sent a letter the following spring, as soon as the weather was good enough to travel to the village and post it.

She received a reply several weeks later from the post-master in her father's village. Her own, unopened letter fell from the center of the slim bundle when she broke the seal. In his accompanying note, the post-master wrote that he regretted to inform her that Dr. Barton had died several years earlier and his widow had sold the house and moved; he was sorry to say that he did not have a forwarding address for Mrs. Barton.

Aila was unable to breathe for a moment and was glad she'd opened the letter in her room, away from her daughters' eyes.

Even if Hannah had believed that Aila had estranged herself from them, she would surely have written and called her back for the funeral. Had Robert intercepted that letter, too?

The initial deception had almost certainly been his way of keeping her father from learning of the lies he'd told, but why keep her father's death from her as well, why deny her the chance to grieve? Had there been some inheritance he'd found a way to divert from her? Or had he secretly, spitefully doled out punishment because she'd failed to bear him a son?

Chapter 9

When the shallows went quiet after the first time they went to hear the vibrations, Nai had assured Manae that the vibrations would occur again. With something to look forward to, Manae had started to eat again, and soon began to recover. Nai wanted her to return to where their shoal lived, but she wanted to heal fully first, to move as well as she had before. She swam near her cave every day and grew faster and stronger, but she couldn't fully correct the strange, jerking motion of her tailfin. She sensed that the others might not welcome her if she risked drawing the attention of predators.

When she was alone in her cave, Manae found herself nurturing a dark feeling, a sensation that had nothing to do with instinct or survival. She thought of the giant, dark vessel that had appeared suddenly behind her and hit her so violently. Nai had explained to her that land creatures had controlled it. She knew her mother and the others had seen these types of creatures before and had even helped them survive when they'd fallen into the ocean, but they didn't belong here. If they couldn't survive on their own, if they needed dangerous machines to traverse the ocean, they shouldn't enter it. Tortoises, dolphins and whales often swam near the surface. She wondered how many of them the land creatures had maimed or killed.

She worked toward healing with two intentions. First, she would hear the vibrations in the shallows again, because when she'd listened to those sounds and sang along with them, she'd found the only peace she'd known since her injury. Her second intention filled her with vengeful satisfaction and drove her to push herself harder toward recovery; she would find and destroy any land creature who entered her ocean.

***

Encouraged by Manae's recovery, Nai attempted to reintroduce her to the shoal. The others circled her to signal acceptance. They all swam to deeper, colder waters, where the frantic back and forth motion of the turbulent waves trapped small schools of fish, making them easy for the shoal to catch and eat. After they ate, they circled around one another, enjoying the rolling sensation created by the rough surface waters above, and pulled Manae in to play with them. She surrendered happily to their affection, reminded of the excitement she'd felt on similar excursions in the past.

Nai halted them suddenly with a short cry. She sensed warm blood in the water. They all drew close in formation around her, pulling Manae in with them so she wouldn't be left exposed beyond the fringe of the group. They knew sharks would appear soon, attracted by the blood.

The first of the sharks swam near them, curious to see if they were the source. Nai screamed, and the shark abruptly turned away. It picked up the scent of the blood again and swam away from them. They followed the sharks at a distance.

An enormous vessel, like the one that had injured Manae, was rolling into the sea as water flooded into a gash in the side. Injured, bleeding land creatures flailed in the water. Manae stared at them. They were strange looking, more like Manae and her kind than she would have expected, but they had two long appendages instead of a tailfin. They waved these appendages wildly in the water, exciting the sharks. Manae recalled her injury and felt sick with fear and panic. She drifted towards the back of the shoal.

Suddenly, the group around her seemed galvanized, and they moved, one by one toward the land creatures. Manae stayed behind, frightened and confused. She saw one of her sisters pull a land creature away from the sharks and wrap her arms and tail tightly around it. Others did the same when they could reach them before the sharks did.

Manae understood her sisters were saving the land creatures, but she remembered the vow she'd made to herself. Despite her fear, she charged forward, moving deftly past the sharks. Instinct drew her to one of the flailing land creatures. She could sense something violent and dark in him, and anger overtook her fear. She darted toward him, sensing her mother's concern as she homed in on Manae. Nai began swimming toward her, but Manae moved as fast as she could, creating a ragged wake, and she reached the land creature before her mother could get close. She tore frantically at the creature, releasing the rage and grief that constantly haunted her. When she finished, she threw his lifeless body to the sharks that now surrounded them.

***

After Manae's violent attack on the land creature, the others in the shoal avoided her. Killing for pleasure violated their ancient code. Nai remained devoted to her, but Manae always hunted alone.

Nai accepted Manae's need for solitude and taught her how to perfect her scream, which would stun predators and give her time to escape. While the others weren't hostile toward Manae, she knew they no longer welcomed her. She saw them sometimes, swimming in groups or pairs, and felt a sad yearning.

She was only happy now when she could listen to the vibrations in the shallows. Her mother always knew when the music would happen, but Manae sometimes went to the shallows on her own during the quiet times to drift along the sand in the brightly lit water.

When the vibrations occurred and Manae and Nai sang along, Manae noticed that the giant transports built by the land creatures would sometimes pass nearer to the shallows. They were too large and deep to come close to the shore, but they came closest then, as if drawn by the sound. Sometimes the transports hit the long ridge of rough rock that stretched out from the shallows below the surface of the sea. When that happened, they sometimes tore, spilling their detritus into the sea.

Her sisters would sense the commotion and swarm in to perform their ritual on the land creatures, while Manae performed hers, her body undulating with its slight jerk from side to side, propelling her through the dark water. She sensed the creatures' fear and panic. She followed the path marked by her senses, and she always paused to decipher the direction of the ones she wanted, to distinguish them from the others. Her targets' darkness and cruel natures radiated below their terror.

Each time, Manae would find her target and wind her way through the current toward him as he struggled against the violent waves. She'd reach out her arms and pull him underwater. She would watch his eyes widen as he struggled to see her in the darkness of the sea. When he saw her face, confusion would cross his features followed by a brief, misguided expression of relief. She'd wrap her arms around his, and she'd sense that he expected her to lift him up to safety. Instead, she would squeeze tightly and pull him further down, deep into the sea, where she would attack, away from the eyes of her sisters.

Chapter 10

One warm day, Karen and Hilary took Wooly down to the beach. They were thirteen and fourteen and, finally allowed to go to the beach by themselves, they went every chance they got. Hilary had read a book about a swimming dog, and they wanted to see if Wooly would try to swim. When they reached the sand, they pulled off their boots and walked toward the water. Wooly followed them. When he felt the water roll over his foot, he jumped, let out a short bark of alarm, and backed away. Then, seeing the girls standing up to their ankles in the water, holding their skirts above their calves, he ventured in again.

This time he went in farther and began to run, splashing in the water and playing in the waves that gently rolled in around him. Delighted, Karen and Hilary chased him in the shallow water. They shrieked with laughter each time he shook his heavy coat and drenched them with sea water.

"We'll bring him every time we come down here!" Hilary said.

Suddenly, Wooly stopped running and stood, staring at a spot in the ocean several yards away, where the water was deeper and darker. His brown eyes narrowed, and he began to bark urgently and angrily, staring steadily at the distant spot. The girls rushed over to him and urged him to move, but he ignored them and continued to bark furiously.

"Maybe it's a shark!" Hilary excitedly scanned the water. Karen began frantically pulling at Wooly, trying to force him back to the dry sand. He resisted, never taking his eyes from the section of the horizon that had caught his attention.

Wooly abruptly stopped barking, ran out of the ocean, and

shook himself off. He trotted to the foot of the path that led up the hill and whimpered at the girls.

"He wants us to go home," Karen said, backing further onto the beach, out of the reach of the tide.

"What do you think it was?" Hilary asked. Without waiting to hear Karen's response, she began to walk toward the rocks. She wanted to walk far out onto the jetty to see if she could spy the shark because she felt certain that was what Wooly had seen. When she started to climb onto the rocks, Wooly barked at her.

"Hilary," Karen called. "We should go home."

Hilary reluctantly stepped back onto the beach and followed Karen and Wooly up the hill.

***

After their sisters went to sleep that night, Hilary and Karen sat on the floor by the fireplace.

"I doubt it was a shark," Karen said, gazing at the dancing flame.

"What do you think it was?" Hilary asked, thrilled to be able to discuss the strange incident on the beach.

"I think he saw the sea woman."

***

Later that summer, Aila noticed Wooly was barely eating his food. She watched as he gave his meal a disinterested sniff and ambled a few feet away to lay down in the cool dirt under the shade of the eaves. He began sleeping most of the day, and his legs began to quiver whenever he stood for long.

She saw that Morgan noticed, too, watched him carefully every day, and she worried for her daughter. Though he was an old dog now, Wooly always danced with joy when he saw Morgan, and he seemed to sense when she felt downhearted, and lavished affection on her whenever she needed it. When she sewed, he sat at her feet, ignoring her sisters' invitations to sit by them instead. She often paused in her work to lean forward and rub his head, his long hair soft against her fingers, and he basked in her attention.

64

Aila knew Wooly would not get better. She could see he was in pain, knew it would get worse for him in the months ahead. In her years as a farmer, she'd learned to spot disease in an animal. She would never have admitted it to her daughters, because she wanted them to understand the business value of livestock and not become too sentimental about them, but she'd wept every time she'd had to put an animal down. Dispatching Wooly would be the hardest because he'd inserted himself into the family, and particularly into Morgan's stoic little heart. As she looked into the rheumy, weary eyes of the tired old dog, Aila resolved to monitor Wooly's condition and decide what to do before October.

***

In early September, while Morgan went to work in the field with Karen, Hilary went to the barn to lead out the sheep. She found Wooly lying on his side on the floor of the barn, panting heavily. She dropped the bucket she'd been carrying and sank down beside him, petting him and murmuring words of comfort. She fetched water for him from the well outside the barn and tried to persuade him to drink. He ignored it and his breathing began to slow to a soft wheeze. Hilary realized what was happening and yelled for Emily and her mother, but neither heard her call. With tears blurring her vision, she placed the dog's head in her lap and stroked his soft fur. He shuddered against her, and she could feel the life drift out of him. Hilary cried out for her mother again, and Aila rushed into the barn.

Aila gently eased the dog's body from her daughter's lap and helped Hilary to her feet. With an arm around Hilary's shaking shoulder, Aila guided her into the house, sat her in a chair and poured her a cup of tea. Hilary sobbed into her hands.

When Morgan and Karen returned for the midday meal, Aila told them what had happened. Morgan rushed to the barn, and Aila followed her, explaining that she had disposed of the dog's body. Morgan whirled around, her eyes filling with tears.

"He was dead when you found him?"

"Hilary found him moments before he died," Aila said. "He

was suffering, and she soothed him. She held him while he passed."

"Why didn't she come and get me?" Morgan moaned.

Before Aila could reply, Morgan's grieving mind began to turn the few facts she had about Wooly's death into an indictment against her younger sister.

"How could she do this to me?"

Aila was taken aback as she watched Morgan's face redden with anger. Morgan ran toward the house and burst inside. Her sisters sat at the table, food before them, waiting for Morgan and Aila to return and join them. The sight of Hilary calmly waiting to eat infuriated her.

"Why didn't you come and get me?"

"It happened too fast. I called for Mother and Emily, but they couldn't hear me."

"He wanted me! Not you! You always hated that I was his favorite!"

Hilary stared at Morgan.

"There was no time, Morgan! He was dying! Would you have wanted me to let him die all alone?"

"Maybe he wouldn't have died if he could have seen me!" Morgan yelled. "But you're so selfish - you couldn't bear to share his last moment with me!"

"You're completely mad!" Hilary shouted back at her. She got to her feet, tears of outrage in her eyes. She stood inches from Morgan and locked eyes with her.

"Girls!" Aila said. "Stop this at once!"

Aila stepped toward them, and they moved apart, but they continued to glare at one another, each silently vowing never to speak to the other again.

Chapter 11

Early one morning, Manae swam up to the shallows without waiting for her mother. The water was finally warmer, and she was anxious to hear the vibrations.

She'd been feeling listless lately and had found herself following the shoal as they hunted and swam. She knew it made them uncomfortable to have her near, but she felt drawn to their collective motion. Now that the vibrations were set to occur again, she could retreat to the shallows and leave the shoal in peace.

The sky was dark when she arrived, and she felt sheltered by the darkness as she settled closer to the rocks than ever before. The first strains of sunlight lit the water while she was resting against a shelf in the rock, waiting. She turned towards the surface and drew back in surprise. A face was peering into the water. It was remarkably like her own, but she realized it was a land creature. She sank deeper into the water, but she couldn't bring herself to look away. This face was different from those of the creatures who fell from the broken vessels. It was round and unlined, with a gentle, curious expression and wide, bright eyes. The eyes met Manae's and widened in surprise.

Startled, Manae swam away from the rocks. She looked up through the water from further away. She could see the land creature now from a distance. Manae saw that there were three of them on the rocks. Two of them were leaning toward the water again, searching for her. She watched in wonder as they opened their mouths and created the vibrations she'd come to hear.

She was staring at them, transfixed, when her mother arrived. They listened to the songs, and Manae watched the land creatures carefully. She could hear something calling to her in one of the voices, a beautiful, beseeching sound. Watching Nai's face register surprise, she could tell her mother heard it as well.

***

Hilary and Karen lingered on the beach after spending the day singing with Aila. Hilary reclined on the sand, digging her bare feet into the grainy softness. Karen lay beside her on her stomach, looking out at the sea.

"Do you think the water feels warmer to her?" Karen asked Hilary, gesturing toward the ocean with her chin.

"I think it must."

"I wish I could see her, too. Tell me again. What was she like?"

Aside from their mother, Hilary was the only one of them who had ever seen the sea woman.

"It was difficult to see her. The water wasn't clear. But I did see a face. It was lovely, but peculiar, not quite human."

"Kind, though? Friendly?"

"Yes, I think so, but she swam away once she saw me."

Karen watched the tide roll in and wondered if the sea woman was nearby.

Chapter 12

M anae swam alone, staying close enough to the surface to pass through the streaks of sunlight filtering into the water. She amused herself by trying to cross through as many of the warm, pale rays as possible. She was moving parallel to a pod of dolphins, staying far enough to not alarm them, but enjoying the protective shelter their presence seemed to provide from sharks.

Her mother had taken her shoal to warmer waters to hunt for fish. She'd wanted Manae to go, too, but Manae knew there were often sailing vessels along the path to those waters, and she wanted to stay away from those land creatures for a while. She was trying to understand her reaction to the face peering into the water. After they'd left the shallows that day, her mother had explained to her that the land creatures on the rocks sang for her benefit, and Manae had compared their kindness to the malevolence she had sensed in many of the land creatures she'd come upon in the water. In destroying those creatures, she had always imagined she was healing herself.

And she *had* healed. Her movements were not as smooth as they had once been, but she was strong again, and she moved with confidence. Her own kind avoided her, but not because of the way she swam. Her propensity to kill for revenge repulsed them, but the first time she'd attacked, a calm satisfaction had briefly replaced the anger and fear she'd felt since the accident, and when they came upon wrecked vessels after that, she'd been unable to resist.

Lately, she'd begun to realize that the vibrations had helped her even more. She'd been prepared to die the day she first heard them, and the strange, beautiful sound—that the land creatures made *for her*—had soothed her and given her something to look forward to.

She rolled quickly in a corkscrew motion, creating a soothing current around her body. She returned to the area where her cave sat, far below, on the ocean floor. She watched the dolphins move on, heard their cheerful songs and chatter. She envied their serenity. She wished suddenly and profoundly that she could regain her own. She would go again soon to the shallows. She had to try to see the singing land creatures. If she could see them once more, maybe she would understand what to do.

***

Karen and Hilary raced toward the hill. It was the end of a long, warm day of chores and they were looking forward to walking on the sand and dipping their feet in the cool water. As they ran, they waved to Aila, who was walking back to the house from the barn. She waved back and didn't try to stop them. She knew they wouldn't be gone for long and, if they got the chance to run and breathe in the salty air of the sea, they would sleep better that night.

When they reached the beach, Hilary was disappointed to find that a low fog had blown in on top of the water, covering the sand in thick, white mist. Ten feet apart, they could barely see one another. Karen hugged herself against the chill and closed her eyes, letting the vapor dampen and cool her face.

"Let's go back up." Hilary stepped closer so she could see her sister's face.

"I'd like to stay for a little while longer," Karen said. "The cool air feels so nice."

"Well, I'm going back. Don't be too long. And don't try to swim!"

Karen watched Hilary walk towards the hill and disappear into the mist. She crossed the beach slowly, letting the sound of the ocean guide her towards the water. When she reached the edge of the jetty, she decided to crawl out onto the rocks a bit to see if the air was cooler over the water. Once she reached the midpoint of the jetty, she sat on the damp rock and put her hand in the icy water. She closed her eyes and thought of the sea woman, wondering if she might be nearby. The thought thrilled her, but it also frightened her a little, and she pulled her hand out of the water. To ease her nerves, she began to sing.

She sang softly at first, a romantic poem set to music, and then, encouraged by the cover of the fog, she sang louder, enjoying the sound of her voice as it rose and dipped along the pretty notes. Singing the flowery words made Karen imagine what it would be like to be in love, and she smiled. She looked down into the water, imagining herself gazing into the eyes of her beloved. She was startled, certain for a moment she'd actually locked eyes with someone. Reflexively, she looked away, but then quickly looked back, wondering if she was finally going to get to see the sea woman. She saw nothing except the churning water.

She wanted to believe, and the moment felt charged with the need for her to say something in case the sea woman was nearby.

"If you can hear me. I would so like to meet you. You have nothing to fear from me. I would never hurt you. I have loved you all my life, and I will always do what I can to protect you."

***

When Nai returned from her hunt with the shoal, she found Manae floating inside her cave. Alarmed at first, because Manae hadn't brooded like this since her injury, Nai was relieved once she sensed her daughter's mood was thoughtful, not somber.

She asked what Manae had done while she was gone. Instead of answering, she asked if it would be possible for Nai to turn her into a land creature in the same way they turned male land creatures to their own kind. Her question startled Nai, and Manae explained that she had come to realize the land creatures who sang to her cared more for her than her own kind did. She had gone to the shallows and one had spoken to her. Though she'd been too stunned to respond, she'd understood what the land creature was telling her, and she'd heard and felt kindness and acceptance. She knew she was different and would always be separate from the shoal, but the land creatures of the shallows loved her. They would welcome her, while her own kind shunned her.

Nai's expression was soft as she regarded her child, who had not looked so hopeful since before her injury. She considered how she might be able to help her. She explained that she could not transform her into a land creature. She didn't know if such a transformation was even possible, though she had heard a story some time ago that one of their kind from a distant shoal had managed to leave the sea as a land creature. But the same story held that she had never been seen again. Nai thought, but did not say, that she felt life on land would be painful and trying for Manae, for any of their kind. Instead she told Manae that when the land creatures were nearing the end of their lives on land, she could offer to change them and they could join Manae and her mother in the sea, where they would be rejuvenated and could live for much longer. She had done this for Manae's father.

***

Manae was disappointed to learn she couldn't change. She'd fantasized about joining her sisters on land and becoming one of them, and the thought of a new life had been exciting. But she accepted her mother's words and considered the alternative her mother had mentioned. She asked how long they would have to wait and why. Nai explained that they would have to come by choice, and they would likely wish to live most of their lives on land. They would probably not be ready to change until they were much older. Manae would have to be patient. She agreed to wait, and to watch them from a distance.

Part 2

Chapter 1

One late autumn morning before the sun rose, Aila went into her daughters' room and gently shook Hilary and Karen awake. Young women now, at seventeen and eighteen, they woke without complaint and pulled on wool-stuffed dresses and thick boots.

After they ate, while Emily and Morgan started on the farm chores, Aila, Hilary and Karen followed the path toward the cliff and made their way down the hill.

The air was getting colder; soon they would have to rely on their store of food and grains to feed themselves. They were well stocked this year, but Aila planned to make one last trip to the village for supplies so they would not have to worry about the impending winter.

They crossed the beach, boots crunching the icy sand. The waves were choppy, and iron-gray clouds lined the horizon. The girls exchanged anxious glances and hesitated before stepping out onto the rocks.

"It will be fine," Aila called to them, without looking back.

They followed her out across the rocks, half crouching, half walking, as waves raced past on either side of them.

"Do you think a storm's coming?" Hilary asked.

"Probably not," Aila said. "The sky is clear where we are."

Karen looked down into the dark, churning, water. It had been years since the foggy day she'd thought she'd glimpsed the sea woman, and she'd looked for her again many times since then but hadn't seen her. She knew she wouldn't be able to see her in such rough water, even if she were right there beside them.

Later in the day, the wind grew stronger, and fog started

rolling in quickly, rushing toward them in low gusts. In the distance, they saw a strange, ghostly shape appear on the horizon. It seemed to be moving toward them.

"What is that?" Karen asked.

"It's a ship!" Hilary said.

Aila's gaze was steady and remained riveted to the sight. After a moment, she turned toward the shore.

"Let's go back home now. I think a storm may be coming, after all. We should get back to the farm."

She led her daughters toward the shore. The wind continued to pick up, and it moaned in their ears as they walked up the hill toward home.

***

Bodies plunged, flailing, into the water. The shoal rushed in to save them. Manae had avoided scenes like this for years now, but it was so close, she felt compelled to swim closer. She felt her old instinct kick in as she swam past her mother and sisters, and she caught the expression in Nai's eyes. Manae could sense her worry, but she couldn't stop.

In the center of the fray, she paused for a moment to decipher her target. She soon sensed the cruelest one, his malevolent nature palpable even under his fear.

Then, she sensed his opposite, a benign, peaceful presence drifting without fear. She had never perceived one so light, and, suddenly, she knew what to do. She rushed toward him, feeling, as she got closer to him, the weight of her long-held anger dissolving from her mind and body. She grabbed him in her arms and swam toward the shore.

Chapter 2

After dinner on the evening they saw the ship, Hilary told her mother and sisters she was going to the barn to check on a sheep that had seemed listless earlier that week. She said she was worried it might be ill. Karen surprised her by asking to come along. Hilary took a moment to consider and then nodded. Lanterns in hand, they left the house and walked to the barn. They went into the pen and wandered through the small flock of sheep.

"Which one is it?" Karen asked.

Hillary glanced around at the animals.

"I'm not sure now," she replied, a distracted expression on her face. Then, she grinned.

"Let's go to the cliffs. The moon is so bright— I want to try to see the ship again."

Karen's eyes widened in surprise. They never left the farm after dark.

"Oh, I don't think we should..."

"We'll be back soon," Hilary assured her. Knowing Hilary would go whether she agreed to or not, Karen nodded. It would be safer if they both went.

They slipped out of the barn and ran down the path to the cliff. The wind had died down to a quiet breeze, but the night air was bitter cold. A strip of shimmering moonlight bisected the dark ocean from horizon to shore. The moon was full, bright, and so large that it looked almost close enough to touch. Karen was staring at it in wonder when Hilary let out a startled gasp.

"Look! Down there on the beach!"

Something the size of a small dolphin or a large fish had washed up on the moonlit curve of sand below the cliff. Karen wondered anxiously if the sea woman was stranded out of the water. She began racing toward the hill to make her way down. Hilary ran after her.

"Be careful, Karen! It could be a shark!"

They rushed across the sand toward the unmoving figure lying between the bottom of the cliff wall and the edge of the frothing tide.

They slowed cautiously as they got closer to it, trying to see it more clearly. Once they were close enough to see that it was a human, Hilary ran over, knelt on the ground and used both hands to roll it onto its back.

"It's a man!" She looked over her shoulder at Karen, then she touched his face and leaned forward.

"He's breathing—he's alive!"

Karen knelt in the sand beside Hilary. She looked down at the man's face. His eyes were closed, and his mouth hung open. In the moonlight, his skin looked pale blue. Though his jaw was wide and covered with the stubble of a beard, he didn't look much older than Hilary and Karen.

"His skin is so cold!" Hilary said. "He'll die out here—we have to bring him back to the house!"

Karen hesitated. They'd lied to their mother about where they were going, and to bring a strange man back to the house seemed like a further violation, but Hilary reached under his arms and directed Karen to lift his legs. She obeyed, and they heaved him up between them. He was heavy with the dead weight of the unconscious, but they were able to make it up the hill without dropping him. Once they reached the top of the hill, they paused to catch their breath, and Karen gave her sister a fretful glance when Hilary said they should move again. They carried him down the path toward the candle-lit cottage.

Morgan and Aila were outside. Karen and Hilary had been gone longer than expected, and, after finding that they weren't in the barn, Morgan and Aila had started to search for them. As Hilary and Karen approached, Morgan squinted, trying to make out what they were carrying, but Aila walked toward them, her expression hardening as understanding set in.

"Is he dead?"

"No, Mother," Hilary said. "But nearly so."

"This man is not our problem!" Morgan shouted angrily, stepping up to stand beside Aila. "You should have left him where you found him!"

"Left him to die?" Hilary stared at Morgan. "Are you that heartless?"

Aila looked uncertain, as they had never seen her before. Hilary and Morgan glared at each other, and Karen stared at the ground.

"Bring him into the house," Aila said, finally, walking away from them. "We'll try to get him on his feet and send him on his way—or we may have to see him die in our house."

Heartened by her mother's mercy, Hilary stepped quickly forward, and Karen nearly fell. She recovered her footing, and they carried the man into the cottage. They lowered him carefully onto the rug in front of the fire.

"By the looks of him, he'll die soon enough," Morgan whispered to Aila.

Aila shook her head, not wanting to hear her daughter speak of death.

"Where was he when you found him?" she asked Karen and Hilary.

"He was lying on the beach," Hilary said.

"Was he the only one?" Aila asked.

"Yes."

"The current runs south and the ship was south of the jetty. It doesn't make sense—unless..." Aila's voice trailed off, and she shook her head. She looked troubled.

What do you mean, Mother?" Morgan asked, but Aila sighed and walked into the kitchen. Morgan rushed at Hilary and Karen.

"What's the matter with you? We don't need another mouth to feed this winter! And this man could be dangerous! Or— what if he dies? Do you look forward to disposing of him? What were you thinking, running off to the beach at night? Upsetting Mother? You stupid, thoughtless girls!"

Karen, who had been gently stroking the man's hand, trying to warm it with her own, began to cry. Hilary, who held his other hand, ignored Morgan's outburst and said gently to Karen, "Will you go and get some more blankets? We have to get the wet clothing off him."

Aila rushed back into the sitting room.

"I'll take care of that," she said, crossing the room swiftly. "Hilary, heat up the kettle, and we'll make a broth. He'll need it if he comes to."

Morgan left the room. When Karen handed Aila the blankets, Aila told her to go and help Hilary prepare the broth.

Aila covered the young man with a blanket and worked beneath it to remove his wet clothes. She laid them by the fire to dry and tucked the blankets around him. His lips and cheekbones were losing the bluish tinge that would have meant certain death if he'd been outside much longer. She searched his face for some sign or indication of who he was and why, against the odds of the long, treacherous jetty and a southbound current, he had washed up—or maybe been placed—on their tiny beach.

***

The cottage had been carefully constructed to defend its inhabitants against the cold winters, with clay between the stones in the walls and a thick tile roof. Robert Reed's grandfather had been a meticulous builder, and Aila knew the house had meant a great deal to him. Though modest, the cottage featured more practical comforts than most of the homes in the villages Aila visited when she sold wool.

As the years passed, she'd often wondered how Robert could have left this place, abandoning it along with his family. She had become so attached to the house and to their way of life that she knew, if he tried to return and forcibly take it from them, she would be willing to kill him if she had to in order to keep it. It had been his home once, but she had kept it up all these years, and it had nearly broken her to maintain this haven for her daughters.

There had been several days, when she had worked herself to the point of exhaustion, her mind hazy and her eyes blurred, when she'd sensed a sudden change in the air and had felt instantly soothed and encouraged. She'd wondered then if the sea captain was sending her a message of support. She sensed he would have preferred her to Robert. She was sure of this somehow.

She wondered now what the captain would have done if a stranger had landed unexpectedly on his beach when the cottage had been his own beloved refuge.

**

The thought of a strange man waking up in their house while she and her daughters slept deeply unnerved Aila, so she and Hilary took turns staying awake to watch over the stranger wrapped in blankets on the rug. They'd agreed to wake the other if he stirred. Hilary did not think to share her mother's concern—she wanted to be the first to see his eyes open so she could ask him who he was and what had happened to him.

**

The next morning, the man woke up. He looked around in dazed surprise and saw Aila and Hilary watching him.

"Hello," he rasped, and winced in pain.

"You have seawater in your throat," Aila told him, standing up. "My daughters found you on the beach below our cottage last night and brought you inside. Are you in much pain?"

"I'm in some pain, ma'am, yes. My ankle hurts... and my head."

He started to sit up, and the blanket fell away exposing his bare shoulder. He quickly pulled the blanket up to cover himself.

"Your clothes are drying there beside you, near the fire," Aila told him.

"Thank you," he said again, holding onto the blanket as he shifted his weight. Hilary, unfazed by his modesty, knelt beside

81

him on the floor. Startled, he backed away from her.

"How did you wind up on our beach?" she asked.

Before he could reply, Aila asked, "Where are you from? We'd like to help you get home."

"I come from Chesley. My name is Henry Northam. I'm a sailor, and we were a few days away from our home port near Chesley when our ship capsized. We hit some rocks and the ship began to take on water. I was asleep below deck and heard shouting. I came up and everyone was rushing around. I remember stumbling, and I must have hit my head and fallen into the ocean."

Emily walked into the room and stared in surprise, stepping backward quickly and bumping into Karen, who caught her. Henry smiled kindly at them and glanced over his shoulders to ensure the blanket was fully covering him.

"I'm Mrs. Reed, Mr. Northam, and these are my daughters," Aila said. "We must begin our day, and you should rest. We'll give you privacy so you can dress while we're out of the house. I'll return soon to give you some broth."

"Thank you, Mrs. Reed...thank you all," he said, giving them a gentle nod.

***

Once the girls and their mother left the house to begin their daily chores, Henry tried to stand to get dressed, but a searing pain radiated through his ankle and lower leg as soon as he put pressure on them. He sat on the floor, grabbed his clothes, which were now dry and warm, and dressed himself under the shelter of the blankets.

Once dressed, he pulled himself up into a chair, careful not to agitate his injured leg. His head ached, and he felt dizzy. Aila had left a pitcher of water for him, and he drank some, the pain in his throat from the salt-water he'd swallowed reminding him to drink slowly. He tried to clear his head. He took a breath, and a coughing fit wracked his body.

He heard the front door whine open, and while he coughed, a blanket was draped over his shoulders, and he gratefully pulled it tight, turning his head to watch through the tears in his eyes as Aila moved toward the small kitchen.

"I'm making you some broth," she said. "It will soothe your throat."

He leaned back in the chair and closed his eyes. He wondered why he hadn't noticed the burning in his chest when he'd first awoken. Perhaps he'd been distracted by the shock of finding himself here in this tidy little home, surrounded by women. Aila handed him a steaming mug of broth, which made him realize how hungry he was. She sat in a chair beside him.

"Drink slowly,' she said. The rich broth warmed his throat and chest as he drank it.

"You nearly died last night." She spoke with the concerned and slightly accusatory inflection of a mother, and, though he was safe and wrapped in a warm blanket in this comfortable little cottage, Henry felt a sudden powerful longing for his mother and his own house. He felt more homesick now than he'd ever felt, even when he'd been out at sea, surrounded by men who were strangers to him.

"You'll want to be getting home," Aila said, as if reading his thoughts. "The day after tomorrow, I'm going to a village several hours from here. I'll take you with me. Someone there will know how to help you get home, and I'll give you some money for your coach fare."

"I appreciate that, Ma'am. I am sorry to have to impose upon you for the fare. I'll take down your address so I can repay you as soon as I get home."

"That won't be necessary, Mr. Northam," she said, standing up. "If you'll excuse me, I have work to get back to."

She went outside, shutting the front door firmly behind her.

***

A few hours later, Henry woke from a nap to a silent house and, with a keen sense of dismay, he realized he needed to relieve himself. He tried again to stand and discovered that the pain in his ankle felt even worse than before. He slid from the chair to the floor and began to crawl toward the front door, hoping the privy would be close by. When he'd almost reached the door, it swung open.

"Are you trying to escape us?" A tall young woman stared down at him from the doorway. She hadn't been with the others at breakfast. He felt foolish lying at her feet, and the blatant hostility in her eyes startled him.

"Hello," he said. "My name is Henry Northam. I arrived here last night. Your sisters rescued me."

"I know." She leaned against the doorjamb, blocking his path.

"Morgan!" Hilary stepped into view outside the door. "Why are you standing there staring at him like a cow?"

Morgan scowled at her.

"Get out of the way so I can help him!" Hilary grabbed Morgan's arm and pulled her out of the doorway. Morgan stumbled backwards, glared at Hilary and stomped off toward the field.

Hilary crouched down beside Henry.

"You can't walk?"

"No. I think my left ankle's broken. The pain is terrible."

"Is the right one sound?"

"Yes, I think so."

"Give me your arm, then."

He obeyed, and she placed his arm over her shoulders. She braced herself against the wall and began to pull him up as he tried to stand on his uninjured leg.

"I don't want to hurt you—I'm sure I'm quite heavy," he said.

She gave him a wry look.

"You were heavier last night with sea water in your clothes. I can lift you. Don't worry."

With a soft grunt, she hoisted him up. His right leg felt shaky, but he was able to rest his weight on it. Despite her assurances, he tried not to lean too heavily on her.

"Where were you trying to go?"

"The privy," he admitted, reddening with embarrassment. He did not see a way around telling her.

"Of course," she said, with a friendly laugh. "I should've realized. Come on, then."

She helped him outside. Between the house and barn, the privy was raised up on wood planks and had a thick door to shield occupants from the wind. It was far less modern than the facilities at his house, but it was clean and fairly warm inside. Hilary waited outside for him. He'd been amazed to learn that she and her sister had carried him up from the beach. He couldn't imagine any of the women he knew being able to do such a thing.

As Hilary was helping him back to the house, they heard a burst of childish laughter coming from the barn.

"That will be Emily trying to catch the chickens." Hilary smiled. "She feeds them and then chases them around."

She helped him back inside and settled him in the chair by the hearth. She poured him some tea and draped blankets over his lap and shoulders.

"I'd better get back to my chores. You should rest."

Henry was surprised to realize how exhausted he felt. With the memory of her friendly smile, he drifted once again to sleep.

Chapter 4

Hilary carried a tea tray to Karen and Henry and sat with them near the hearth. He'd been with them over a week, and the three of them had fallen into a routine of having tea together every day after the girls finished their morning chores.

"I wish I could help you with your work," he said. "I feel like such a burden. As soon as I can walk, I'll help—or try to make my way home."

"You're not a burden to us. And it wouldn't be safe to try to travel this time of year," Karen said.

"And we'd miss your stories of life at sea if you left." Hilary loved hearing about his life, so different from hers. The youngest of three sons, he had lived with his widowed mother and his brothers on their estate, not far from the ocean. He'd ridden out to the beach every chance he could get as a child and taught himself to sail a small boat he'd built and kept near the shore. Two years before he washed up on their beach, he'd convinced his eldest brother, Charles, to allow him to join the Royal Navy.

"Will you return to your post once you heal?" she asked.

"Yes, if they'll have me back. Though, it may be a while before I'll be able to sleep easily on a ship again. I wonder if I'll always be thinking of the wreck."

"You must have been so frightened," Karen said.

"Not as much as you'd expect, but only because it all happened so quickly. I was asleep in my bunk, and, when I heard the commotion, I ran up on deck. Before I could make much sense of it, I was in the water. It was almost like a dream—I must have hit my head pretty hard. The next thing I knew, I was here, safe in your cottage."

"It's remarkable you made it to shore," Hilary said, considering how strange it was that he'd been the only member of his crew to wash up on their beach. She, Aila and Karen had gone back to the cliff several times in the days after they'd found him to check for others.

"It is, and I'm so thankful you found me." He frowned slightly.

"What are you thinking about?" Hilary asked, leaning forward.

"I think I can almost remember—I'm beginning to—or imagine, perhaps—something more," he said, leaning forward as well. "I remember moving through water quickly. Perhaps I swam?"

The girls exchanged glances.

"But I'm sure I was moving very fast," he said slowly, searching his memory.

Hilary stared at him with growing apprehension. She believed she knew how he had made it to shore. She and Karen had suspected when they found him. He didn't seem to have fully worked it out, and Hilary suddenly hoped he wouldn't recall the truth.

"Maybe a dolphin pulled you to shore!" she suggested, her eyes catching Emily's surprised glance. Emily had been sitting quietly nearby, but Hilary could tell she was listening intently. Though Emily, who hadn't yet mustered the courage to even speak to Henry, was unlikely to burst forth with information about the sea woman, Hilary's eyes implored her to keep silent.

Unaware of the silent communication between the sisters, Henry considered Hilary's theory.

"Maybe it *was* a dolphin. That would explain the speed. The strange thing is, though, the more I think about it, I recall a feeling of being carried, held. How could that be?"

"One of your shipmates?" Morgan said, suddenly and somberly, from where she sat sewing at the table in the alcove. Emily and Hilary stared at her. The suggestion was ghastly, hinting that Henry might have been rescued by someone who had then drowned. Morgan kept her gaze on the dress she was mend-ing, but Hilary could sense her dark satisfaction as Henry's face clouded over with grief and guilt.

***

Hilary slept poorly that night. She felt sorry for Henry, and she also felt strangely culpable. She thought of how his ship had seemed to turn toward them that day, to move closer to where they'd been singing, as if drawn to their songs. On the face of it, it didn't make sense —their voices surely couldn't cross such distance —but sometimes when she sang, a strange hypnotic sensation did seem to surround her, to lull and comfort her so much that she felt reluctant to leave the damp air and the hard perch of the rocks at the end of the day.

***

Karen had seen the heartache in Henry's eyes. She'd kept quiet about the sea woman, but, lying in bed that night, she felt terrible for him. The thought of a shipmate dying while trying to save him would probably torture him forever. Once she was sure she could trust him, she would tell him the truth. She would find a moment to be alone with him, swear him to secrecy and tell him then about the sea woman. She imagined a look of relief crossing his handsome face, and she smiled to herself in the dark.

Chapter 3

On the day she planned to take Henry to the village, Aila woke to the howl of a fierce wind. She rushed to the window and her heart sank. Thick snow covered the ground outside, and more snow was falling fast. It was the beginning of a storm, much earlier in the season than usual.

Aila hurried to wake her daughters. They dressed quickly and rushed to work. Emily and Karen led the sheep into the winter barn and began to gather the stores of feed. Morgan and Aila boarded up the weaker spots in the barn walls to shore the structure against the wind. Hilary brought the cows into the winter barn, and then went to pump water into large jugs. Her sisters would help her carry them to the house. Next, Emily, on Morgan's shoulders, used a long, heavy branch to push snow off the roof. Aila and Karen brought in stores of coal and firewood, piling it all in a corner of the main room.

The cupboard was soon bursting with the grains they'd brought in. The stores of provisions piled in various sections around the house made their stockpile seem abundant, but they all knew the winters could be long and it was easy to underestimate what was needed for the five family members as well as the animals.

**

The preparations whirled around Henry, who felt miserable about his inability to help them. He tried several times to ignore his injuries and get up to help, but fell each time, searing pain grounding him. He sat by the fire and, when the women finally came in, Karen apologized to him for not being able to feed him sooner. Morgan glared at her.

Before he could protest that he would never have expected

them to forgo what needed to be done on his account, Morgan gave him a sharp look and said, coldly, "Karen, we need to focus on doing what *needs* to be done, not playing servant to this stranger."

"Clearly, he isn't enjoying himself at our expense, Morgan. And Karen was only being cordial—leave her alone," Hilary said.

"I'll be on my way as soon as I am able," Henry assured Morgan, who ignored him. Aila sighed deeply. Usually, once the first heavy snow of the season fell, she halted her trips to the village, and they all settled in for winter.

"I'd hoped to take you today, but there's no way we can make the journey in this weather. It's early in the season for a storm like this, but it may be the start of our winter. Let's hope this storm is followed by a thaw."

***

To Aila's disappointment, after the first storm abated, the weather remained frigid and other storms followed, obscuring the roads and preventing travel. Winter had indeed come early.

Chapter 5

Once Henry could put weight on his leg, he insisted on helping with the chores. He was thinner and weaker than he had ever been before, and he felt humbled by the Reeds' strength and determination. They never complained about the work they had to do or the small portions of their rationed food.

Even this harsh winter, which had surprised them by coming so early, hadn't found them completely unprepared. They were so well-aware of what needed to be done, they'd simply started earlier and worked faster. Except for Morgan, who seemed to resent him more with each day, they welcomed Henry's help, but even Hilary and Karen had laughed good-naturedly at his initial attempts at chivalry. They didn't expect him to do things for them they could do themselves, and it seemed ludicrous that he should offer, rather than choose an open task.

When it came time to slaughter one of their cows to provide meat for the winter, he offered to do it, to spare Aila the trouble and the sadness he imagined she might feel at having to kill one of her own animals. He had seen the girls treat their livestock with affection, almost like pets. But when he asked Aila to allow him to do it, she stared at him in surprise

"Do you have experience slaughtering livestock?" she asked him.

"Not much," he admitted, unsure if his hunting experience would be a fair example.

"Then why would you want to attempt it?"

"Well, so you wouldn't have to do it. I imagine it might be painful for you to kill your own animals."

"I'd rather do it," she replied. Her subtle nod acknowledged the kindness of his gesture as she dismissed the offer. "I can put the animal down quickly and avoid its misery, which seems better to me than the chance of it suffering at the hands of someone with less practice."

Her explanation moved him, and from then on, Henry did whatever he could to help. He cooked in turn with the girls, learning quickly and making few mistakes. He cleaned, learned to mend fabric, cleared the roof and tended to the animals. He slept deeply each night, his energy spent by the labors of the day, and he was humbled to learn that, to conserve energy since their store of food had to last them through the winter, the girls actually worked less in the winter than in other seasons.

***

In the evenings, they all sat by the fire, and Henry became better acquainted with the family, especially with Hilary and Karen.

Karen was the mildest of the girls and reminded him of the girls in his social circle. She was soft spoken and seemed to daydream often.

Morgan remained aloof towards him, holding tightly to her resentment.

Emily spoke to him much more often than she had at first. She peppered him with sweet, childish questions about the many horses and dogs his family kept. She loved his stories about fox hunts, especially those in which the fox eluded the dogs and hunters. She asked him questions about his childhood, what games he and his brothers had played, and what books they'd read. She was fascinated by his stories of governesses and schools. She knew no other children her own age and could hardly imagine being surrounded by enough to fill a class. Henry tried to temper Emily's wistfulness by explaining that not all the boys in his classes were worth knowing, and some were quite rotten. She loved to hear the stories of the rotten boys most of all, and she would giggle in disbelief as he told her tales of their mischievous pranks and subsequent punishments. She was charmingly relieved to learn that Henry had always been a dutiful pupil and good citizen.

Henry knew Aila was uncomfortable having him in her house. A strange young man living in a house with five women was not ideal, was even unseemly, but he didn't think it was the main reason for her discomfort, since their way of life was far removed from the laws of conventional society. He couldn't be sure what bothered her about his presence, and he could not seem to get to know her well at all. Even as they passed many days in such close quarters, she became no more familiar with him, and he imagined he would be driven off in her wagon and set on the street of some village with a stranger's farewell, even if many months passed before they parted.

Hilary was the one he could imagine considering a close friend. He felt he knew her well already. He felt a kinship with her and a delight in her presence that reminded him of the joy he felt in the company of his beloved eldest brother. He loved her forthright, fearless nature. She was strong, like her mother, but she was also joyful and boisterous. She loved to laugh and tell stories. She was affectionate with Emily, who clearly responded to her warmth and love. Hilary had cheerfully taught him how to do all the tasks necessary to keep the farm running and survive through the winter. She was a patient and thorough teacher, and he knew she wanted him to succeed so the others would see him through the same friendly eyes as she did. When he did leave, he would miss her.

***

Late one evening, when her mother and sisters were asleep, Karen slipped from the bed she shared with Hilary. She crept to the door into the main room, her heart pounding. Henry was lying on the rug beneath a blanket, but she could see by the firelight that his eyes were open. He looked up in surprise as she crossed the room and sat beside him on the floor.

"Is anything the matter?" he asked.

She smiled at his concern.

"No. I wanted to speak with you alone."

He looked puzzled, and she regarded him for a moment while

she considered exactly what to say.

"I wanted to let you know you were not rescued by a man from your ship."

"How could you know that?" he asked, gently.

The softness in his deep voice caused a stirring lightness in her chest.

"It was a sea creature—a—a benign sea creature. A woman, really, with a face and arms like a human, but with the tail of a fish. Before you protest, I can tell you Hilary has seen her, too."

He stared at her. As a sailor, he'd heard many stories of sirens and mermaids, told with passion and conviction by older sailors who had crossed the seas many times. He had listened with the skepticism of a modern young mind, never having seen any of these romantic creatures himself, but Karen's intense belief mirrored that of the some of the sailors he'd known.

"You've seen it—her?"

"Yes."

"How amazing." He smiled, not sure if he believed her, but grateful to her for trying to make him feel better.

Karen sat beside him, watching his face. She was leaning toward him, and he was suddenly intensely aware of how close she was, the sleeve of her soft white sleep shift brushing his arm. Her long, fair hair was loose, spilling over her shoulders and down her back. Her large dark blue eyes gazed into his. He could reach his hand out and gently touch her cheek, and he sensed she would allow it, welcome it. But, in the same moment he considered it, he dismissed the idea, ashamed of himself and afraid for her. She sat here so close beside him, and her innocence was so complete she saw nothing untoward in it.

He drew himself up into a more formal posture, shifting subtly away from her.

"Thank you for telling me this, Miss Reed," he said, smiling gently. "Now, I don't want to get you into any trouble with your mother, so I think you should go back to your room."

She looked startled, as if woken abruptly from a dream. She averted her eyes from his and bowed her head. Then she moved away from him, stood quickly and walked toward her room without looking back.

Chapter 6

Hilary and Henry finished their work in the barn and stepped outside into the cold afternoon air. The snow was thick on the ground, but the sun was shining.

"Do you feel well enough to walk to the cliff?" she asked.

"Yes."

The trek was harder in the snow than it would have been on grass, but when they finally reached the cliff's edge, the view was a glorious reward.

The ocean glimmered, and the snow-covered beach surrendered its shore to the sapphire waves rolling over it and back out again. The jetty looked like an unfinished bridge to the horizon.

"It's beautiful." He looked down at the beach. "Is that where you found me?"

"Yes." She pointed to the spot between the waves at the bottom of the hill. "Right over there."

"I still can't believe you and Miss Karen carried me up. It's even farther than I'd imagined! And the path looks so uneven."

"It's not bad when there's no snow. We've walked it so many times—we've worn a pretty smooth trail. And you can refer to my sister as 'Karen'. We are not so formal here." She grinned.

"Do you go down there a lot?"

"When the weather's warm. The air feels so nice by the water —and the sand is so soft. If you'd like, when spring comes, we can try to go down there before you leave."

"I'd like that."

He was surprised to feel downhearted when she mentioned his departure. He stared out at the sea and wondered if any of his shipmates were down there somewhere beneath the rolling waves. He looked at Hilary.

"Karen told me a mermaid rescued me." He saw her eyes widen. "Please don't be mad at her for telling me. She thought it would make me feel better. I thought she must have been making up a story at first, but she was so sincere—and the more I think about that night, I find myself believing it might be true."

She looked at the ocean.

"Will you tell me – is it true?" he asked.

She met his gaze, and he was struck by the storm in her eyes.

"It's true."

"Karen said you've seen her. What was she like?"

"I never told Karen this, but it frightened me. I was on the jetty, and she suddenly appeared in the water. Her face looked almost human. She had long waves of hair and large eyes. I was so startled—I had to stop singing when I saw her."

"You were singing?" He smiled at the thought of her sitting on the jetty singing sweetly to herself.

"Karen didn't tell you I was singing?" She frowned.

"No, she only told me you saw her once."

"Oh." She looked down, then back toward the house. "We should get back to the farm."

He offered her his arm. When they reached the end of the path, near the cottage, they stepped apart, and he noticed her anxious expression.

"What's wrong?" he asked gently.

"Nothing."

She jogged ahead of him into the house and began busily preparing dinner. Bewildered, he followed and watched her from the doorway.

After dinner, she claimed she wasn't feeling well and went to bed early instead of joining her family and Henry in the sitting room.

***

Hilary placed a blanket over the horse's back. She'd been in the barn for hours, walking the cows, sheep and horses, one by one, back and forth down the long narrow barn. She hadn't spoken to Henry since dinner the evening before, but his confused expression after she'd left him in the doorway had been in her mind all day.

In the few weeks he'd been with them, she'd gotten to know him, and she felt guilty for avoiding him. She knew he felt more comfortable with her than with the others. The one brief barrier to their friendship had been his initial rigid sense of decorum, and she chuckled to herself whenever she recalled finding him on the floor that first day, trying to drag himself to the privy on a broken ankle instead of calling for help.

If she could find him, laugh with him about the usual everyday things they always joked about, the strangeness would disappear. She left the barn and went through the house and out the back door. He was in the storeroom behind the house, measuring out buckets of food for the animals.

"Oh! Hello," she said, as if she'd wandered in instead of searched him out.

He looked up and smiled when he saw her. She smiled back at him.

"I've finished exercising the animals. Can I help you feed them?"

"Thank you." He pushed two of the filled buckets toward her and lifted the other two. They carried the food out of the house, toward the back of the barn.

"Are you feeling better today?" She noticed the way he squinted slightly when he was concerned.

"Yes," she said. "I was tired yesterday."

"I want to apologize. I didn't mean to tease you—about singing. I didn't think it was funny. I found it rather sweet—I am sorry." He looked so uncomfortable that she would have teased him if she weren't so anxious to change the topic.

"It's fine. Really. I'm embarrassed, so maybe we could agree not to talk about it?" she said, with a friendly laugh. She pressed her lips together and opened her eyes wide, pulling a face she'd often used to amuse Emily and Karen, and he laughed in surprise.

"Fair enough. My father always said a wise man knows when to let a topic die."

"Did he really?" She laughed.

They walked into the barn and started pouring the buckets of grain for the animals.

"He did – honestly. He was a great conversationalist—and a wise man himself."

His smile didn't falter, but sadness clouded his eyes.

"Were you very young when he passed?" she asked gently.

"I was fourteen. It was sudden—that was the thing of it. He was there one day and gone the next. Hunting accident." He shook his head. "My brother, Nathaniel, blamed the game keeper and wanted him prosecuted, but Charles, my eldest brother, wouldn't allow it. Good thing, of course, it wasn't the poor man's fault."

"That must have been hard for you. What a terrible shock."

"Yes. I miss him. Were you quite young when your father passed?"

"I barely knew my father." She considered pretending he'd died but felt it more punishing to state what a coward he'd been. "He left us when I was a small child."

"He left—do you mean he abandoned you?"

"Yes, he ran off with some other woman, married her, though he was already married to my mother, and left us all here to die. My mother took over for him and provided for us all these years."

"I can't believe a man would do that to his family!"

The look of disgust on Henry's face mirrored her emotions whenever she happened to think of her father.

"Has he ever written your mother, sent her money?"

"No, but I know she worries he might come back someday and try to take the farm back and turn us out."

She'd never seen Henry angry before, she realized, as she watched fury contort his handsome face.

"I promise you, when I leave here, I will find him and make

sure he never takes this place from your family. Tell me every-thing you can remember about him."

***

Storm winds howled outside, confining everyone to the house. Hilary and Henry sat on the rug by the sitting room fire. Aila, Karen and Emily sat reading in chairs behind them. Henry had been telling her about his mother's and sister-in-law's frequent, day-long trips to fashionable dressmakers and their shared obsession with clothing and elaborate hairstyles.

"That sounds so dull!" Hilary laughed, shaking her head in disbelief.

"Hilary!" Karen looked scandalized, but Henry laughed.

"No, no. I agree with her!' he said. "—And that's on a regular day. When there's a party or a ball, it takes them even longer."

"I can't believe it! But does it make enough of a difference to warrant all that time and energy? They must look quite spec-tacular." Hilary's eyes sparkled.

"They actually do. My sister-in-law is very pretty, anyway, but she does seem to choose gowns that make her look quite stunning. My brother met her at a party, and he could hardly take his eyes off her the whole evening. It's the colors, I sup-pose—she often wears blues that match her eyes and it makes a lovely impact." He looked at Hilary's eyes. "If you were to wear a gown of forest green, I'm sure it would have the same effect."

She blushed, and then, he did, too. She laughed to break the strange tension, but she felt confused and uncertain.

***

For days afterward, this new feeling forced her, even as she tried to ignore it, to notice the softness in his eyes when he looked at her and the strong curve of his jaw when he smiled. She felt warm, joyful, and uncomfortably fragile, as if she might start to cry at any moment. She gravitated toward him, though she fought it from the moment she realized what was happening to her. She did not want anyone in the house, least of all him, to suspect what she was feeling. She considered, but quickly re-jected, the notion of confiding in Karen. She was afraid to say

100

the words, which would give them even more gravity and more control over her than she'd already lost.

Something else prevented her from telling Karen. She'd been part of many of their conversations around the fire, the third party in what was, initially, an equal friendship between the three of them, but since Karen had told Henry about the sea woman, she had become more and more reticent, choosing to read or sit near Aila instead of talking with Hilary and Henry. She seemed melancholy and preoccupied lately, and Hilary wondered if she regretted confiding in Henry. She wanted to reassure Karen that they could trust Henry, but she worried saying so might somehow push Karen further away.

***

The snow burned her fingers, and Karen considered climbing back up the hill. She was halfway down to the beach and her heavy dress was wet from snow drifts up to her waist. She was far enough down the hill to be out of sight of anyone at the house now, but if she went all the way down to the beach, she'd have to make her way through more snow, and she'd be drenched by the time she got there.

At least she'd made a path for herself she could use again to climb back up. She could go back now and hide in the barn to dry off. She felt the familiar urge to do what was expected of her, to climb back up, and she almost gave in. But being in the cottage, even in the barn, felt so stifling, now. And out here, even though the cold was terrible, it felt fresh and she finally felt free.

Since the night she'd told Henry about the sea woman and he'd backed away from her, she felt the sting of humiliation every day, every time she saw him. And recently, she'd noticed the way Henry and Hilary looked at one another, and her embarrassment was joined by a bewildering, hollow feeling. Even as she sat in the same room with them, day after day, she felt left behind and forgotten. Some days she was furious at Hilary. Other days, sadness clouded her mind, and her sleeves were stiff by the afternoon with tears she'd had to hide as she worked.

The beach was the only place she could go where no one else

could see her. Maybe if she could cry and let these awful feelings out, they would go away. She continued making her way down the hill as the icy wind slapped her cheeks.

Snow covered the sand, but was lighter on the damp jetty, so she walked to the rocks and brushed the snow aside. She sat on the rocks and watched the waves until she felt calm. Then, she stood and walked further out, kicking the snow into the water. It didn't make sense to be jealous of Hilary—when Henry left, her heart would break.

But, in those first days after they'd found him, Karen had hoped something exciting and romantic, something like what she'd read about in books, might happen to her. Before then, she'd always accepted that she'd remain on this farm for the rest of her life. Now, instead of going about her days and not thinking about what lay ahead, she could see that her life would only ever be working the farm and anxiously negotiating her family's moods.

Her tears felt hot against the chill of the wind on her face. She kicked the snow harder, and she slipped. Her ankle rolled, and she fell sideways, landing on an edge of the rock that sloped into the water. She was on her knees and starting to slide sideways toward the water. Heart racing, she scrambled to get her footing and pull herself up from the slope. She made it up and sat on the rock for a moment, catching her breath.

She felt a charge in the air, like the way she could always tell, without looking up from the book she was reading, when her mother entered the sitting room. She looked down into the water. The sea woman was staring up at her. She heard words somehow inside her head, but as clearly as if they'd been spoken. The sea woman was asking if she was hurt.

"No, no. I'm not hurt," Karen said. Dazzled, she forgot her sore ankle and the chill of the wind. "Can you understand me?"

The sea woman nodded and asked why she was on the rocks alone.

"I came here because I was feeling sad and being near the ocean always makes me feel better. I thought it might help."

Karen looked into her eyes. They were like pale blue crystals floating below the surface. Her face was strangely colorless, and more youthful than Karen had expected.

The sea woman told her she understood; she came to the shallow water to be near land when she was sad. She asked Karen what troubled her.

"I feel very alone, even when I'm with my family. And I've only ever lived here on our farm, and I realized I'll never leave, never marry or live anywhere else. I think I'd like to, but, then, I don't know if I'd want to live somewhere else, to be around a lot of other people. I wonder if this makes sense to you."

It did, the sea woman told her. She had been injured and no longer felt accepted by her shoal.

"You were injured?" Karen recalled the story of the sea woman's daughter. "Was it you who met my mother?"

The sea woman explained that her own mother had met Aila.

"I know who you are! I'm so happy to meet you and so glad you're well! My mother told us, years ago, that you couldn't swim back then, and your mother was beside herself. My name is Karen."

Manae told Karen her name and thanked her for singing. The songs had given her something to look forward to when she was at her worst.

They talked a while longer, each sharing stories about what their lives were like.

When Karen's teeth started to chatter, she told Manae she would have to get back to the warmth of her house, but she asked if they could meet again the next day and how she could find her. Manae said she would stay close by and watch for her when the sun was at this same place in the sky. They said good-bye and Karen watched Manae disappear beneath the dark waves. She retraced the path she'd made in the snow and made her way home in a daze, warm with excitement, despite the wet cold. For the first time in a long time, she was looking forward to the next day.

Chapter 7

As winter began to cede to spring, the weather grew steadily calmer. One afternoon, Hilary saw her mother and Morgan exercising the horses on the long road beside the farm, getting them ready to ride out to the village soon. Tiny buds of green appeared on bony tree branches, and the road was mostly clear of snow now. The horses trotted happily, finally free of the barn, but Hilary's heart sank as she watched them.

Every other year, she'd been delighted to see the signs and little rituals that meant she'd soon be able to venture farther than the house or barn and spend more time outside again. But this year that freedom would demand a trade—she'd have to part with Henry.

They'd become such good friends, and she couldn't remember ever enjoying herself as much before he had become part of her life. She remembered basking in the warmth of the sun in the summer, enjoying the sensation of the cool waves washing over her feet, and talking and laughing with Karen. She'd loved curling up and reading a book, losing herself in the pages. These things had all been diverting, but nothing like how she felt when she was with him. Before, happiness had been a steady, comforting feeling. Now, she felt a jumping joy full of promise and excitement. The feeling was new to her and exhilarating, and she knew it would leave with him when her mother took him away.

As she listened to the distant stomping of the horses' hooves on the dirt, she worried about what life would be like without him. She let herself imagine for a moment that he might decide to stay, and the upswing of hope she felt frightened her. No, it was impossible. Even if he *would* choose to remain here in their small, rural house, rather than go home to his servants, elegant parties and fine manners, Aila would never allow it.

And, if he stayed, he would eventually learn that Hilary, his dear friend, had climbed with her sisters onto the rocks that autumn day to sing, as loudly as she could, songs that had lured his ship toward the rocks hidden treacherously below the surface of the water. He would hate her if he knew, and it hurt to even imagine the look in his eyes. No, she couldn't keep him here with her. But she really didn't know how she was going to bear letting him go.

***

Aila smiled at Morgan as they rode the horses back toward the barn.

"It feels good to be outside, even though it's still cold," Morgan said.

"Yes. This winter felt especially long." Aila patted the horse's neck.

"I'll be glad when it's just us here again. I can't seem to turn a corner in the house without tripping over Hilary and Mr. Northam huddled together deep in conversation or laughing at some private joke. Last week, I saw them coming back from the cliff, arm in arm, walking slowly, as if it were a warm summer day instead of the end of winter." She shook her head.

"They are too familiar," Aila agreed. "Even your father and I were married at least a year before we spoke so plainly to one another. I'd expect Henry to know better if what he's said about his background is true."

"Do you suspect he's lying about his family's wealth?"

"He's never come out and said that he's wealthy, has he? His stories about the horses and the house, and his speech and manner would suggest so, but, then, I've been fooled before." Aila smiled sadly.

"Well, I'll be glad to see the back of him." Morgan opened the barn door.

"I'll be taking him soon. I just hope Hilary will be able to take it in stride when he leaves."

Though he seemed as enamored with Hilary as she was with him, Aila knew he wouldn't stay, even if she would have allowed it. And, if Henry wasn't exaggerating his lifestyle as Robert had, his family would never allow him to bring home and marry a farm girl like Hilary. He must have known this, and he had no right to look at Hilary the way he did, to speak to her always as if she was the only other person in the room.

At least it would be spring and there would be so much work that Hilary wouldn't have much time to mourn his absence, though this knowledge was a small comfort when she worried about her daughter's heart.

Aila was almost certain the sea woman had delivered Henry to their shore, and it troubled her. Over the years, Aila had seen ships come as close as Henry's had, and possibly there had been similar wrecks, but no one had ever washed up on the beach. She would get Henry out of their home as soon as she could, but she worried she was overlooking something else.

Chapter 8

O ne day in late March, Aila announced over breakfast that she would be leaving for the village the following morning.

"I expect you'll be glad to get home to your family," she said to Henry.

Henry met Hilary's eyes across the table, and the urgency in his expression caused her heart to race.

***

They were busy for most of the day, stuck working apart or with one of her sisters too close by for them to have a private discussion. Finally, a moment came when they were leaving the barn and Emily, with good natured frustration at their slow pace, darted ahead to help prepare dinner, leaving them alone together on the path.

"Can we walk to the cliff?" Henry asked. Hilary knew her mother would be annoyed if they were late, but she decided, if she was meant to part with him forever tomorrow, she deserved to have one last walk with him.

The weather was mild as they made their way to the cliff.

"Shall we go down to the beach?" he asked.

They walked down the hill, stumbling and laughing lightly, but both more subdued than usual. When they reached the soft sand of the beach, they stood side by side and stared at the sea.

"This is where you found me," he said, with a gentle, grateful smile.

"Yes. I'm so glad we were walking up there."

They were quiet for a little while before he spoke again.

"Do you think she's nearby now, the sea woman?" he asked.

"I don't know. I can never tell. We can go out on the rocks and look into the water."

She gestured toward the jetty.

"No." He shook his head. Then he took her hand.

"Hilary, will you come with me tomorrow?"

She stared at him in surprise His eyes held her gaze.

"I'm asking you to be my wife. Will you marry me?"

Tears filled her eyes, and her chest tightened. Pure joy washed over her, followed by a sad realization. To take the journey with him would mean leaving everything she knew behind. But, she saw the softness in her eyes, now so achingly familiar, and felt a rush of certainty and excitement.

"I will!" she said, and his face lit up with delight and relief. They laughed and embraced for the first time. Then, he gently kissed her lips. The wonderful, lightening response of her mind and body to the warm pressure of his arms around her and his lips on hers took her by surprise. A sudden wave crashed at their feet and soaked their boots. They laughed in surprise, incapable, in that moment, of dismay.

"Shall we go and tell them?" he asked. "You'll have to prepare for the journey!"

The journey. She tried to imagine arriving with him at his home, a larger, far grander house than her cottage but she could only envision the illustrations she'd seen of fine homes. It didn't matter. In a few days' time, she would be there, able to see it for herself. They rushed back up the hill and across the field to the house.

***

The force of their joy preceded them, like a giant living thing. Aila felt it in the air, sensed what was coming moments before they entered the house together. She was at the spinning wheel at the back of the storeroom when they entered, and she kept working furiously, even as they walked up beside her.

"Mother," Hilary said at the same time as Henry said, "Mrs. Reed."

Their eagerness, and the way they stumbled over one another, made them seem so childlike to Aila, and she braced herself to hear what they had to tell her and to respond as she knew she must.

"Ma'am," Henry said. "I have asked Hilary to become my wife, to travel back home with me to be married at the chapel near my house. Unless you prefer that we marry here before we travel – in the village chapel perhaps?"

"Hilary cannot marry you," she said, as stonily as she could manage. "I won't permit it."

"But, why not, Mother?" Hilary cried out.

"I need you here on the farm to help us. You know that."

"I can send money," Henry said. "So that you could hire a lad to help."

Aila gave him a sharp look.

"If it were as simple as that, I would have hired someone myself, years ago. I don't need more money. My answer is no. Let that be the end of it."

She kept her eyes on her wool and tried not to look at their stricken faces.

"Hilary, I know you have more work to do," she said. "Please see to it."

Hilary turned and ran out of the house.

"If you won't allow her to leave, may I stay here?" Henry asked softly.

"No, that wouldn't suit us or your family. You must go home to them. And you and I both know, with Hilary's upbringing, your family wouldn't accept her as your wife. I won't send my daughter to a place where she isn't welcome, Mr. Northam. And, even if I were to let her go, even if your family did accept her, she isn't accustomed to your way of life. She's used to being free to speak her mind, to run in the fields, to—"

"I would take care of her, Ma'am," he pleaded. She shook her head.

"I gave you my answer."

"Yes, ma'am." He looked at the floor and then walked off.

***

Henry found Hilary in the barn yard among the chickens, who

were warily venturing outside after their winter internment in the barn.

"Hilary," he said.

Her eyes shimmered with tears. "I will go with you. I don't care what my mother said! If you still want me to?"

"Yes!" he cried, overjoyed. "I was so afraid I'd lose you."

They embraced and held one another tightly before stepping apart.

"We'll leave before dawn, before they all wake," she said. Then she had a thought. "Do you think we could bring Karen and Emily with us? If they'll come? I hate the thought of leaving them."

"Of course, we can! We can give them such an education—and fine dresses! Emily will have beautiful dolls and a pony of her own!"

"We'd have to take two of the horses—and some of Mother's money," Hilary said, uncertainly. She was furious at her mother, but she didn't want to steal from her.

"Yes, but, don't worry—I'll send money to replace it all—and more."

***

Inside the barn, Morgan and Emily stared at each other in silence, shocked by what they'd overheard.

"You can't go," Morgan whispered to Emily.

"I would like to play with other children."

"Don't concern yourself about it because she can't take you away."

***

Once she could elude Morgan, Emily ran toward the field in search of Karen. She saw her standing in the distance among the grazing sheep. Emily raced through the long grass toward her. Karen watched her rapid approach with alarm.

"What's the matter?" she asked as soon as Emily was close.

"Henry has asked Hilary to marry him!" Emily was breathless from her run. "And they're going to take us with them to his home! They said I'll have a pony and we'll have fine clothes!"

"Emily," Karen placed her hands on her sister's shoulders. Emily looked up at her, expectantly. "I can't leave. I don't want to leave."

The attention of the household had been so focused on Henry in the past weeks that Karen had been able to slip down to the rocks almost every day and spend time with Manae, whose descriptions of a simple life of infinite motion in the sea had painted a vivid picture in Karen's mind. Manae and her kind were not tethered to the ocean floor. They could soar above it, up to the edge of their atmosphere, where their world met hers. They could skim the soft sand of the ocean floor with their hands as they glided along, far beneath the waves. They were unaffected by weather. There were no winters to trap them indoors as prisoners of the elements.

She dreamt at night of gliding along beside Manae through her blue-green world, where the weight of things, of labor and expectations, were unknown. And once summer came, Karen would swim with Manae. Though she would have to leave the water at the end of the day, she could spend hours pretending to be free, like Manae. The anticipation had encouraged her through the short, heavy days of late winter and sustained her through the aftermath of saving Henry.

"But, Karen, we can have a better life! Receive a proper education. Maybe get married someday."
Karen shook her head gently.

"None of those things matter to me, Emily. I have all I need here."

"But I can't leave without you," Emily said, tears welling up in her eyes.

"I don't want you to leave," Karen said. "But I don't know if it would be better for you to stay either—this is such a surprise. I do know for certain that I can't go. And I'm surprised Mother has consented."

"She hasn't," Emily said. "She's forbidden Hilary to marry Henry, but they're going to marry anyway!"

"Hilary's going to defy Mother? I can't believe she'd do that!

Oh, Emily, I don't think you should go! You might never see us again!"

"I hadn't thought of that," Emily said, sadly.

She turned from Karen and trudged back toward the farm, the afternoon sun bright around her small silhouette.

***

That evening when everyone was asleep, Hilary lay awake in her bed. She was imagining her new life with Henry when she suddenly became aware of a shadow beside her. She started as the shadow closed in quickly. It was Morgan.

"What are you doing?" Hilary whispered. She glared at Morgan, who glared back.

"I know what you're planning. You think you can sneak out of here and take Emily and Karen, as if you have the right!"

Hilary fought a rising sense of panic—how had Morgan found out? She considered denying it, but she realized Morgan was stubborn enough to wait up all night to catch her in a lie. She stood and crossed to the far corner of the room. Morgan followed.

"What of it?" Hillary's voice was a shrill whisper. "I'm old enough to decide what I want to do, and Emily and Karen deserve a proper education, not to be stuck here forever!"

"What makes you think you know what's best for them?" Morgan hissed. "You've never lived anywhere else! You don't know what you're going to face out there and you want to drag them along, so you don't have to be alone when you realize what a mistake you've made!"

"What do you know about making mistakes? How could you know life isn't better somewhere else? You've never left this farm, either! You don't even read books! You have no idea what else is out there! I know what I'm facing, and if I didn't think I could give my sisters a better life, I wouldn't dream of bringing them!"

"It doesn't matter," Morgan said. "Because you're not bringing them! And you aren't leaving!"

"You can't stop me!"

Morgan returned her sister's fiery glare, and then, a small, calm smile crossed her face.

"Do you honestly think Henry will even want you to come with him once I tell him how you sang as loudly as you could out there on the rocks—and lured his shipmates to their deaths?"

Hilary flinched.

"No, Morgan. Please don't. Please, please don't."

"You're giving me no choice."

Hilary sat on the floor, her mind working frantically. She looked up at Morgan.

"I'll go alone. We'll leave Emily and Karen behind. Please don't tell him, and please don't try to stop us."

Morgan shook her head.

"No," she said. "You stay, too. I'll hold my tongue if you promise not to leave."

Hilary stood. She struggled to keep her voice calm.

"Please don't do this, Morgan. You and I have never gotten along. I know you don't like me. Imagine, if you let me go, I'll be out of your way. I won't be a bother to you any longer."

Morgan's face softened at Hilary's last remark, and Hilary felt her heart lift with hope.

"Hilary, I'm not trying to punish you. But you can't leave. You know how much it will hurt Mother if you desert us like Father did. You are so like him already."

Hilary felt stricken. She was about to protest when she saw Morgan's expression harden again. Morgan turned, walked back to her bed. Hilary climbed into her own bed beside Karen. As moments turned to hours, she knew that, though Morgan was lying there silently, she would not fall asleep.

***

Just before dawn, Hilary heard a light tap on the floor outside their room. Both girls stood, one miserable, one grim. Hilary put out a hand to stop Morgan.

"Please. Let me tell him alone. I promise this isn't a trick."

Morgan looked doubtful, but she relented with a quick nod.

For a wild second, Hilary considered grabbing his arm and bolting for the door, but she knew Morgan would race after them and shout her damning truth.

Henry was waiting beside the hearth. In the moonlight filtering through the window, his eyes were shining with excitement.

"Are you going to wake Emily and Karen?" he whispered. She shook her head sadly.

"Henry, I can't go with you."

He stared at her in confusion and alarm.

"Why not? What's the matter?"

"I can't disobey my mother and abandon my sisters."

"I love you," he said. "I don't want to leave without you."

She knew he could understand her loyalty to her family and wouldn't pressure her if she insisted on staying behind, but she could sense his confusion. They'd been so hopeful and optimistic hours before.

"I love you," she said. "But I can't leave."

Dejection clouded his features.

He took her in his arms, and she leaned on his chest. They held onto each other tightly, until they heard the others waking.

***

When Aila walked into the sitting room in the morning, Henry and Hilary were sitting opposite one another in the chairs by the hearth. They were silent, eyes downcast. When she looked up and saw Aila enter the room, Hilary stood and went into the kitchen to prepare breakfast.

"Are you ready for the journey, Mr. Northam?" Aila asked.

"Yes ma'am. Can I help you load your wagon?"

He was as courteous as ever, but Aila noticed a dullness in his voice.

"We'll eat before we load the wagon. Then we'll be on our way," she said.

After breakfast, Hilary, Henry, and Karen helped Aila prepare the wagon and hitch the horses. Aila climbed up onto the bench, lifted the horses' reins, and gestured for Henry to join her. He started for the wagon, but stopped and turned back to face Hilary, who stood beside the house with her eyes fixed on the dirt beneath her feet.

He walked over to where she stood. He lifted her hands and kissed them gently. When she looked up at him and saw the tears in his eyes, she began to sob. He fought the urge to embrace her.

Instead, he gently stroked her damp cheek. Then, he turned and walked quickly to the wagon. He climbed aboard, and Aila snapped the reigns to move the horses as soon as he sat. Then, they were off, riding away. Hilary imagined the exciting new life she had almost gotten to live racing away with them.

Chapter 9

After Henry left, Hilary worked as hard as she could, not pausing to rest. She didn't talk to any of her sisters but pushed herself silently through the day. She could not bear to consider the pain that was waiting, so patiently, to overwhelm her as soon as she stopped.

When Aila's wagon appeared on the horizon that evening, Hilary caught herself hoping wildly that Henry might be there sitting beside her, having somehow convinced Aila to allow him to return. But as soon as the wagon came into focus, Hilary could see that Aila was alone.

She turned and ran, first toward the field, which seemed too wide open, and then toward the cliff and the beach, but that was the last place they had been happy together, alone, and that was where he had asked her to marry him, where she began to hope, to believe she could be with him forever. She stood, perplexed, her mind frozen with grief, and then turned again and ran for the far side of the barn.

She slumped against the stone wall and pulled her knees to her chest. She released the anguish she had been holding back, allowing it to flow out of her in gasping sobs. It hurt, even as it escaped her, and she knew she had so much more pain within her and she might never feel better. She rocked and wailed until her eyes burned and her face ached. When she felt spent, she heaved herself up and made her way into the house to lay by the hearth, in the spot where he had slept during the months he had lived with them. She would sleep there every night.

***

Days and weeks passed, and Hilary seemed to retreat further into herself. She refused when Karen tried to coax her to visit the beach. She went outside for walks or into the barn while the rest of them gathered around the hearth. She came inside after they had all gone to sleep, and she slept in the main room, where he had slept, away from them.

***

Life in the cottage upon the hill was changing for the worse since Henry had left. Karen did not blame him, but she didn't know how to make it better. She felt stifled and overwhelmed by the tension in the house. She went down to the beach more often to seek the solace of her sea sister.

One afternoon, she lay on the rocks, looking into the ocean while Manae drifted lazily in the water beside her. She apologized for always complaining about her life.

Manae told her, in her strange manner of communicating, that she knew of a way to help Karen.

"Really? How?" Karen asked.

Manae told her that her mother could change Karen into one of their kind, and she could live in the ocean with them.

The suggestion startled Karen. Manae had told her that the Sea Women could transform a human man, but she hadn't considered the possibility that a woman could be changed. Manae's stories of life under the waves had enchanted Karen for months, and she had fantasized often about what it would be like.

"Would I be able to turn back into a human?"
Manae didn't know, but she had heard stories that only one had ever changed from her kind to human, but no one knew if she survived. She'd never returned.

"Would I be able to swim here and talk to my mother and sisters, the way you talk to me?"

Manae thought so and asked if Karen would truly consider changing. She was so excited and hopeful that Karen felt nearly ready to do it at that moment.

"I'll consider it," she said, with a smile. "I certainly will."

They parted when the sky began to darken, and Karen spent the evening thinking about Manae's offer.

Without making a dramatic change, she would never escape

the sensitivity and discomfort that seemed to plague her life. She didn't want to run away to some village, populated with strangers, who would have their own conceits and conflicts. Nor could she imagine going off to live by herself unless she could live near the sea and spend time with Manae. She lay awake all night, and as she made her way toward a decision in the deep blue of the earliest morning hours, she felt her fear give way to exhilaration.

***

One afternoon, while they worked side by side in the field, Karen said to Hilary, "You may fall in love again someday."

Hilary stared at her.

"I think that's unlikely, Karen. I don't think I'll ever be able to stop loving Henry, as much as I wish I could. And short of pulling another one out of the sea, none of us are likely to meet another man, let alone fall in love with one." She stabbed at the soil with her spade. Then, she smiled at Karen, appreciating her sister's attempt to cheer her. Karen smiled back, happy to see a hint of Hilary's old, jovial self.

"Do you remember the sailors who were on the ship with Henry?" Karen asked.

"What about them?"

Hilary's smile had turned to a wary frown. This was a dangerous topic.

"They've not all died."

"What do you mean?" Hilary stopped working and glanced toward the cliff as an image of unconscious men sprawled out all over the beach flashed through her mind.

"No, they're not down there. I've been spending a lot of time down on the rocks. I've been able to communicate with a sea woman, like mother did—"

"The sea woman spoke to you?"

"Not the one who spoke to Mother. Her daughter. She told me that her kind rescue drowning sailors."

"Are you telling me they saved Henry's shipmates?"

Hilary felt hope bubble in her chest. If it were true, she could

118

find a way to write to Henry, and maybe he would forgive her for her part in luring the ship onto the rocks.

"Yes, but not the way they saved Henry," Karen said. "They can transform men into creatures of the sea, like themselves. They must do this because they can only bear daughters and must mate to do so. They rescue drowning sailors and transform them so they can mate with them."

"They—?" Hilary stared at her sister.

"Have you seen any of the men they changed?" she asked, a strange, cold sensation passing through her.

"No."

"But they do live, survive?"

"Oh, yes. Manae told me that they're quite happy. They form packs and roam the sea together."

Hilary frowned. She wasn't sure Henry would forgive her if he knew his shipmates had been turned into sea creatures, even if they were alive. She wondered if he would even believe it. Thinking of him, something odd occurred to her.

"I wonder why they didn't keep Henry."

Karen blushed.

"He was meant to be a gift – for us."

Hilary giggled, embarrassed and amused by the implication.

"How interesting," she said. The strangeness and mystery of Karen's news ignited a remnant of her former curiosity about life.

She looked at Karen.

"You said we might meet men someday. Is that because they can be turned back into humans? Is that what you meant?"

Karen shook her head. She opened her mouth but hesitated a moment before speaking.

"No," she said. "They probably can't be turned back. But the Sea Women could transform a human woman."

Hilary's eyebrows rose.

"Are you suggesting we might let them change *us*? Karen, we couldn't!"

Karen smiled.

"Imagine," she said, her eyes sparkling with more excitement than Hilary had ever seen. "No more work, no chores. Just gliding through the water and playing every day! There's a kind of palace the Sea Women have built at the bottom of the sea. They live there when they want, but they're free to explore the entire ocean."

"You sound as if you've given this a lot of thought."

Hilary was frightened by the fervor in her sister's voice. She recognized the sound of a decision made.

"We would never be able to see you again," she said. Karen smiled gently.

"Of course, you would. I'll stay close by. You can sit on the rocks and call for me and I'll come. And you can always change, too, later, if you aren't ready yet. I'll help you," she promised.

"You really want to do this?"

"Yes, I really do."

"When, Karen?"

"Very soon. I wasn't sure until Henry left. Everything has changed so much, and I can't bear it here any longer."

Hilary wrapped her arms around Karen and hugged her tightly. Karen returned the embrace, warmed by her sister's support.

When they stepped apart and returned to work, the mood of the afternoon had changed for Hilary. She felt dazzled, the air around them seemed shimmery and soft. She wouldn't try to stop Karen and she wouldn't tell anyone, especially Morgan, about Karen's plans.

***

The air was unusually hot for spring on the morning Karen rose before anyone else. She slipped out of the bedroom she shared with her sisters and placed a folded letter on the breakfast table. Then, she walked outside. Wearing her nightgown, her feet bare, she walked to the hill. She gazed at the field on either side of her and studied the well-trod dirt path before her.

When she reached the clifftop, she stared down at the ocean and smiled. She walked down the hill. She moved quickly as her anticipation grew. She climbed onto the rocks, walked out to the farthest point, and took in a long breath of salty air. She saw the signs of sunrise in the sky and watched for a little while, imagining it would look quite different through the watery filter of the sea.

She sang for her sea sister. Manae and the sea woman appeared, moving in languid, looping circles below the surface. Karen stepped off the rocks and plunged into the sea, where they circled her. She went under, fighting the instinct to rise to the surface and gasp for breath. She began to panic at the discomfort of being unable to breathe, but Manae took her hand, and the sea woman held her firmly by her upper arms, leaned close, and, like a mother to a beloved infant, gently kissed her lips.

**

Aila saw the letter first. She was in the kitchen preparing breakfast when she spotted it sitting on the table. Her daughters were walking into the room as she unfolded the letter and began to read. Her face went pale, and she dropped the letter and raced out the door.

"Mother!" Morgan shouted in alarm, chasing after her.

"What's wrong?" Emily asked, looking at Hilary, who put a calming hand on her shoulder. Hilary sighed sadly.

"We'll wait here," she said. She smoothed her sister's hair.

**

Running down the hill, Aila tripped on a rock on the hill and stumbled. She barely noticed the pain as she got up and ran toward the beach.

"Karen!" she screamed, running into the water, pushing against the rolling waves. "Karen!"

"Mother! What are you doing?" Morgan cried, racing after her.

"Karen!" Aila shouted again, then turned to Morgan.

"Oh, Lord!" she moaned, peering frantically into the water. "Help me look for her! Karen!"

Morgan felt the chill of understanding flow through her, and she fought desperately to rise above the devastating sensation so she could help her mother, who could not stop screaming

Karen's name. Morgan climbed onto the rocks and scanned the water. Seeing nothing, she joined her mother in the water. Aila was combing through the waves with her hands.

"Mother," she said gently, "She may have come down here hours ago."

Aila turned to face her. They were waist deep in the sea, waves rolling in around them, and breaking against their chests. The anguish on Aila's face was more than Morgan could bear. For the first time since her childhood, she embraced her mother, using her strong arms to hold Aila tightly. They let the waves rock them until, finally, Morgan led her sobbing mother home and settled her in bed.

Chapter 10

Aila decided one summer morning that they would go to the rocks together to sing. They were all hoping to see Karen in the water.

Emily and Hilary held hands as they climbed onto the rocks behind Aila and Morgan. The return to the ritual was comforting after so many turbulent months. They sang, letting the rising sun warm their faces.

In the first weeks after Karen left, Aila had said she would never set foot on the beach or the rocks and never again sing for the sea woman, who had taken her daughter.

But, once her pain progressed from agony to regret, Aila had gone back to the beach. At first, she'd searched desperately for Karen, staring into the water for hours, while Morgan stood watchfully beside her. Then, gradually, Aila had stopped searching and simply found comfort in standing on the sand.

Hilary told them of Karen's friendship with the sea woman's daughter, and Aila began to believe she would see Karen again someday. And she stopped blaming the sea woman, who had understood her grief and loneliness all those years ago.

They didn't see Karen that warm summer day, and Aila cried that night, but her tears were a gentle release that brought her relief, instead of stirring up her sorrow. She and her daughters were healing. She noticed that Morgan and Hilary spoke civilly to one another, instead of bickering all the time. It touched her to see how they both comforted and cheered Emily. Morgan's gestures were brusque, as was her nature, but it somehow made her efforts sweeter to behold. Aila wondered sometimes if she had somehow unwittingly traded one daughter for another. If she had allowed Hilary to leave with Henry, would Karen have stayed? Or would she have lost them both?

***

That summer, Aila watched Hilary for signs of grief, knowing she'd had to trade one heartache for another. But Hilary stayed calm, even while the others broke down at times, including Morgan, who was remorseful because she'd always treated Karen so harshly. Hilary moved back into the girls' room, but she slept on Karen's side of their bed, like a ghost prone to haunt the last resting place of the most recently departed.

Aila remembered Hilary's childhood fantasies of planned adventures, shared with her sisters in the stories she'd told for their entertainment. She had never stopped to consider that Hilary might have actually believed she would go to those places or do those things.

Before Henry came, Aila had never told her daughters they couldn't leave, but she had never imagined they would want to. She felt the weight of realization and regret. She couldn't undo what she had done. But she paid closer attention to her daughters from then on, trying to understand them, so that she might make better decisions if given the chance—for each of them.

***

The following autumn, they did not go to the rocks to sing. The family had gone to the beach nearly every day of the summer, though for Hilary, the memories of Henry the waves and sand evoked were painful. Once, as they'd sat on the rocks singing for Karen, Hilary caught sight of the spot on the beach where they'd found Henry, where he had asked her to marry him. The little stretch of sand looked so still and empty it made her heart ache. She wondered if he'd forgotten her yet.

When Hilary tried to imagine her future, contemplate the empty sameness of it, she grew weary. She kept her feelings to herself, but she took comfort in remembering that she had not always felt this way about her life. Maybe one day she would feel better, hopeful, again. Perhaps she would be able to go to the beach without reliving her brief past with Henry. Maybe she would see Karen, who would tell stories of her life beneath

124

the waves that would somehow open doors of promise that felt closed to her now. She knew that in the coming winter she would miss Henry and Karen terribly, and she braced herself for it, hoping spring would bring renewal.

***

The following spring, Hilary and Emily walked out into the field when the warmth of the sun began to thaw the frozen fields and bring the trees back to life, coaxing buds onto branches and luring the first birds of spring out to sing. They laughed and ran, thrilled to be outside again in the fresh air.

During the past winter, Hilary had started half-heartedly making up stories with Emily, hoping to distract herself from the loneliness she dreaded, but soon found herself having fun, laughing, and nearly believing their stories. She was impressed by how much her younger sister was growing, and their camaraderie reminded her of her friendship with Karen.

As the warm scent of heather and grass swirled in the breeze around them, Hilary looked at her youngest sister and felt sorry she had taken Karen for granted, that she'd been too caught up in her own concerns to try to keep Karen from believing she would have a better life away from them. She wouldn't make the same mistake with Emily.

Chapter 11

K aren wondered if she would eventually become like the others. They lived in a dream-like state, fully content, drifting through the water together, each with her own rhythm. Unlike Karen and Manae, they didn't communicate frequently; instead, they followed each other by instinct.

She hadn't seen her own face since Nai had transformed her, but she could see her tailfin and the webbed skin between her fingers. Her face felt smoother and narrower, and she imagined she looked something like Manae. The males of their kind looked more human than the females, and, though the sea women were beautiful, she hoped she still looked somewhat human so her mother and sisters would recognize her when she returned to visit them.

She was anxious to see them, but Nai recommended that she adapt to life in the ocean before going back. A few of the men had tried too soon to visit the shores of their human lives and had perished trying to breathe the air their transformed bodies could no longer tolerate.

Karen sensed Manae's fear that she would feel compelled to return to her family when she saw them, but Karen had no desire to go back. She loved her new life.

She was finally where she belonged. She could glide along the ocean floor, lost in pleasant, hazy thoughts, and marvel for hours over the vibrant colors of the coral and sea life. Fish were easy to catch, kelp and seaweed abundant to pick. She no longer had to work until her muscles ached, and her body, freed from the heavy dresses she'd worn all her life, felt wonderfully light and graceful.

Manae showed her how to survive and revealed to her how limitless the ocean was. She taught Karen how to navigate back to the cave they used most often for shelter, but they were not tied to any location. Together, they swam north to where the ocean was cold, and gigantic whales passed above them in rhythmic formation. They carefully avoided sharks and orcas as they passed through deeper, darker waters. They swam south, to places where the water was warm and clear. Karen forgot about trees, wind and snow. All she wanted was this endless buoyant freedom with Manae.

Chapter 12

Hilary and Emily were in the barn yard tending to the new baby chicks when they heard hooves pounding the earth in the distance. They looked at each other, surprised. Aila was home, out in the field with Morgan, and no one ever rode out to their isolated farm.

Hilary walked toward the front of the barn, where she could see the road. She lifted a hand to shield her eyes from the bright afternoon sun. The sound grew louder, and she could see a large, ornate carriage approaching. Aila and Morgan were also watching it from the field.

Hilary saw Aila moving toward the house, walking at first, then running. Hilary's heartbeat quickened. *Father!*

Hilary ran out to the front of the house.

"He won't take this farm from us," she said, when Morgan and Aila joined her.

She wondered how—and why—her father would dare try to justify taking back this land from them. Had his fine family turned him out and sent him running back here? Or had greed compelled him to try to snatch this home from the family he'd betrayed?

"It doesn't matter how many he's got in there with him," Morgan said, grim-faced. "They'll regret making this journey."

She held the neck of a heavy shovel, and Hilary regarded her older sister with sudden, fierce pride. Hilary ran to the barn and returned with a scythe, which she handed to her mother, and a long stick, which she held herself.

Emily had followed her out of the barn and stood back, near the door of the house. She was astonished by the sight of them, standing shoulder to shoulder, weapons ready.

The carriage was racing toward the house, seeming to grow larger as it gained ground.

Soon, the long and elegantly appointed coach stopped in front of their house. The driver jolted in alarm when he saw the armed women staring at him.

"State your business!" Aila said.

"Ma'am, my name is John Pritchett. My master, Sir Charles Northam, wishes to speak with you."

He climbed down from his bench, keeping a wary eye on them as he hurried to open the door of the coach, which was being rattled by an occupant who was anxious to get out. With the driver's help, the door burst open and, to their astonishment, Henry hopped out.

Hilary covered her mouth with her hands. Tears sprang to her eyes when she saw the expectant look on his face and the softness in his gaze. He looked stronger and fuller now, and his clothing was the finest she had ever seen, but his exuberant smile was the same as she remembered.

The driver helped a young woman in a blue silk dress out of the coach. She had fair skin and her pale hair was carefully arranged atop her head in curls. The woman stood beside Henry and regarded them with wide, curious eyes and a warm smile, as another man, dressed as finely as Henry, stepped down from the carriage to join them.

"Mrs. Reed," Henry said, facing Aila. "May I present my brother and sister in law, Sir Charles Northam and Lady Helena Northam?"

Aila bowed respectfully, and they nodded to her. Henry turned to his brother and sister-in-law.

"Here are Mrs. Reed's daughters: Miss Reed, Miss Hilary Reed, Miss Emily Reed, and..."

He stopped and looked at Hilary.

"Where is Karen?"

"She has left us, Mr. Northam," Aila said.

"Oh! I'm so sorry to hear..."

Aila could hear the sad confusion in Henry's voice.

"We've made peace with it," she assured him, gently. "What brings you back here?"

"I am sorry to call unannounced. But I had no address for you —I was able to find my way back by memory. I have something for you. And my family wanted to meet you."

"Your home is lovely," Lady Helena said.

"Thank you," Aila said.

"Miss Hilary. We owe you a great debt," Sir Charles reached his hands out to Hilary. He took her hands in his. "Thank you for rescuing my dear brother."

Behind his stoic, trained expression, she could sense great emotion.

"Is it really true that you and your sister carried him up a hill?" he asked.

"Yes. The hill is over there." She gestured to the clifftop in the distance.

Sir Charles smiled.

"Amazing."

He turned to Aila.

"Mrs. Reed let me explain why we have come. My brother has told me that you are afraid your husband may attempt to re-claim this property."

She looked at him in surprise, realizing Hilary must have con-fided in Henry.

He went on before she could speak, "My brother and I contacted your husband and convinced him it was in his best interest to sell the property to us. He refused at first, but we reminded him that neither the law nor his benefactors would look kindly upon the fraud he has perpetrated by passing off an-other woman as his legal wife and an illegitimate son as legitim-ate in order to secure a piece of his family's fortune. He sold the property to me, and, as a gesture of my deep gratitude, I have le-gally granted ownership of this land to you. I am pleased to tell you that you are now the legal owner of your home and land."

He handed Aila a document, and she read it in stunned si-lence. Though her mind was racing, she forced herself to concentrate and make sense of the words on the page.

"Thank you," she said, finally.

She looked at Henry, who wore the beaming smile of an excited child. She smiled warmly at him.

"Would you all like to come inside for tea?" Aila asked.

"That would be lovely!" Lady Helena said.

***

Over tea, the visitors told of their journey, which had been long, requiring multiple stops and stays in the country homes of relatives and friends along the way. Lady Helena was keenly interested in Hilary, watching her almost as much as Henry did. He could barely take his eyes from her face. Hilary glanced at Henry several times, but kept her eyes mostly on her dish, trying to steel herself against the disappointment that would come with his departure.

When she did meet Henry's eye, the expression of hopefulness she saw there reassured her that his feelings hadn't changed. Hilary caught Morgan's eye and gave her a searching look. Morgan returned her gaze and sighed with resignation.

Near the end of the meal, Henry stood.

"It gives me such pleasure to see my dear friends and my beloved family seated here together, along with the woman I love."

Hilary looked up, surprised.

"Mrs. Reed," he said, looking at Aila. "May I speak with you privately?"

Aila stared at him for a moment. "Yes."

They stepped out of the house into the cool air.

"I respect your concerns about Hilary leaving the life she has known here," he said. "I have spoken at great length with my mother and my brother, who is here with me today to attest to what I am going to tell you. I will admit that, at first, they shared your concerns, but I've convinced them, as I hope to convince you, that I can provide Hilary with a life that will ensure her happiness. If you will allow me to marry her, Hilary and I will live in a house on the far end of my family's estate. We will

131

live a peaceful, quiet life with a small farm of our own. We will have help, but Hilary will have full charge of the farm if she wishes. She and I will be expected to attend formal affairs at the holidays, but otherwise, we will be left to live as we see fit. My family have consented to our marriage, if you'll allow it, and if Hilary will have me."

He saw her shoulders stiffen.

"I will respect your refusal if you still feel you must. I came here fully prepared to be refused by both of you, but intent on thanking you properly for rescuing and caring for me. The ownership of this land is *not* contingent upon your permission. Nor was it intended to be a bribe to convince you. It is a gift to thank you. But I love your daughter, so I feel I must try once more to persuade you to allow me to ask for her hand."

"In the past year, our lives have changed a great deal, Mr. Northam," Aila said. "After Karen left us, it occurred to me that my hopes for my daughters were possibly mine alone. I'd never considered that they would have hopes and plans of their own. I believe Morgan is devoted to our quiet, busy lifestyle. But, Hilary longs for a different life. She loves you, and I do believe that if she tells me she is ready to go with you today, then she truly is. If she wishes to accept your proposal, she has my blessing to do so."

The smile that lit his handsome young face was so joyful and pure, she felt reassured, despite her reservations. They returned to the house, where the others sat at the table. Henry walked over to Hilary.

"Your mother has given her consent," he said, kneeling before her. "Will you marry me?"

Hilary gasped, surprised and delighted. She looked up at Aila. "Truly, Mother?"

"Truly." Aila smiled.

"Yes, I will marry you!" Hilary exclaimed, grinning at Henry.

Lady Helena clasped her hands together and smiled.

"May she leave with us today?" Sir Charles said to Aila. "They can be married in two weeks' time in the chapel on our estate.

We can send a coach for you if you'd like to come for the wedding. It's about five days ride."

"Very well, she may leave with you," Aila said. "But I don't think we'll be able to make the trip to attend the wedding. We've too much to do here on the farm."

Hilary looked at Emily, then at Henry, who nodded.

"Mother," Hilary said, her heart racing with the fear that she might forfeit her mother's permission by asking for too much. "May Emily come with us?"

"If she is unhappy, we will bring her back home to you," Henry promised.

Aila was not as shocked by the request as she would have been a year earlier, but it surprised her. Of all her daughters, Emily was the one who reminded her most of herself as a young girl. She thought Emily would be content to stay at the farm, but she realized she could as easily picture Emily working on needlepoint in the front room of her parent's home, strolling with friends in the village, or attending the quaint dances she herself used to enjoy.

"I'll need a moment to consider," Aila said. She stood and reached her hand out to Emily. They walked outside.

"Emily, if you wish to go, I will allow it, but on the condition that they do promise to bring you back to us if you are unhappy there."

Emily looked up at her mother, surprised and touched.

"Will you be sad if I leave?" Emily asked, thinking of how Karen's departure had hurt Aila. "Won't it be a hardship for you and Morgan to do the work of five?"

"I've been thinking of pulling in the farm a bit, so it isn't so much work for us. With two of us to feed, it will require less work anyway."

She smiled at her youngest daughter, and Emily smiled back.

"Do you want to go?"

"Yes. I would like to go with Hilary and see what it's like to live in such a place. I'm grateful you will allow me to come back."

"Of course," Aila said, with a fond smile. "You're a good girl, Emily."

They walked arm in arm back to the house.

The travelling party would have to leave soon to make their next stop before too late in the evening. Morgan and Aila walked them to the coach. Hilary turned suddenly to Henry.

"May I have a few moments more, before we leave?"

"Of course," he said. "Have you forgotten something?"

"Yes," she said, and turned and ran toward the cliff. She raced down the hill to the beach and walked out onto the jetty.

"Karen!" she shouted, her voice echoing with joy. "Karen! Henry came back for me! I'm going to marry him!"

She looked out at the sea. She didn't see Karen, but she felt certain her sister could hear her.

"Please watch for Mother," she said. "Let her see you. She comes for you all the time. I will look for you whenever I am near the ocean! Good-bye, Karen!"

She turned and ran back up the hill.

Chapter 13

Karen had been withdrawn and thoughtful in the days since they'd heard Hilary's call, and Manae worried that she missed her life on land and being part of the changes in her sisters' lives.

With Karen beside her, Manae had been happy and free, fully able to let go of the loneliness and anger that had once fueled her desire for revenge, and she knew she could resist the temptation to attack, though she wasn't sure whether her restraint was due to the peace of mind Karen brought or her fear that, if Karen witnessed her attacks, she would be appalled as the others had been.

She asked Karen what was wrong. Karen explained that, now that she was ready to see her family again at the rocks, her sister was leaving, and she didn't know if she would see her again. She knew Henry's house was near the water, but how would she find her, even if Hilary went to Henry's beach to call for her?

Manae took her to Nai, who reassured Karen that she would be able to find Hilary again. Distance in the water was different from the way Karen described it on land. Because they were connected by blood, she would be able to sense, even miles away, when her sister was in the sea. As a sea woman, Karen would also be able to feel and hear familiar voices as they travelled through the water. She and Manae would be able to find Hilary's new home as soon as she went into the ocean or called her from the shore.

Chapter 14

Hilary rested against the velvet arm of the carriage seat and smiled at Henry, who sat across from her, framed by the tufted fabric wall. Lady Helena had taken the middle seat between Hilary and Emily to give them the view of the countryside, farms and villages as they made their way south, but Hilary would have been content to sit anywhere. They'd been riding for three hours, and she found herself even appreciating the occasional uncomfortable jolt when the carriage hit rougher patches of road. One wouldn't include those details in a dream.

They would be spending the first evening of their trip at the home of some friends of Lady Helena's and were over an hour from the house.

"Charles, is that Littleton?" Lady Helena pointed to a cluster of buildings in the distance. Sir Charles glanced out the window.

"Yes, I believe it is."

"Shall we stop there for a stroll? There is a shop Lady Bertram wrote about in one of her letters. I'd love to stop in."

"Certainly, my dear. We could all do with some fresh air."

He told the driver to take them into Littleton.

As they entered the village, they passed tall, gracefully adorned buildings. There were pubs, coffee houses, a bookstore, a dress shop and a grocery, all well-marked with printed signage. Streets were bustling with fashionably dressed people. The men wore tall hats and complicated outfits with jackets, vests, and breeches. Women in fine dresses and silk bonnets walked in pairs along the streets.

When the coach stopped beside an inn, the coachman opened the door and the men stepped out first, turning to help the women down onto the street. Emily gazed around, and Hilary felt nervous as she noticed the curious glances from passers-by. She was suddenly aware of her plain, brown dress and her dirty, worn boots.

Lady Helena turned toward Emily and Hilary.

"Miss Reed and Miss Emily," she said, her eyes shining with excitement. "I should like you both to accompany me to a dress maker here in the village. I hear from my friend, Lady Bertram, that she does excellent work. Will you join me?"

Hilary noticed Emily's eyes widen with excitement. She would have preferred to remain with Henry, but it would be rude to refuse Lady Helena, who had been exceedingly kind. She had kept up constant conversation in the long carriage ride, intent on putting the sisters at ease.

"Yes, thank you," Hilary said.

"I'm so glad!" Lady Helena said. "I insist you allow me to treat you to some lovely new gowns."

Hilary fought to hide the sudden irritation she felt. She glanced at Henry and saw the happy, expectant expression on his face. She would have to put her pride aside and make some effort to adjust to his way of life.

Henry and Sir Charles opted to visit a coffee house across the street and promised to meet them at the inn in an hour.

Hilary and Emily followed Lady Helena into a shop with elegant black-paned windows. The shop keeper approached them, and the look of pity and concern in her eyes as she regarded their old dresses made Hilary's cheeks feel hot, but Emily, distracted by the beautiful dresses surrounding them, didn't seem to notice.

When Lady Helena introduced herself to the shop keeper, the woman curtsied and declared it an honor to have Lady Helena in her shop.

"I'd like to order some dresses for myself and for my sisters-in-law," Lady Helena said.

"Well, that's wonderful, Lady Northam!" The shop keeper smiled. She summoned her assistant from the rear of the shop to begin fitting the ladies. Lady Helena suggested they work first with Hilary, but Hilary demurred, so they began with Emily. The dressmaker took her measurements and Emily giggled when she had to stand behind the curtain in her undergarments.

The shop keeper offered to alter and sell them some dresses she'd already made. Emily chose two. Lady Helena was impressed with her choices, and Emily flushed with delight at her praise.

Hilary did not care which dress she wore. She hoped she could wear something with few adornments. This stipulation politely requested, she gave the decision over to Lady Helena, who chose for her a series of lovely, understated gowns in dark, rich fabrics and simple, elegant patterns.

Most of the gowns would take a few days to complete, but the dressmaker offered to alter one gown for each of them immediately, so they could have one to wear around the town.

When the fittings were done, the shop keeper seated them in her small parlor and asked her young servant to bring them some tea while she made the alterations. Before she went to her work room, she gently informed Lady Helena that her sister was a hairdresser and offered to summon her to do a simple style for the girls. Lady Helena was thrilled with the idea.

The shop keeper's sister arrived with a bag of tools and ribbons. Emily took the first turn again. Hilary hoped the dressmaker would finish her alterations before her turn so they could make the excuse of being short on time. She watched as the woman brushed and twisted Emily's fair hair into a style like Lady Helena's, pulled back and up except for wispy face framing curls. The style suited her, but Hilary was surprised at how different Emily looked.

The sun was low in the sky when they walked back to meet the men. They were coiffed and dressed, ready to ride on to the home of Lord and Lady Bertram, where they would stay for the next several days.

The new dress was more confining than Hilary's old sack of a dress, but she was grateful to learn from Lady Helena that fashions had changed from several years before when all well-dressed ladies wore tight corsets and towering hairstyles. Hilary smiled when she caught Emily glancing admiringly at her own reflection in the dusty glass of every shop window they passed.

Sir Charles and Henry were waiting for them in front of the inn. They were engaged in conversation, smiling and laughing with the easy comfort of brothers who enjoyed one another's company. Hilary noticed what a striking pair they were, both so handsome and well-dressed, and it occurred to her that Henry would have seemed so foreign to her if she had seen him like this before he washed up on their beach. She thought of her mother venturing to villages like this to sell and trade wool and goods from their farm. She dressed as plainly as her daughters. Did people regard her with curious glances as she passed them in her wagon? Would Henry have done so? As if he could hear his name cross her mind, he looked away from his brother and saw them. His eyes widened with joy at the sight of her, and he smiled.

"You both look lovely!" he said, walking to meet them.

"Indeed, you do," Sir Charles said. He smiled at his wife, acknowledging her success in transforming the two farm girls into proper young ladies. She smiled back, satisfied with herself and encouraged by Emily's enthusiasm. She took her husband's arm, and they led the little party toward the coach.

***

They spent many days travelling, enjoying brief stays at the homes of the elegant friends of Sir Charles and Lady Helena. During these visits, Hilary and Emily kept mostly to themselves, awed at the splendor of the houses and the manners of the hosts, and unable to reconcile themselves yet to having such a vast amount of leisure time.

Finally, the small party found themselves on the last stretch of road before reaching their home. During most of the ride, Lady Helena had led the conversation, telling the girls about the house where they would live, the kinds of diversions that could be found and, with a gleam in her eye, sharing some benign, but amusing stories about neighbors and family friends the girls had yet to meet.

Emily was more interested in this information than Hilary, who was nervous as they drew closer to their new home. But, whenever she met Henry's eyes, his warm smile soothed her anxiety. She could hardly believe they would be together now, always, and she was looking forward to their wedding, which he'd promised her would be a quiet affair.

Lady Helena was talking to Emily about her plans for a new carriage, and she was wondering aloud whether a team of all white horses might be too showy and, also, impractical, for then they would have to convert the cottage back into a second barn. Hilary looked up at this. Henry had mentioned that they would live in the cottage. She wondered why Lady Helena didn't know.

"Here we are, at last," said Sir Charles, gesturing out the window. Emily let out a soft gasp. Hilary leaned forward so she could see it as well, and she involuntarily mirrored her sister's reaction. The white stone house gleamed in the afternoon sun. Roman columns lined its facade, and four stories of tall windows towered over the nearby treetops. Identical, slightly shorter wings stretched out from either side of the center section.

"It's ghastly, isn't it," Henry said, grinning. Lady Helena shot him an annoyed look. For her, the stunning edifice was a source of pride. It had been most helpful in persuading her father to allow her to marry beneath her family's position in the peerage when Sir Charles was her young heart's desire.

They rolled up to the front of the house, where a line of servants in blue livery awaited their arrival. Lady Helena laughed as a gust of wind threatened to steal her hat and, following her out of the carriage, Hilary watched her stroll past the servants as though they weren't there. A well-dressed older woman had come out of the house, and Lady Helena rushed up to kiss her on both cheeks. They stood together outside the front door, watching as footmen helped Hilary and Emily down, and as the gentleman offered their arms. Emily took Sir Charles's arm shyly, and Hilary followed suit, holding tightly to Henry.

"Mother," Sir Charles greeted the older woman, leading Emily up the stone steps toward her. Henry followed with Hilary.

Charles introduced the young ladies to his mother, and she murmured a greeting and peered at them curiously. She gave the sisters a tentative, not wholly welcoming smile before she turned to lead the party indoors.

The front hall was a further marvel to Hilary and Emily. The floor was a gleaming sea of marble, and life-sized statues lined the expansive hall like a frozen army. Lush, gilt-framed paintings adorned the walls.

Sir Charles and Lady Helena suggested they all retire for a rest and meet in the drawing room in the afternoon. A servant led Emily and Hilary up the sweeping marble staircase and down a series of long hallways to their rooms, which were large and well appointed; each had a bathtub, a canopied bed and a tufted settee.

"Would you like to sleep for a while?" Hilary asked Emily.

"I'm afraid I'm too excited to sleep!"

Hilary noticed that Emily had already picked up a manner of speech from Lady Helena, who prefaced many of her sentences with the words "I'm afraid". She smiled, recognizing that the imitation was unintentional.

"I am, too. Let's sit in your room and talk."

They curled up on Emily's settee. A young maid brought biscuits and tea. They thanked her profusely, which seemed to confuse her, and she hurried out as soon as they excused her.

"This is so strange," Hilary said with a sigh. "I never really imagined Henry in a place this grand."

"I've never imagined any place this grand at all!" Emily said, and they both laughed.

"Do you think you'll be comfortable here?" Hilary asked. She hadn't formed a clear picture in her mind of what their lives would be like but, during the journey, she'd imagined the house would be older and smaller; fine, but not of this scale. Gazing out the window, she saw a long, wide expanse of green field behind them and, in the far distance, some buildings backed by a small forest. The barn and the cottage. Even the cottage looked different from how she'd imagined it. She'd thought it would be closer, maybe a minute's walk to the main house, but the building looked distant.

"Lady Helena and Sir Charles are so kind," Emily said. "But Lady Anne didn't seem glad to meet us."

"I noticed that, too. I imagine she planned a different sort of wife for Henry."

"But you're here now, and she's already agreed to it!"

"Don't worry." Hilary grinned. "I don't care whether she likes me or not."

Emily laughed, refreshed by the spark in Hilary's eyes.

"Henry's done so much to reunite us," Hilary said in a softer tone. "He wouldn't do all of this on a whim. We love each other, and I know I can count on him—whatever his mother thinks of me."

***

When they went down to the drawing room after resting, they found Lady Anne and Lady Helena seated on a pair of identical sofas. Sir Charles sat in an armchair near the large window, perusing a newspaper. Henry wasn't there yet, and Lady Helena excitedly motioned for the girls to join her.

"Hello, girls!" She called. She turned to Lady Anne and said, "They look quite well!"

Lady Anne offered a tight smile in response.

"Sit by me, Miss Emily." Lady Helena patted the seat beside her.

As Emily crossed the room toward her, Lady Helena gestured at the open seat on the sofa beside Lady Anne.

"And you sit there, Miss Reed."

Hilary walked over and perched uneasily beside the older woman.

"Have you both rested?" Lady Helena asked.

"Yes, thank you," Hilary said. Emily smiled at Lady Helena,

142

who beamed back at her.

"Doesn't Miss Emily's new hairstyle suit her perfectly?" Lady Helena asked Lady Anne. Lady Anne peered at Emily and bobbed her head slightly in grudging agreement.

"Thank you," Emily said, softly. Lady Anne kept her gaze on Emily.

"Do you play the piano, Miss Emily?" she asked.

"No, Ma'am, I never learned," Emily said, blushing.

"We must arrange lessons," Lady Anne said. "Do you sew?"

"Yes Ma'am."

Lady Anne nodded her approval. Hilary sat quietly. She would have spoken directly to Lady Anne, but she was unsure whether it was proper for her to speak first to the older woman.

Henry bounded into the room, smiling widely at the sight of all his favorite people gathered in one place, and sat on the far end of the sofa, beside Hilary. She returned his smile and felt her anxiety lessen.

"Oh, Henry, you are too exuberant," Lady Anne said with a sigh.

Her words were chiding, but her tone was resigned and affectionate. Henry, the youngest, was her favorite.

Hilary noticed that Lady Anne started to look at Henry several times but looked away when she realized she'd have to look at Hilary also because of the angle of where they each sat. She thought it likely that Lady Anne had permitted their marriage because she was incapable of denying Henry anything, but that did not mean she would ever be happy with his decision.

Chapter 15

Hilary and Henry planned to marry in an ancient stone chapel on the grounds of the estate two weeks after they arrived, but Lady Anne mentioned to Henry that she hoped his brother, Nathaniel, would return from his travels abroad in time for the ceremony, and asked that they postpone the wedding until he arrived. Hilary recalled Henry once mentioning that Nathaniel was very like his mother in demeanor and point of view. She wasn't eager to have two people present on her wedding day who would likely view the occasion with regret.

The delay was especially frustrating because Hilary was looking forward to moving to the cottage at the back of the farm after they married. There, she and Henry would be free from the many rules and expectations that weighed on her in the manor house. She had planned to give Emily a room in the cottage, but in the four weeks since their arrival, she'd noticed that her sister seemed to be adapting well to life on the estate. Emily had become a pet of Lady Helena's. She had also wandered into the good graces of prickly Lady Anne, who, intent on turning her into a proper young lady, enjoyed bestowing gems of advice on Emily. At least, Hilary thought, her younger sister was welcome.

As she and Henry strolled on the path of the estate's maze-like flower garden, Hilary decided to broach the subject of the wedding and the subsequent move to the cottage.

"Have you or your family heard from your brother? I'm beginning to feel uncomfortable living here without being married, like a guest who's overstayed her welcome" she said. He smiled at her directness.

"We still haven't gotten an update on when he'll arrive, but we've already waited so long for him. I think we can move ahead with the arrangements and be married in two weeks," he said. "I don't want to wait any longer, either. Will that cheer you?"

"Very much."

"Then, I'll arrange it. And we'll move down to the cottage right after. I know you are anxious to return to your milkmaid ways," he teased her, with a grin.

She chuckled and squeezed his arm with affection, marveling at how quickly she had become used to this leisurely lifestyle so far removed from her "milkmaid ways".

It would feel good to be able to do some work again, once they were in their cottage away from the eyes of the manor house occupants. If only for the satisfaction of completing something, since her contribution was not needed here, she thought she would take care of a small flock of sheep and perhaps tend to a small garden.

**

Two weeks passed and they were still unmarried and living in the main house. Henry seemed to have forgotten their conversation, and Hilary began to grow anxious. As they walked down to dinner one evening, she stopped him before they reached the dining room.

"Have you decided when we will be moving to the cottage?" She couldn't bring herself to ask about the wedding again. It felt demeaning to have to pester him.

He looked instantly sheepish, and she wondered if he had forgotten about their conversation.

He took her hands in his.

"I'm afraid we'll have to wait a little while longer. Mother has asked that we stay here in the house for a bit, and she seemed so downhearted when I mentioned moving. I couldn't bring myself to insist."

Hilary sighed in exasperation.

"Really! It's not as if we'd be far away!"

"I know, my love. But you must remember that she nearly lost a son. She's always been quite fragile. We must try to be patient with her."

Hilary thought Lady Anne was less fragile than her son imagined, and she felt the sore ache of defeat in her chest as they crossed the threshold into the dining room, where Lady Anne sat in conversation with a man of her own age. Yet another Lord, Hilary assumed, from the seemingly endless supply of titled old friends who came by to fill out the dinner table.

Hilary sat to the right of Lady Anne's friend at dinner. She was glad he was too absorbed in what her mother-in-law was saying to turn and try to force polite conversation with her. She watched Emily glide into the room, arm in arm with Lady Helena. They wore rich silk gowns, pale pink with gold lace on Emily, a deep peacock blue with silver beading on Lady Helena.

Hilary's gown was a simple plum-colored silk, one of the gowns Lady Helena had bought for them on the journey to the manor. She wondered if Lady Helena and Emily had gone to a dressmaker without her, and she was hurt for a moment, until it occurred to her that the pink dress was likely a cast-off gift from Lady Helena's own closet. She reminded herself that, even if they had gone out together, leaving her behind, it wouldn't have been a gesture of exclusion. They would have wanted to give her and Henry time together, as newlyweds.

"How splendid you both look," Lady Anne said to Emily and Lady Helena. The gentlemen at the table murmured comments of agreement. Hilary met her mother-in-law's eye and the cold enmity in Lady Anne's narrowed gaze startled her. Lady Anne looked away quickly and colored slightly. Conversation began to flow again around the table.

Warmed by the buzz of friendly chatter, Hilary wondered if she'd imagined the strange animosity in her mother-in-law's stare, but then the gentleman beside Hilary asked if she liked to ride horses. Before Hilary could reply that she did enjoy riding very much, Lady Anne leaned into their conversation and, touching her friend lightly on the sleeve, said, "Miss Reed will not know how to ride. I'm afraid she has limited experience in the customs of polite society."

Hilary's face grew hot and she glared at her mother-in-law. She was about to reply that she did ride quite well, but Lord Appleton cleared his throat uncomfortably and shifted slightly away from her.

"Oh, I see," he mumbled, looking down at the table, and he seemed relieved to turn away from her as Lady Anne launched into a story about the recent travels of a shared acquaintance. Hilary tried to keep her expression neutral and finished her meal in silence. If she spoke, her voice might betray her anger, and she would not give her mother-in-law the satisfaction of knowing she'd upset her.

***

Trees arched above them like the ceiling of a grand corridor as Hilary and Emily rode through the forest toward the beach. Henry had told them that his horses knew the way, and Hilary was impressed by their surefooted persistence over the uneven forest floor.

"I'm glad we're finally going to see the ocean again," Emily said. "I didn't realize how much I would miss it."

"Me, too. I wish we could let Karen know where we'll be." Hilary thought it would be nice to have one more ally close by.

They saw the ocean ahead, framed by the trees like a painting. At the sight of the familiar deep blue water, Hilary felt some of the tension of the past several weeks slip from her shoulders.

"I can't believe Lady Anne suggested that you couldn't ride," Emily shook her head as she watched Hilary gracefully dismount onto the beach. They tied the horses to a tree.

"I'm sure I can ride better than she can. Perhaps I should challenge her to a race!" Hilary laughed.

They walked to the edge of the frothy tide, careful to keep their boots dry. Emily took a deep breath.

"Oh, that wonderful smell!"

"It reminds me of home." Hilary sighed.

"Do you miss it?"

"I suppose I do, more than I thought I would. You know I never expected Lady Anne to be happy about Henry wanting to marry me, but I didn't think it would be this hard. When they all came to the house, it seemed like the way had been cleared for us. She's already given him her permission. She won't risk alienating him by coming out and forbidding the marriage now, but I think she is going to do everything she can to convince Henry not to go through with it."

"But, he loves you! He won't go back on his word!"

"I don't know, Emily. She's constantly belittling me, especially when he's around. Just little jabs, insinuations. He doesn't even seem to notice. He doesn't defend me or tell her to stop. I've just been avoiding her, which helps, but now I worry about what she's saying to him in private, what he's thinking about me. Sometimes, I wish I'd never come here. But, other times, when he and I are together..."

"That is what you must focus on! Don't let her make you feel uncertain about him. Why don't you talk to him about it, ask him to tell her to stop?"

"I feel like that's what she wants me to do, so she can accuse me of being petty or going against her. I just want to scream at her sometimes!" Hilary nudged the water's edge with the tip of her boot, watching it darken the leather with wetness.

"Even if we do get married, will this be what my life is like forever? Having her constantly trying to change his mind about me? I don't know if I can live like that."

Chapter 16

Invitations to a society ball arrived one morning by messenger.

"Shall we go to the ball?" Henry asked Hilary as they all sat together in the drawing room.

Hilary had been half-listening to Lady Helena and her visiting friend discuss whether it would be proper for Emily to attend the ball. The serious tones they used to discuss the frivolous subject amused her.

Startled by his question, she brought her full attention back to Henry.

"Oh, no," she said quickly. "I'd rather not!"

The thought of spending an evening trussed up in a gown and jewels in a room packed with people like Lady Anne made her shudder. Henry grinned, amused by her hasty refusal.

"I thought you might feel that way, and I am in complete agreement. Those things are terribly dull. I would much rather spend a quiet evening with my lovely wife."

Lady Helena overheard him and frowned at them.

"But you must go! I insist! It will be no fun without you!"

Hilary smiled at Lady Helena, who could be so childlike in her exuberance or petulance but was always genuinely kindhearted.

"Perhaps next year we'll go," Hilary said. "I don't feel quite up to it yet."

Lady Helena's friend nodded, as if she understood completely, and Hilary wondered irritably what Lady Helena had told her about the two wild girls from the north who had come to live with them.

She and Emily had recently received a letter from Aila, who

had arranged for them to be able to send letters to her, as well, in care of a post office in her favorite village. They were glad to read that Aila and Morgan were faring well on the farm, and they enjoyed the brief updates about the animals and their small crops. Reading her simple, straightforward well wishes, Hilary imagined she could hear her mother's voice, and it had made her feel homesick. It also made her feel protective of her mother and their way of life. She hated to imagine Lady Helena, whom she considered a friend, disparaging her family and their lifestyle.

She let go of her suspicion once she saw kind resignation on Lady Helena's face.

"Very well," she said with a small pout. She shook an admonishing finger at Hilary. "But I will hold you to your word next year!"

***

Lady Helena and Lady Anne discussed the ball at dinner one evening and decided to go into town to visit their favorite dressmaker.

"What will Hilary wear?" Lady Anne asked, as if the thought had suddenly occurred to her. "She must come, too, to have a new gown made."

For a moment, Hilary felt warmed by Lady Anne's unexpected inclusion. But, then, the implication dawned on her. She looked at Henry, who was deep in conversation with his brother and hadn't heard his mother.

"Henry and I won't be going to the ball," she told Lady Anne.

Lady Anne stared at her. Hilary hesitated, uncertain if she was waiting for further explanation. Lady Anne turned her gaze to Henry who sat opposite her, talking with Charles.

"Henry," she said, her voice shrill. He stopped talking and looked at his mother.

"Yes, Mother?"

"Is this true? You're not planning to attend the ball?"

Lady Anne's wide-eyed expression and hurt, pleading tone was a departure from the chilling glare she'd given Hilary mo-

150

ments before.

Henry glanced at Hilary's face quickly before meeting Lady Anne's beseeching gaze.

"Well, Mother, we hadn't decided officially, but we are rather against it. Hilary is getting settled here. We thought the ball might be a bit too much excitement."

Lady Helena dipped her chin, as if she could see the wisdom in Henry's explanation. Hilary noticed with interest that Lady Anne bit back whatever she had been about to say when she observed Lady Helena's supportive reaction. Instead, she nodded once and turned her eyes to her food. Hilary was relieved to see the matter put to rest.

***

The following morning, Hilary looked out her bedroom window and saw Henry and his mother walking together in the garden, heads bobbing in animated conversation. Lady Anne appeared to be earnestly working at making a point, and Henry was nodding in agreement. Hilary sighed deeply.

***

"There you are!"

Henry found Hilary in the sitting room with an open book on her lap and hurried over to her. She had been staring out the window, thinking how happy a flock of sheep would be to claim the expanse of grass between the great house and the small, quaint cottage. She looked up at him.

"Will you go to the ball with me, my dear?" he asked with a soft, teasing smile, meant to cajole her.

"I will go if you want me to." She did not want to be petulant, but she was hurt.

"I do," he admitted. "Only to keep the peace with my mother."

"Why must we give in to her every wish?" she asked, suddenly overwhelmed by her frustration. He sat beside her.

"She hates me, Henry."

"I think she feels intimidated by you," he said, "and she doesn't know how to manage it."

"Intimidated by me? I don't believe that! She thinks you've made a mistake in marrying me. She wanted you to marry a grand lady, and she sees me as a savage."

"You have such strength and energy. It overwhelms her," he said.

"Are you suggesting I change? Do you want me to be some meek and obedient little miss, agreeing to everything she asks, even while she stares at me as if she wishes I had never come here?'

She felt her anger rising.

"No, not at all!" He held her hands. "I love you and want you exactly as you are! But perhaps, as a small compromise, you could attend this ball. I believe it will go far in improving things between you and my mother. I wouldn't ask if I didn't."

She wondered sadly how many more compromises he would ask her to make.

"I'll go," she said. "But I refuse to wear some ridiculous confection of a ball gown."

"I appreciate it, my love."

He smiled and leaned in to kiss her gently. Against the will of her stubborn heart, she returned his kiss.

***

On the day of the ball, Lady Helena and Lady Anne began to prepare in the late morning. Hairdressers twisted and pressed their curls and worked painstakingly to perfect their ornate hairstyles. The ladies suffered the pulling, tugging and occasional poking of their heads without complaint.

Emily bustled around the room, trying to be helpful. She was excited for them and hopeful that one day she would be allowed to go as well.

She was holding a bowl of fruit for them when Lady Anne looked at her suddenly.

"Emily, where is your sister?"

Emily blushed under Lady Anne's direct gaze and let her own eyes drop to the floor in deference, a gesture which tended to satisfy and soften Lady Anne.

"She has gone riding with Sir Charles and Lord Henry," Emily said.

Lady Anne sighed, but Lady Helena chuckled and winked merrily at Emily.

"I wonder whether Lady Ascher will wear her blue silk," Lady Helena said, rolling her eyes skyward. "She *always* wears her blue silk."

"Lord Featherston must have told her it suited her," Lady Anne said with a smirk. The ladies began to speculate about others in their social circle. To Emily's relief, Lady Anne seemed to have forgotten about Hilary's absence.

***

That evening, Sir Charles, Lady Anne and Lady Helena sat in the drawing room waiting for Hilary and Henry. Lady Anne was about to complain that Hilary would force them to be late, having returned from riding less than an hour earlier, when Hilary entered the room on Henry's arm. She'd twisted her long, dark hair into a simple knot at the crown of her head, and she wore a simple, but elegant gown of dark green silk. Lady Anne pressed her lips together tightly, but she could find nothing critical to say. The party said good-bye to Emily and rode off for the city as darkness fell over the fields and trees along their path.

***

When they entered the ornate ballroom, Hilary saw the crush of finely arrayed men and women filling the room. It felt like they all turned to watch as she entered. To calm her nerves, she told herself they were staring at Lady Helena, who was radiant, jewels at her throat and in her hair sparkling in the candlelight.

As they crossed the room, Hilary worried that, despite her exquisite dress and her well-born husband at her side, her humble origins were obvious to everyone she passed.

At their table, Lady Anne found a friend to gossip with, and with his mother comfortably situated, Sir Charles led Lady Helena off to dance.

"Would you like to dance?" Henry asked Hilary.

She'd recently learned the complicated dance steps that were

153

popular at balls and dances, but she hadn't had much practice. She wasn't eager to dance in front of a room full of people, but she realized her other choice was to sit with Lady Anne.

"Yes." She took his offered arm.

She danced better than she'd expected, and Henry was gracious during the few times she'd knocked into him because she'd been watching her feet. Having to keep time to the music and remember the steps kept her mind nicely occupied.

After three dances, Lady Helena led her off to find some refreshment, taking her arm and leading her companionably through the hall. When they returned to the table, they spotted Henry and Sir Charles standing near a large window, away from the crowd. The two men were deep in conversation, their expressions equally grave. In response to something his brother said, Henry glared toward the entrance to the ballroom.

Hilary followed Henry's gaze. When she saw who he was looking at, she gasped.

An older gentleman stood in jovial conversation with a younger man, and a woman stood beside them, her eyes darting around them room as if seeking opportunity. The older man had a florid complexion and graying dark hair. If Henry and his brother had not been watching the threesome with such consternation, Hilary wondered if she would even have noticed him, if she might have passed the night without having to endure the sickening sensation that was twisting her stomach. With rapidly rising anxiety, she realized she was looking at her father.

Before she could force her gaze elsewhere, she saw the man spot Sir Charles and Henry. His smile faded, and his red face turned purple. She could not look away from him. He was grotesque. She saw only traces of the father she remembered. She'd been so young when he'd left them that her memories were fuzzy, comprised of shapes, scents and feelings, but she could recognize his face. It matched some long-forgotten picture in her mind. She remembered him as strong and lean, a smiling, outsized presence. She remembered his hand ruffling her hair and how the rooms of their small house had seemed to come alive when he was in them.

Now, bloated and ungainly, he looked as if he'd been stuffed into the expensive blue waistcoat he wore. His shoes had shiny silver buckles and, if she hadn't recognized him, she would have taken him for an important man. Amid her shock, she supposed, having achieved his goal of being reinstated in his family's line of inheritance, he actually was a wealthy man of some importance to this society. What would they all think of him, she wondered bitterly, if they knew the truth?

Henry had caught sight of her and was rushing to her side, which brought her father's gaze to her face. For a moment, their eyes met. His were blank, he was staring at a stranger.

He looked back toward Sir Charles and said something to the woman and young man beside him, who were chatting happily. They looked bewildered as he spoke, and they reluctantly followed him as he turned to leave the room. Henry guided Hilary to a chair at their table. She sank down, her heart racing, her hands shaking. Henry gave her some wine to drink and took her hand. He watched her face carefully, his eyes full of concern.

"Whatever is the matter?" asked Lady Anne irritably, taking in Hilary's white face and shallow breathing.

"She'll be alright," Henry said, not taking his eyes from his wife's face. "She isn't used to such crowds."

Lady Anne gave a disdainful huff and returned her attention to her friend.

"I would like to leave," Hilary said quietly to Henry.

"Yes, of course we'll leave. Right now. I'll let my brother know." He gently squeezed her hand and walked toward his brother and Lady Helena.

Hilary watched, warmed by the bond of friendship Henry shared with his older brother. Sir Charles nodded, and appeared to agree they should take their leave. Lady Helena looked perplexed.

A sudden movement at the entrance of the room drew Hilary's gaze, and she saw her father striding toward Henry and

Charles, his face grim. His companions had followed him back into the room, but they waited back by the entrance, watching him with apparent confusion.

Without thinking, Hilary stood and walked toward Sir Charles and Henry. Her father reached them before she did, but she was close enough to hear him speak in a fierce whisper.

"I was going to leave when I saw you two," he said, his voice strained with anger. "But I've decided I won't let you intimidate me. You've received my share of our bargain, and I fully expect you'll keep yours. I won't be glared at as if I do not have the same right to stand in this room as you! I won't be chased out of places where I belong!"

"Oh, you left the place you really belonged readily enough!" Hilary said. Startled, he spun to face her.

"Madam, I don't believe I've had the pleasure of making your acquaintance, and I will thank you to remove yourself from this private conversation!" he snapped.

"You've made my acquaintance! Nearly twenty years ago."

He looked puzzled and alarmed.

"You must be mistaken."

"You also knew my sisters, Karen, Emily and Morgan," she said, her voice strident with anger. At the mention of Morgan's name his eyes widened in recognition, and it made Hilary feel sick to wonder if he even remembered her name or the names of her younger sisters.

He stepped away from her and looked between her, Henry and Sir Charles.

"Are you..." he said, sputtering. "Are you conspiring against me? Is this some kind of trick?"

He glared at Sir Charles.

"I won't be blackmailed!"

"They aren't blackmailing you, you old ghoul!" Hilary shouted, her temper getting the best of her. People turned to stare.

"How dare you accuse them, as though your conscience is clean, and you are some fine gentleman? How can you live with yourself? What kind of greedy monster leaves his wife and children for dead so he can become wealthy?"

His face went red with indignation, then paled quickly, as he realized people nearby might have overheard her.

"Please," he said, holding his palms up. "Please stop shouting."

"I never expected to see you again," she said. "And I desperately wish I hadn't."

He stared at her, his mouth agape and his expression pained. He started to speak, but no words came out, and she looked away from him, unable to bear seeing her memories of a strong, handsome father reduced to the pathetic, puffed-up fraud before her.

"Leave us, Mr. Reed," Sir Charles said.

Robert Reed closed his mouth and marched away, through the buzz of curious gossip. He led his bewildered companions from the room.

Before Henry could console Hilary, Lady Anne grasped her elbow and was leading her briskly to a small salon beyond the dance floor. Inside the salon, there were soft velvet sofas where ladies could escape the noise of the music and rest for a moment. The room was empty when they entered. Lady Anne, her eyes flashing with anger, turned to face Hilary

"I cannot believe you would willfully disgrace us in this way! You ungrateful...When I think of all my sons and I have done for you! Elevating you from some wild drudge into a society most outsiders would give anything to join!"

Hilary stared at her in disbelief.

"All *you* have done for *me*?! How can you have forgotten? I saved your son's life! You should be grateful to *me*! I never needed or wanted your clothes or your manners or your house! I came because I love Henry, because he asked me to be with him!"

Lady Anne's jaw dropped, and Hilary held her gaze, prepared for anything the woman might say to her. But Lady Anne was silent, as Hilary's words sunk in.

Hilary noticed Henry standing in the doorway. She braced

herself for what he might say, expecting him to be angry at her for raising her voice to his mother. She wondered if he would agree with Lady Anne and send her away. She was too furious and annoyed to care. Henry crossed the room. He stood beside Hilary.

"She's absolutely right, Mother," he said, his tone firm. "She saved my life. If you love me, you should thank her, treat her with kindness."

Lady Anne looked at Hilary and then back at her son.

"I never look at it that way," she admitted softly, looking down. "I can't bear to think you nearly died, Henry."

She looked at Hilary.

"You are correct," she said. "I should be – that is, I am - grateful, very grateful, to you for saving Henry."

She looked lost, confused by the realizations flooding her mind, disturbing the pattern of the way she expected things to be. She shook her head, as if to make sense of it.

"Though, I do wish you would try to follow our rules," she said, her voice soft and tentative. "It would make it all much simpler."

Hilary sighed. She sat on one of the sofas, suddenly exhausted. She felt tears forming in her eyes.

"Henry, can we please go home now?" she asked.

"Of course," he said, offering her his arm.

He kissed his mother's cheek and walked with his wife through the hall and out into the crisp evening air.

***

The next morning, Hilary woke to find a servant delivering a tray of breakfast for her with a note asking her to meet Henry in the garden later that morning.

"How are you feeling, my darling?" he asked, when she found him.

"I feel better."

She smiled. She was tired despite a deep sleep, and her face ached from crying. Once she'd gotten into bed the night before, grief caught up with her, and she wept, mourning the small hope

158

she'd always secretly harbored that her father had once loved her, even a little bit.

"If you'll still have me, I've arranged for us to be married the day after tomorrow. In two days' time we'll be moving into the cottage," he said, a broad smile lighting his face.

"Do you mean it?"

"Yes, I promise!"

She threw her arms around his neck, and they held one another tightly.

***

Later that day, she told Emily.

"Will you come with us to the cottage? We can fix up a wonderful room for you," Hilary said. Emily smiled

"Thank you, but you too should have some time to yourselves. I'll be fine here."

Hilary wasn't surprised. She gazed at Emily. She looked lovely in her pale pink dress, with her soft, fair hair swept up in a simple, becoming style. She looked as though she'd been born to this life, and she was clearly content. Lady Helena doted on her, and, though likely nicer to Emily at first in order to discomfit Hilary, Lady Anne seemed genuinely, if grudgingly, fond of her.

Recently, Hilary had heard the two ladies discussing the possibility of formally presenting Emily at court, so that she might find a husband. They were concerned that finding a suitable husband for Emily could prove difficult, since she hadn't the rank in society to attract an heir, nor a large dowry to attract a second or third brother from a good family. She was, they agreed, exceptionally pretty, which would be of some help. Hilary hoped they would wait at least another year to begin such a campaign. She wanted Emily to live free of that particular care for as long as she could.

***

Henry and Hilary were married in the small chapel two days later and, after the ceremony, they rode to the cottage at the far end of the property. Despite its small size, it was exquisitely furnished, and Hilary adored it from the moment they stepped

159

inside together.

Chapter 17

A month after their wedding, Henry found Hilary behind their cottage feeding their small flock of chickens.

"I have some news."

"Tell me," she said.

"My brother Nathaniel is returning after all. He will be here next week."

Hilary smirked.

"Lady Anne must be delighted."

***

Nathaniel arrived a week later than expected, to the frustration of his mother, who abhorred tardiness and was anxious to have all her sons under one roof. Lady Anne had arranged for a small feast the week before, on the day he was due to arrive, and she had been annoyed to have gone to the trouble to have him delay.

The carriage rolled onto the drive in the afternoon. The ladies were in the drawing room. Lady Helena and Lady Anne were discussing an upcoming garden party they were planning to attend. Hilary and Emily sat side by side at the piano forte, where Emily was teaching her older sister to play.

Hearing the commotion of the arriving carriage and the servants rushing out to greet it, Lady Anne rose and peered out the front window. Once she saw her son step out of the carriage, she smiled widely and hurried to the entry hall.

Nathaniel strode into the house and met Lady Anne in the hall.

"Mother,' he said, leaning in to kiss her cheek. "You look well."

"How was your journey, Nathaniel?" She took his arm.

"Oh, it was long. My friends badgered me to stay in town a week longer than I'd intended. Lady Hollingsbrook needed an extra man for her fete for the Duchess."

Impressed, she raised her eyebrows. As they crossed into the drawing room, Nathaniel caught sight of Emily. His gaze lingered on her appreciatively for a moment, and Lady Anne pretended not to notice.

Spotting Lady Helena, he crossed the room to greet her. He bent and kissed her cheek.

"You look lovely, sister dear," he said.

She accepted the praise with a radiant smile.

"Welcome home, Nathaniel! We'd begun to doubt you'd ever arrive!"

He grinned at her

"Nathaniel," Lady Anne said. "This is Mrs. Northam, Henry's wife, and her sister, Miss Emily Reed."

He strode over to kiss their hands in turn.

"How lovely to meet both of you."

He stared at Emily, who blushed and looked down.

"It is good to meet you, as well. Henry speaks of you often," Hilary said. He flashed a quick, dismissive smile in response and joined Lady Helena on the sofa.

He leaned back, with his arm along the back of the sofa, a sprawling gesture that reminded Hilary that this had been his home long before it had become hers. She glanced at him while he chatted with Lady Helena about his journey.

He had pale, watery eyes, and his hair was a faded brown, lighter than Sir Charles's and darker than Henry's. His chin seemed to drop straight down in profile, with a pad of fat blending jaw into neck. His vest pulled tight across his stomach, and the rims of his eyes were an unhealthy reddish pink. Hilary suspected he denied himself little, especially in the way of food or drink. He did not resemble his brothers at all. He favored his mother while Sir Charles and Henry more closely resembled their deceased father, the handsome, formidable baronet, whose portrait hung in the hall.

"So, you fished my poor brother out of the sea?" Nathaniel asked Hilary.

"Not quite. He was on the beach when we found him."

"Ah, was it both of you then?" He looked at Emily.

"No, our other sister was with me that evening," Hilary said, leaning forward slightly to shield Emily from his gaze.

He stood, finished with the conversation.

"Where are Charles and Henry?"

"Charles is in town, and Henry has gone riding," Lady Anne said.

"I am too tired from my journey to ride. But perhaps Miss Emily Reed would accompany me on a stroll through the gardens?"

Emily's eyes widened, and she hesitated to respond. Hilary knew Emily wasn't sure if it would be proper for her to walk alone with a man she'd recently met. Hilary wasn't worried about propriety, but she didn't like the way he was looking at her sister.

"My sister was teaching me to play a new song," Hilary said. "I'm afraid I am doing quite poorly, and, if she leaves me now, I'll never grasp it."

Hilary saw a look of relief pass over Lady Anne's face. Clearly, she didn't relish the possibility of a match between her second son and Emily.

"Yes, do let them continue, Nathaniel," she said, standing. "I shall take a stroll with you."

Nathaniel stared coldly at Hilary, a forced smile on his lips.

"Very well, Mother."

Hilary and Emily turned their attention to the music book.

"I suppose it must be quite difficult to learn many things when one has been raised in savage environs," Nathaniel said haughtily.

Emily's face went pale, and Hilary seethed at his rudeness. She met Emily's eye with a pointed look, asking her silently to ignore the remark and focus on what they were meant to be doing.

"Really, Nathaniel!" Lady Helena exclaimed, angrily. "You are such a child when you don't get your way!"

He smirked.

"Forgive me, ladies. I apologize if I have offended you." He looked at Emily.

A slow smile spread across his lips, and Hilary fought the urge to jump up and poke his eyes. She doubted he would stare at Emily that way, and she knew he wouldn't have insulted them, if Sir Charles or Henry had been present. She wondered how long he intended to stay.

Henry had mentioned that Nathaniel was looking for a wife and had set his sights on a local heiress. Feeling guilty for wishing the misfortune of Nathaniel's company on a stranger, Hilary, nonetheless, hoped the heiress would marry him quickly and move him into her family home.

***

Once his brothers arrived home that evening, Nathaniel seemed to forget about Hilary and Emily, and the strange hostility he seemed to feel toward them dissipated.

When they encountered him in the days following his arrival, he was neither friendly nor unfriendly. He mostly ignored them, speaking to them only when necessary, and, on such occasions, he was courteous. Hilary wondered if she'd mistaken harmless sarcasm for animosity when they'd first met. Perhaps she'd been expecting him to dislike her because Henry had told her he was so similar to Lady Anne. Though she and Henry's mother had gotten along better since the ball, Hilary could well remember Lady Anne's contempt for her.

But, since he had only been rude to her and Emily that first day, she was able to allow that Nathaniel might have been exhausted and irritable from his long journey when he made his rude comment. She did notice that he seemed to enjoy speaking out of turn and saying things that bordered on shocking, even in the company of his mother, though he always stopped shy of angering her. In response to his outrageous comments, Lady Anne always assumed a look of resigned exasperation that was clearly familiar to her sons.

The family dynamic became clearer to Hilary the more she observed them together. Charles, the eldest, was the wisest and most admired. For the well-being of his family, he'd taken control of the estate when their father died, and he was serious and commanding, but he was also fair and kind. Nathaniel, the middle son, relished his role as the rogue and seemed to fancy himself much more physically attractive and charming than he actually was. Henry, the youngest, was the idealist and the favorite, always affable and eager to please everyone.

Chapter 18

A month had passed since Nathaniel's arrival, and Emily was enjoying a respite from his presence. He hadn't insulted her or Hilary again after the day he arrived, but the way he stared at her and the teasing tone of voice he used when he spoke to her made her skin crawl.

Luckily, this week, he, Hilary and Henry were away, visiting the home of family friends and attending several parties with them. Emily felt sure Hilary was enjoying herself. She got along well with this set of Henry's friends, who were frequent dinner guests at the house. Emily missed her sister, but she was happy to have a chance to relax without the pressure of Nathaniel's unsettling attentions. She hoped he would become smitten with another guest at his friends' house and forget about her.

She joined Lady Helena and Lady Anne in the drawing room.

"He hinted to me that he has hopes of Miss Eleanor Woodford," Lady Helena was saying to Lady Anne, who smiled with satisfaction.

"She is a lovely girl, and the Woodford's are a fine family. She would make a suitable match for Nathaniel," Lady Anne said.

Emily had spent enough time with Lady Anne to understand that her approval of a potential daughter-in-law meant that the young lady held a certain rank in society, likely a bit higher than the Northams' own. Lady Helena, as the daughter of an Earl, outranked the family and most of their social set. Lady Anne clearly hoped for another such marriage in the family—perhaps to offset Henry's decidedly more modest match.

***

A few days later, the ladies were having tea, when they heard a commotion outside the house.

"What is that noise?" Lady Anne asked. Emily rushed over to the window.

"It's Nathaniel!" she said.

He was standing in the courtyard, shouting instructions at a footman. Beside him, a saddled horse whinnied and shook its mane. Nathaniel's clothes were spattered with mud from riding, and his face was red from exertion. He turned away from the footman and stomped up the steps to the house. Emily looked away from the window, and the concerned expression on her face alarmed Lady Anne.

"What is it? Is he hurt?"

Emily shook her head. "I don't think so."

They heard his footsteps in the entrance hall. Lady Anne hurried out to meet him. Emily and Lady Helena looked at each other. Rushed, muffled words filtered in from the hall. Then, they heard a loud clatter, as something heavy hit the marble floor.

"No! She'll not have me, Mother!" Nathaniel shouted. "It seems I am not worthy of that stupid cow's affection!"

He was striding past the open doors of the drawing room when he noticed Lady Helena and Emily. His face twisted in disgust.

"Your sister was quite a success at the party!" he said to Emily. "*She* was welcomed like a bosom friend by our hostess! Never mind that she was practically feral until my brother found her! Bloody hypocrites!"

His hatred seemed to rush at her like fire, and she felt tears spring to her eyes. He stalked off, and his mother hurried after him.

"You mustn't let him upset you, dear," Lady Helena said, taking Emily's hand and patting it soothingly. "He can be so awful, but he really doesn't mean what he says. He's been this way for as long as I've known him. Reacts terribly when he's disappointed. This mood of his will pass, and I'm certain he'll apologize."

***

As Emily approached the dining hall later that afternoon, Nathaniel rushed at her from the shadow of a statue. He grabbed her arm and leaned close to speak into her ear.

"You are quite pretty for a low-born drudge." His breath smelled of ale. She struggled to free herself from his grip.

"What?! Are you too fine a lady to be touched by my hand? You forget yourself, Miss Emily. You're a worthless waif, here at the benevolence of my family... and, as your benefactor, I think I'm due some payment from you. Some private companionship might help settle your debt... I'll want to collect quite soon."

She stared at him in horror. He dropped her arm and grinned at her before striding past her into the dining hall.

***

Emily slipped out of the house and made her way through the woods to the beach. She ran the whole way, and when she arrived, she sat on the sand, hugging her knees to her chest and shivering in the cold damp air. She worried vaguely about how to explain the sand that might stick to the heavy fabric of her dress. She wished this beach were more like the one near her mother's cottage, with a cliff and caves, where she could seek shelter until Hilary and Henry returned. Hilary would be furious when she learned of Nathaniel's threats. Emily was almost reluctant to tell her, for fear of how aggressively Hilary would retaliate.

For now, though there were no caves, at least, she could sit right against the small hill that backed the beach and hide from the sight of anyone on the path from the woods.

She felt hunted. She wished she could call for Karen, but she was afraid to shout, even though she doubted Nathaniel was near. He was probably still having luncheon or somewhere with Sir Charles or sauntering around the small town where his family was regarded with great respect.

Alone now, and, as safe as she could be without Hilary to protect her, she relaxed a little bit. The sensation of letting go of her fear was almost painful and she began to cry. She hugged herself and sobbed and then, sweating despite the chill in the air, she crawled to the water's edge and placed her hand in the cool foam. Her tears fell into the water the receding tide washed her tears out to sea. She pressed her wet, sandy hands to her face to soothe her cheeks.

Calmed by the water, she returned to her hiding place against the small hill to think about what she could do to stay safe. If she could convince Lady Helena that Hilary's absence was making her homesick, maybe Lady Helena, intent on comforting her, would keep Emily by her side for the evening. Then, tomorrow, she could persuade Lady Helena to send her to Hilary. Emily knew Hilary would help her get back to Mother and Morgan—and before Nathaniel knew anything about it, she would be gone and safe.

***

Karen and Manae were swimming north, returning to the waters they knew best. They'd spent several languid weeks soothed and enchanted by the warm waters of the southern seas. They'd marveled at the colorful fish and the giant, vibrant coral formations teeming with strange and delicious creatures.

Manae was delighted by Karen's enthusiasm. With Karen beside her, she saw her surroundings through new eyes and enjoyed them as much as Karen did. Only the growing presence of sharks in the warm waters had persuaded them to head north.

They were enjoying the thrilling sensation of cooler water, a sign that they were getting closer to home, when Karen started in alarm and stopped swimming. Manae circled back to her, afraid she was hurt. She looked around for an eel or other small predator that might have stung her. The drawn, anguished look on Karen's face convinced Manae that something was horribly wrong. She touched Karen's cheek to get her attention and, when they locked eyes, Karen told her she could sense that her youngest sister was in danger. They must go to her, Karen insisted, not considering that they couldn't help Emily on land.

Manae focused on the current. She sensed a violent struggle, miles away— a whale fighting off an orca. She sensed her sisters calmly navigating the seas to the north. Slowly, vaguely, she was able to register the signal that had reached Karen. It was human, terrified and desperate. In answer to Karen's anguish, Manae began swimming towards the signal. Karen followed. They would reach the area after nightfall. Then, they would wait and see what could be done.

Chapter 19

Emily slipped back into the house, unseen, through the servants' entrance. She made her way up the back staircase, stepped quietly into the hall and ducked into her bedroom. She removed her damp slippers and changed from her sandy dress into a clean rose-colored gown she knew Lady Helena liked. Flushed from the long trek home from the beach, she sat on her bed for a moment, trying to slow her breath.

She didn't want to linger alone in her room for too long in case Nathaniel was searching for her. She stepped out into the hall and made her way quickly to Lady Helena's suite of rooms. She knocked softly on the door. Lady Helena's maid, Finley, opened the door and peered out at her.

"May I speak with Lady Helena?" Emily asked, shyly deferential to Finley's age, commanding height and long-standing position in the household.

Though Emily was the sister-in-law of the baronet's brother, she felt uncertain around the servants, worried they would resent her if she put on airs. She always showed them respect and courtesy, and, because of this, they all liked her. Finley nodded briskly, but not unkindly, and went to ask Lady Helena if she would see Emily.

Emily heard Lady Helena's bright, musical voice exclaim happily. Finley returned a moment later and led Emily into the room.

"Hello Emily!" Lady Helena said. She wore a pink silk dressing gown and reclined on a one-armed sofa with a book on her lap.

"Good afternoon, Lady Helena," Emily said, smiling despite her anxiousness. Lady Helena gestured to a petite blue sofa beside the window, and Emily sat, grateful to be able to rest. She closed her eyes briefly and considered confiding in Lady Helena about Nathaniel.

When she opened her eyes, Lady Helena was staring at her with a worried expression.

"What's wrong?" she asked. "You look troubled."

This was Emily's opportunity to tell what Nathaniel had said to her. She looked at Lady Helena, whose hair had been done for breakfast and would be rearranged again for dinner, her dainty satin slippers hovering above the floor, their soles clean and impractical for anything besides walking clean-swept floors from one amusement to the next. A person with a good heart and kind nature, she might believe Emily, but, as a born aristocrat with a life-long association to the Northam family, she might not.

"Please don't think me ungrateful when I say this, My Lady," Emily said, sadly. "But with Hilary gone, I feel terribly homesick. I haven't been able to sleep properly since she went away, and it makes me miss my mother and sister very much. I'm afraid I'm making myself quite ill."

As she spoke, genuine tears sprung to Emily's eyes.

"Please forgive me," she said to Lady Helena, who was sitting up now, watching her with concern.

"Oh, my poor dear! What can I do to help you? I know—you must stay with me! Be my companion until your sister returns. We'll play cards, tell stories and keep each other amused. How does that sound?"

"Oh, thank you, that sounds lovely!" She would be safe until she could get away to find Hilary.

They talked and played cards until it was time to dress for dinner. Again, Emily dressed quickly, her heart skipping a beat with every noise from the hall outside her bedroom.

***

Later that evening, she and Lady Helena went down to dinner together. Nathaniel was there, with friends of Sir Charles's, who had ridden over to join them for dinner. Emily sat between Sir

Charles and his friend, and Nathaniel was between Lady Helena and the other man's wife.

She was able to avoid his stare until he asked pointedly, "Whatever is bothering our dear Miss Emily Reed? She is so quiet this evening."

To Emily's relief, Lady Helena spoke for her.

"She is missing her sister. Nathaniel, you mustn't tease her!"

"Very well. I promise to let her be," he said, putting his palms up in an exaggerated show of surrender, but Emily could hear the jeer in his voice.

***

When the visitors had gone home and the household was preparing to turn in for the evening, Emily's eyes welled up with tears as she considered the danger of returning to her room alone. She would have to try to find a hidden closet somewhere in the servant's hall and hope to make it through the night undiscovered.

Lady Helena saw her anxious expression.

"My dear, why don't you stay in my rooms this evening, so you won't be lonely? I have sisters, too, and this will remind me of being in the nursery with them," she said with a kind smile. Emily gratefully accepted. After they turned in, even though Lady Helena snored with surprising verve, Emily was able to sleep through the night.

***

The next morning, Emily rose, feeling well-rested and optimistic. She was thrilled when Lady Helena suggested they go for a ride later that morning and then go into town. While they were out shopping together, she would ask Lady Helena to send her to see Hilary.

The gentlemen joined them at breakfast, and Lady Helena told them of her plans for the day, inviting them to join. Emily blanched at this, but knew she would be safe, since Lady Helena would stay close to her. She could talk to her about going to Hilary when in one of the dress shops, where the men would be unlikely to follow them.

173

"Why don't you let me ride with Emily," Nathaniel said. "I can show her the way to town on horseback. The meadows there are beautiful this time of year. I know you are not fond of that ride, Helena, but she may be."

Lady Helena made a face at him.

"It's too rough for me— and you ride too fast!"

She glanced at Emily whose face had gone pale at Nathaniel's suggestion.

"It might be good for you, Emily," Lady Helena said. "Some exercise might help you feel better. I think perhaps you should go with Nathaniel."

Sir Charles spoke then, surprising Emily. "Helena, don't coerce her. She may not wish to go on such a rough ride, either."

Emily met his eyes, and she saw genuine concern in them. He was watching her closely, and she sensed he was trying to understand what was bothering her. She wished she could tell him. He could put an end to it for certain. But would he believe her over his brother?

"I don't think I'm ready for anything too challenging," she said softly. "I'm not a confident a rider yet."

"Well, fine then, Charles," Nathaniel said, as though conceding defeat. "I'll take her on a gentler path around the grounds here."

"Wonderful!" said Lady Helena. "That should refresh her."

With a sinking sensation, Emily realized Nathaniel had successfully altered their plan.

"Will you ride with us, too?" she asked Lady Helena, who shook her head.

"I don't think I will after all. I can plan out my shopping while you ride, and then we'll all go into town together in the coach. Nathaniel is an experienced rider. You'll be quite safe in his care. I'll accompany you to the stables, though, so I can tell Lewis which horse to give you."

Lady Helena walked with Emily to the stables. Sir Charles had detained his brother for a moment, but Nathaniel, practically singing with satisfaction, called after them that he would be along shortly.

The groom brought out the horse Lady Helena had requested, and Emily mounted, sitting carefully side saddle. Lady Helena sneezed at the dust the horse kicked up and waved it away from her face. She bid Emily a good ride and walked back to the house to get away from the clouds of dust.

The groom went back into the stable to prepare Nathaniel's horse and Emily was alone for a moment. This was her one chance to escape.

Heart pounding, she prodded the horse, and he began to trot away from the stable. She hiked her skirt, threw her leg over the horse so she was no longer seated side-saddle, leaned close to his neck, and urged him to run faster. He broke into a gallop. She guided him through the woods and down through the field. She stopped him once they reached the beach. She climbed down and pushed him to run back without her. He wouldn't go at first, but, finally, he trotted off.

She slipped down onto the beach, shaking with adrenaline and fear. She watched the waves rolling in and wondered what she had done. She didn't care if they were furious. They would send her home to her mother, and that would be fine with her. She realized she could have kept the horse and tried to ride him home, but then she would be a thief and could be hanged for it. She could survive, here on the beach, until Hilary returned. She and Henry were expected back in a few days, but if Emily were missing, they would probably be called back and arrive before tomorrow.

Slowly, she calmed down. As her adrenaline gave way to exhaustion, the steady sound of the waves lulled her into a soft sleep.

***

"Here you are!" Nathaniel's voice cut through the fog of sleep, like a living nightmare.

Emily's eyes flew open, and she saw him looming above her on the small hill. Despite her sudden terror, she was briefly grateful he'd felt the need to yell out in self- satisfaction. He could have easily snuck down and been upon her before she woke. The realization made her throat to constrict in panic, and she jumped up and backed away from him toward the water.

"Where do you think you're going to go?" he asked, laughing. He jogged down the hill toward her.

She ran into the ocean, and he stood on the shore and stared in disbelief as she waded deeper in and farther away from him, until the water was up to her shoulders. Her dress felt unbearably heavy and her boots felt like stones tied to her feet.

"You must be mad!" he said. "But that won't deter me."

An ugly grin crossed his face.

"I tried to save the poor girl from drowning," he said, in a dramatic tone of voice, as if rehearsing for the stage. "She was so desperate, you all saw her, but who could have known she was going to try to take her own life? Shame about my ruined clothes, but I had to try...Maybe I will save you. Let's see how you behave!"

He began wading toward her. Waves splashed against her face as she started to cry, furious and terrified. She was in as deep as she could go without being submerged. She tried to move sideways, thinking she might be able to make it back to the beach while he was in the water, but he was coming at her too quickly, and soon his arms grabbed hers, pulling violently.

Though he held her arms, she clawed at his hands and fought to stand her ground against the forceful waves and the shifting sand beneath her boots. He cursed at her as they struggled, and she felt strength well up in her. She'd drown before she let him defeat her.

Then, she felt something brush her back, startling her. She looked down and saw the shimmering black and gold tail of an enormous fish glide past them in the cloudy water. She gasped.

In his hateful fervor, Nathaniel didn't notice. He jerked her arms viciously and she screamed in pain. Then, she felt his grip loosen as, beneath the water, she saw a pair of hands slide over his hands, working to pry them off her. She felt him tighten his hold in resistance for a moment, but then his hands were pulled from her arms. The pressure of his grip subsided, and she realized she was free.

Instinctively, she began stumbling toward shore. She heard him scream, but she did not look back. She moved as quickly as she could against the current, desperate to make it back before he did, to run and find a hiding place before he got out of the water.

When she reached the shore, she dared a quick look back, terrified he was right behind her, but he was gone. The surface was unbroken, and the tide rolled in, undisturbed. She scanned the shoreline in case he'd swam in either direction and was now making his way out of the water farther up the beach, but she saw nothing except the sand and the sea. She stood for a long moment, numbly watching the calm, constant tide.

***

Karen reclined beside Manae on the ocean floor in the shelter of a small reef. The attack had taken a lot out of Manae and she needed to rest. She was exhausted and disoriented, but aware of the comforting weight of Karen's hand on her back.

As she came out of the fog that always followed her bouts of violence, she felt relieved to see Karen beside her. Karen was watching over her with concern in her eyes along with something else, something Manae couldn't decipher. This troubled her and she struggled to become more coherent so she could ask Karen what was wrong.

Karen asked how she was feeling, if she was hurt. When Manae said she was only tired, Karen told her she was grateful to her for saving her sister. They held each other's gaze, as the sea gently rocked their bodies. The pain and fear in Karen's eyes when they found her sister under attack and the urgent malice radiating from Emily's assailant had evoked Manae's dormant fury.

She had set upon the land creature in a violent rush, pulling him away from Emily and dragging him into the depths of the sea, where she'd torn at him until the sharks began to appear. Karen had watched the whole attack, and Manae suddenly understood that what she saw in Karen's eyes was triumph. She

177

had underestimated her gentle friend.

Karen was looking at her now with a tenderness that told Manae she didn't have to worry about scaring her away. Together, they rose from the ocean floor and began to swim north, toward home.

Chapter 20

Once her shock subsided, Emily began walking. She was damp and exhausted, and she had to get warm. She entered the woods, and made her way back toward the estate, staying under the cover of the trees as she approached the back edge of the property.

She left the woods once she reached Hilary's cottage. The sky was growing dark, and the servants had finished their work and returned to the main house. She was grateful to find the kitchen door unsecured, and she slipped inside. She shed her damp clothes in the kitchen and hurried up the stairs. In Hilary's bedroom, she found a nightdress to wear. Then, she wrapped herself in blankets and climbed into the bed.

***

The sound of footsteps on the stairs woke her. She jerked upright, her heart racing, afraid Nathaniel had somehow emerged from the sea and found her here. The bright morning light hurt her eyes and she was about to stand, though her legs were aching, when Hilary entered the room.

"Emily! Thank goodness! What's happened?"

Hilary wrapped her arms around her sister.

"They sent for us and told us you'd gone missing! I was so worried!" Hilary said, beginning to cry with relief. Emily sank into her sister's embrace and exhaled.

"I was lost," she said. "The horse took off and I couldn't control him."

The lie tasted bitter as she told it to her sister, who was watching her face anxiously.

"They said Nathaniel went searching for you. But he hasn't returned. Did he find you?"

Emily opened her mouth to lie again, to say he had not, but instead felt desperate to confide the truth to her sister.

"He threatened me! I ran away because I was afraid of him, of what he intended to do!"

She sobbed and went on in a rush.

"He began stalking me as soon as he returned from your friends' house. He said I owed him for his family letting me stay here. He kept trying to catch me alone. I tried so hard to avoid him, but then they were going to let him take me riding alone! So, I ran, but he caught me on the beach! He chased me into the water. I would have died—I would have died rather than let him —but somehow I got free and then..." She tried to remember what had happened. She recalled the giant fishtail and the hands that had covered his beneath the water.

"Where is he now, Emily?" Hilary asked. Her voice was steady, but her eyes were wild with anger. Emily thought for a moment, piecing together what she could recall.

"I think Karen saved me," she said. "I think she pulled him away from me and took him out to sea."

Hilary gasped.

"Did you see her?"

"I didn't see her face, but I did see a tail— and hands. I saw someone pull him off me in the water. As soon as I was free, I ran to the shore. I looked back to see if he was following me. But he never came out of the water."

Emily shook as she spoke, reliving the terror of the day before. Hilary hugged her close.

"It's over now, Emily. Don't worry. And if he did survive, he'll pay for this. He will never harm you again."

They were sitting quietly, side by side, when Henry found them.

"Emily! Thank the Lord! Are you hurt?"

"She's fine," Hilary said. "She lost control of the horse. When she got him to stop so she could get down, he ran off. She got lost in the woods and had to find her way back and was walking most of the night. She's exhausted."

"Thank goodness you're safe!" he said, kneeling in front of Emily. "Oh, I'm so relieved!"

She smiled at him.

"Emily, did you see Nathaniel? He went to try to find you. We've been looking for you both in the woods, but we've seen no sign of him."

"No," Hilary answered for Emily. "I asked her. They didn't cross paths. Maybe he's returned home by now. Are you going to go back to the house?"

"Yes, maybe you're right. I'll go up there."

He headed for the door.

When they could see him through the window riding off toward the house, Hilary faced Emily.

"I trust Henry, but I'm not going to tell him what Nathaniel did yet in case he did make it out of the ocean. If Nathaniel does return, I'll take care of him myself."

"I don't want you to take that kind of a risk for me!"

Hilary shook her head, determined.

"I'm wondering if you should go back to live with Mother and Morgan. It may be safer for you there, whether he returns or not," she said.

Emily had been happy here until Nathaniel had returned and now that he was probably gone, she had thought she might be happy here again. But she knew Hilary was right.

"Don't worry about it now, Emily. We'll discuss it once you've recovered. Now you must rest."

⁕

Hilary and Emily were having a small meal in the cottage's dining room, when they heard Henry's horse approaching. It had been several hours since he'd left for the main house, which Hilary had taken to mean that Nathaniel had not returned. She walked to the front hall to greet him and saw the worry in his eyes.

"They've found Nathaniel's horse," he said, slumping into a chair. "Down by the sea, waiting for him... why on earth would he have gone into the water?"

He was shaking his head. Hilary put her arm around him.

"I am so sorry for you, Henry," she said, holding him tightly. "This is so difficult for all of us. Will you come in and take something to eat? It may help."

He shook his head

"No, I can't. I don't know what to do."

Hilary heard the helplessness in his voice, and she felt sorry for him. She wondered how one family could produce two fine men like Henry and Charles and a monster like Nathaniel.

"How is your mother taking the news?"

"Not well. She collapsed when she heard. Helena is with her now."

"Can I do anything to help?"

"I don't know—I can't think. I'll go back up soon to talk to Charles. I wanted to let you know I may not return until quite late tonight. Will you and your sister be all right?"

"Of course. We'll be fine," she said, rubbing his shoulder.

He kissed her cheek and stood slowly. She watched him walk upstairs to change his clothes.

She returned to the dining room where Emily sat. Jonathan, the footman who came from the manor to serve them each morning and evening, placed a teacup before her. The look of concern on his face touched her. She knew the servants would have heard that Emily had gone missing. She felt a sudden chill as she realized they might also know about Nathaniel's ill-intentioned pursuit of Emily. Many things were seen by the servants passing silently through the halls and hidden passages of great houses. She glanced at Jonathan as he pulled out her chair for her.

"Thank you, Jonathan," she said. He nodded solemnly.

Emily was looking at her expectantly, anxious for news. Hilary caught her eye and then glanced toward Jonathan who stood behind her. Emily lowered her chin, a subtle gesture that showed she understood her sister's meaning, but her eyes remained wide with concern. They ate in silence, interrupted only by the sound of the front door opening and closing as

Henry left for his family's house.

***

They retreated to Hilary's sitting room after dinner, once Jonathan and the cook returned to the main house for the night.

"They found Nathaniel's horse on the beach."

Emily gasped.

"They have no way of knowing you were there," Hilary reminded her, touching her arm. "It seems to them like he was looking for you and may have decided to wade into the ocean. That can be explained away by something he thought he saw. You left nothing behind?"

"Nothing." Emily shook her head. Her horse had returned to the house, and her dress and boots were all she'd had with her. Hillary had hidden the clothes under a loose floorboard in her room while Emily slept. They smelled of the ocean, and Hilary intended to wash them as soon as she could do it without anyone seeing.

"Will you send me home soon?" Emily asked. She sat on a delicate dove-gray settee, a gift from Henry's mother that Hilary rarely used because she saw it as Lady Anne's attempt to convert her into someone who would sit and do hours of needlepoint work to pass her time.

"I think we'll wait a little while to send you home," Hilary said. "It will be safer for you to go home, where you won't have to worry about keeping the secret, but, until we know a little more, I'm afraid it may look suspicious to send you off. For now, we'll say you are recovering from your ordeal, and I'll keep you here, so you don't have to go back to the main house. After a few weeks pass, it will seem natural to send you back to Mother."

Hilary sat beside Emily on the dainty sofa. She saw worry cloud her sister's eyes.

"Everything will be fine, Emily. You've done nothing wrong. Nathaniel got exactly what he deserved. I wish we could tell them all the truth and expose him for the beast he really was. Please try not to worry. Trust me to take care of this."

"I do. I have always trusted you—and Karen."

They smiled at one another.

"I wish I had seen her face," Emily said. "She was so close, and I missed her, after all this time. And now, it wouldn't be wise to go back to the beach to look for her."

"No, it wouldn't. But perhaps when you get back to mother's house you can look for her there."

"Will you go up to the manor house tomorrow with Henry?" Emily asked.

"I don't know. If he wants me to, I suppose I will. But I have no idea what to say to them, since they are grieving someone I despise."

***

Henry returned late the next morning, surprising them by arriving in a carriage. Hilary watched from the front window and frowned when she saw Lady Helena and Sir Charles climb out of the carriage as well. A small mercy, Lady Anne was not with them.

Hilary ushered Emily quickly up to one of the bedrooms and asked her to get under the covers and pretend to be asleep. She was walking back down the stairs when Henry entered, followed by his sister-in-law and brother.

"Hello," she said. "I was checking on Emily."

"How is she feeling?" Lady Helena asked, her eyes red-rimmed and full of concern. "May I see her? Oh, I owe her such an apology! This whole terrible ordeal is all my fault!"

Tears spilled from her eyes, alarming Hilary who was confused by her words and unsure how to react.

"Darling," Sir Charles said to Lady Helena. "It's not your fault. I keep telling you. I'm certain Emily bears you no ill will."

"I was supposed to ride with her," Lady Helena said to Hilary. "But I selfishly changed my mind when Nathaniel volunteered. I went back into the house and left Emily. Nathaniel was detained and she was left alone, so when her horse bolted, no one was there to help her, no one saw where it took her!"

She began to cry again, and Hilary fought back irritation.

"You couldn't have known that would happen," she assured

Lady Helena. "But Emily is sleeping now. Perhaps you might visit with her later?"

"Of course," said Lady Helena, miserably. Hilary turned to Sir Charles.

"How is your mother this morning?"

He sighed.

"She is not well, I'm afraid. But I'm glad to hear that your sister is recovering. I look forward to seeing you all at the house as soon as she feels up to it."

***

The weeks following Nathaniel's disappearance passed slowly for everyone on the estate. Lady Anne retreated to her rooms for most of each day, coming out only to share meals with the family.

When Hilary and Henry brought Emily up to the house for breakfast several weeks later, Lady Anne refused to acknowledge her. She blamed Emily for being a poor horsewoman, for inspiring Nathaniel's chivalry and causing his disappearance. She didn't speak her feelings, but her animosity toward Emily was clear.

After the uncomfortable meal, Emily retreated to the cottage, and Hilary went out to ride across the estate with Henry, hoping Emily might nap if left alone. Hilary had heard the gentle creak of floorboards nightly since the incident, as Emily paced late into most evenings, unable to quiet her mind and fall asleep until early morning, when she was finally exhausted.

Before she left to ride with Henry, Hilary had reassured Emily that Lady Anne did not know or suspect what had really happened after Nathaniel had left the house. While another sort of person might have taken some consolation in the possibility that her son had died performing an act of bravery, Lady Anne most resented losing the one family member who relished their position in society as much as she did.

***

Alone in the cottage, Emily tried to rest, reclining in the sweet little bed in the smallest bedroom in the cottage. Hilary had offered her a larger room, farther down the hall, but she preferred this nest-like little sanctuary,

Through the round window beside her bed, she saw the wide green lawn and the imposing main house. It would be a lovely view for a child if this room someday became a nursery.

She sighed, exhausted. The soft light of the late afternoon had muted the fear that dogged her every night in the darkness, but when she closed her eyes, her mind seemed to speed up, churning with anxious thoughts.

She would ask Hilary to help her return to their mother's house. Enough time had passed. Aila and Morgan would welcome her back, and she longed to be near them.

She was surprised to feel an ache in her chest at the thought of leaving. It felt like turning back halfway through a journey, but she couldn't stay at the estate, where her presence would continue to upset Lady Anne. And if anyone in the family ever found out what had happened to Nathaniel, they would despise her. He would always be family to them and would surely always come before her in their hearts, regardless of what he'd done.

She cared for all of them, especially Lady Helena and Sir Charles. Now, she felt uneasy around them, stalked by the threat of suspicion. Sometimes, she imagined them cloistered in the library, discussing Nathaniel and deciding she must have been to blame. When she'd gone up to the house for breakfast earlier that day, the halls themselves, once welcoming and easy to cross, had felt cold and closed off. She wouldn't have dared to climb the imposing marble staircase to visit her old room. This was no longer her home, and it would be best for everyone if she returned to her mother's house.

***

Emily was in her room, waiting for Hilary to return from her ride with Henry that afternoon, when someone knocked on the door of the cottage. She heard the muted rumble of voices as Joseph opened the door and greeted the visitor. Moments later, she heard fast, heavy footfalls on the steps and then a light rap at the door of her room.

"Yes? Who's there?" she called out. The door swung open and a young maid peeked into the room. Her full cheeks were pink from exertion.

"Lady Helena is asking for you up at the house, Miss. I'm to tell you she's sent the carriage for you."

Confused, Emily stared at her for a moment. She wished Hilary would return. What if they wanted to interrogate her about Nathaniel? But, if that were the case, the summons would more likely have come from Lady Anne, or even Sir Charles. And if she refused to go, it might seem suspicious.

"I'll be down in a moment," she said, and the girl stepped out of the doorway, closing the door. Emily smoothed her hair and walked down the stairs and out into the waiting carriage.

The sun was beginning to set as she rode toward the house. From the carriage window, she spotted the silhouettes of two riders galloping against the orange sky. Hilary and Henry were heading back toward the cottage along the opposite side of the great lawn.

At the house, she entered the marble hall and went up to knock on Lady Helena's door. Finley ushered her into the room. Lady Helena was relaxing on the settee by the window. When she saw Emily, she stood and hurried over, taking her by the hands and kissing her cheek.

"Hello, my dear friend! I'm so glad you've come! I have the most wonderful news!"

***

"A baby!" Hilary exclaimed, when Emily relayed Lady Helena's news to her later that evening. After dinner, Henry had retired to his study to read, and Hillary and Emily sat on the bed in Emily's room. Since Emily been staying with them, Hilary had taken to sitting and talking with her awhile before going to her own room to sleep. The ritual comforted Emily, reminding her of when they'd shared a bedroom at home.

"Yes, she is overjoyed!"

"It's wonderful news for them. Sir Charles must be thrilled," Hillary said. She noted her sister's anxious expression. "Why do you look troubled?"

"She asked me to come back and stay at the house and be her companion, but I've been thinking I should go home soon."

Hillary put a hand on her shoulder.

"I understand. You need to find peace. I'll miss you terribly, but I want you to feel happy and safe."

Emily looked into Hilary's eyes, struck by how soft they could be when she was in a gentle mood. The spark that usually blazed there was absent, and all Emily could see was concern.

"I really want to stay, actually, but I feel so terrible for what happened."

Hilary looked startled. "*You* feel terrible? Emily, it wasn't your fault!"

"Sometimes, I think of what it would have been like for them if I'd never come here. Nathaniel would be alive. Instead of grieving, everyone would be happy because of Lady Helena's news. She wants me to be with her to cheer her and keep her spirits up because it's so depressing up there lately. I want to help her, but I can't help but feel that their grief is partly my fault. I'm glad he's dead—and I feel guilty for thinking that. I worry for Karen, for how she feels after taking his life. I remember how pleasant things were before he took an interest in me, and I wonder if I somehow encouraged his attentions, if it was partly my fault."

The fire was back in Hilary's eyes, and her jaw was tight.

"Emily, *none* of what happened was your fault! You did nothing to encourage the terror he inflicted upon you. He was evil. If he were here right now, if he walked into this room, I would kill him myself to protect you, and I would not regret it. And Karen would do it a thousand times over if she had to. You are completely innocent! He's the one to blame—and he got what he deserved. You must believe that!"

Her sister's passionate response blanketed Emily, and finally, mercifully, she did believe it.

***

Emily slept soundly that night, and when she woke up the

next morning, she decided to stay.

Chapter 21

As her pregnancy progressed, Lady Helena kept Emily by her side. She much preferred Emily's pleasant demeanor to Lady Anne's somber moods.

Lady Anne no longer held Emily responsible for Nathaniel's disappearance, since she had adopted the view that he had been remarkably heroic and noble, which fanned her pride and soothed her. But, she moved through the house like a wraith in a dark dress, and she did not engage much with anyone, joining them only when custom demanded.

Emily noticed that Lady Helena seemed to be almost afraid of Lady Anne, becoming nervous and retreating to her rooms if she heard the older woman approaching. Emily worked to be cheerful, even when she felt tired, and she fought the lure of the drowsy melancholy that permeated the once-vibrant house.

At first, Emily and Lady Helena were aware they sometimes laughed a bit too enthusiastically at one another's jokes, and their smiles were often buttressed by intention rather than emotion, but gradually, the gloom began to lift, and they fell naturally into their old way of enjoying one another's company. Emily enjoyed being attentive to Lady Helena, watching with excitement as she grew larger with her baby. Lady Helena was convinced she would give birth to a boy.

"To cheer my poor mother-in-law, perhaps we'll name him Nathaniel," Lady Helena mused one afternoon, as they sat sewing together in her sitting room. A bitter chill shook Emily at the mention of the name, and, without thinking, she said, "No!"

Lady Helena looked up, startled.

"Forgive me!" Emily said, thinking quickly. "It's just— I expected you would name him after Sir Charles. I didn't mean to speak out like that!"

Lady Helena laughed heartily.

"Oh, but you're right! I suppose we should name the boy after his father!" Lady Helena said, and she winked at Emily. "Charles, he shall be."

Chapter 22

D read weighed on the occupants of the room like a physical burden. The doctor's forehead shone with sweat, and Emily mopped it for him in between her ministrations to the laboring Lady Helena. Finley, who was supposed to be aiding Lady Helena, had been too tentative and slow, overcome by the distress of her mistress. Now, she hung back uselessly while Emily and Hilary helped the doctor.

Where the familiar face of a trusted maid had reassured many new mothers in the doctor's care, Finley's presence offered no comfort to Lady Helena, who was barely conscious. Fever blurred her vision, clouded her mind and convulsed her body. Lady Anne had long ago lost her nerve and left the room. She was fretting somewhere in the house, while Sir Charles paced in large circles in his study, desperately anxious for his wife. He had not understood the danger, the trauma she would have to endure. He felt sick with fear and guilt.

In the birthing chamber, Hilary's hardy confidence bolstered the doctor. He was grateful for the help of Hilary and Emily, who flanked the bed, showing no fear. Their young faces were fierce with resolve as they tended to Lady Helena and directed the maids in replenishing supplies.

The blood was what had unnerved Lady Helena's maid and rendered her useless. She'd seen a woman give birth before, and bleeding was something she'd expected, but she'd never seen it like this. The doctor knew the torrent of deep red and the greying of the young woman's flesh were terrible signs. He was deeply relieved when the infant was born at last. It cried and breathed, and he handed it quickly to the Emily so he could concentrate on trying to save Lady Helena.

Emily took the tiny, wailing baby into her arms and saw that it was a girl. She cleaned the baby gently and wrapped her small, wriggling body in a soft, clean blanket. The baby's healthy cries seemed to echo in Emily's heart, filling her with a tender relief that was almost painful. She smiled gently at the little face.

"Hello," Emily whispered.

Hilary helped the doctor, who was working frantically to normalize Lady Helena. Finley seemed to have recovered from her inertia. Seeing an opportunity to make up for her earlier uselessness, she hurried over to help Emily with the baby. She peered down at the bundle Emily held in her arms, and she gasped loudly. Emily, Hilary and the doctor stared at her.

"What is it?" The doctor asked, keeping his eyes on Lady Helena.

"It's deformed!" Finley said. "There's no nose, Doctor, and the face isn't shaped right!"

Emily looked down at the baby in her arms. Now that Finley had mentioned it, she could see that the child had no nose between her slate blue eyes, and her right eye sat a little bit lower than the left. But Emily saw only beauty in the tiny face.

"Is she breathing?" the doctor asked.

"Yes," Emily said.

"Then please take her to the nurse to be fed, and I will examine her when I can." He looked at Lady Helena, whose skin was ashen, and shook his head. "And please send for Sir Charles!"

***

Emily left the room with the baby in her arms. She dispatched a maid who was lingering in the hallway to summon Sir Charles for the doctor. The maid hurried off, and Emily entered the nursery where the nursemaid waited.

The nursemaid crossed the room swiftly to receive her charge. Emily placed the infant in her arms. The woman looked down at the baby and halted suddenly.

"Oh…" she said in a soft, anxious voice. "I don't know if I can… Miss…What's wrong with it?"

The nursemaid stepped backward, her eyes fixed on the

baby's face.

Emily fixed the nursemaid with a hard look

"You must feed this child. Now. I won't see her starve because you are squeamish."

The woman began to protest weakly, but Emily's determined insistence silenced her, and she reluctantly accepted the baby. She fed the baby, with Emily sitting close by to make sure she finished the first crucial feeding.

As soon as the baby had been fed, the woman quickly held her out for Emily to take. Emily accepted the child gently and gave her a soft smile before turning her attention to the agitated nursemaid.

"Please, Miss. I don't think I can do it again!"

"Then you must find someone who can – right away! She'll need to be fed again soon!"

Relieved, the woman stood and said, "May I go, then? To find someone?"

"Yes but be back within the hour with someone who will feed this child!"

The woman nodded and hurried from the room. There had been plenty of recent births among the poorer women of the parish. Not all of them could be as weak-minded and squeamish as this one. Emily felt sure she would find someone as quickly as she could because she wouldn't want to be in the bad graces of the Northam family, and she certainly wouldn't want to be seen as the person responsible for the child's death.

While she waited for the nursemaid's replacement, Emily held the baby and hummed a soft tune. She gazed at the small, sleeping face and felt a wave of peace wash over her, despite her worry for Lady Helena. It astounded her to think anyone could look at this tiny, innocent child and see anything bad or frightening. The baby was breathing soft, hearty little breaths. Emily felt sure she would survive.

Chapter 23

While Lady Helena recovered slowly from giving birth, Emily had taken on the role of supervising the baby's caregivers. The new nursemaid was a mature, efficient woman. She immediately accepted the child into her arms when she was brought to the house on the night the baby was born. She patiently ensured that the baby fed well and completely, pausing often to make sure the baby could breathe.

A nanny had been hired as well. The nanny, a young woman named Agnes, was strong, pleasant and unfazed by the baby's unusual appearance. Emily was devoted to the infant and did not want to hand her off to someone else completely, but she quickly came to trust the young nanny. Both Emily and Agnes were looking forward to taking the baby to meet Lady Helena. Agnes dressed her in a tiny satin gown for her first meeting with her mother.

Family visitors to the nursery had been scarce, except for Hillary who came to help Emily every day, and Henry, who came often to check on them. Lady Anne did not visit at all.

Visiting the nursery one morning after leaving Henry and his mother in the sitting room, Hilary confided angrily to Emily that Lady Anne had said she would be relieved if the child would die, "for the good of the pitiful creature".

Sir Charles had visited his daughter in the nursery once. He entered the sunny little room in good spirits after learning that his wife would recover, but he'd looked stricken when he saw the baby's face and had found an excuse to leave shortly after arriving.

***

Despite the negative reactions of the baby's father and grandmother, Emily felt sure Lady Helena would be enchanted with her little daughter now that she was finally well enough to meet her. The baby was as sweet and good natured as an infant could be, happy and uncomplaining, even during examinations by the doctor, who came to the nursery often to check her progress. Emily thought she was breathtakingly beautiful, especially when she smiled.

Finley met the small party of Emily, who carried the baby, Agnes and Hilary at the door of Lady Helena's rooms. Finley had suffered great personal shame for her initial reaction to the baby, and she kept her expression respectfully composed as she opened the door and greeted them.

Lady Helena was sitting up in bed, waiting, with a bright smile on her pale face. The doctor had gently warned her of the child's irregular appearance, and she had replied, laughing, "But aren't all infants rather hideous?"

"Meet your mother, my dear girl," Emily said, smiling so tenderly at the infant that Lady Helena thrust her arms out, anxious to share Emily's obvious joy. Emily placed the baby gently in her mother's arms, and Lady Helena cradled her carefully. Lady Helena looked down into the eyes of her daughter.

Watching this first exchange, Emily was struck by the procession of emotions that crossed Lady Helena's face: first bewilderment, then sadness and, finally and worst, disappointment. Emily looked away and wished they could have left mother and daughter alone for this moment, so these initial intimate reactions could have passed unobserved by outsiders before they moved on to the look of love she knew would follow. She did not want shame to cloud Lady Helena's memory of meeting her daughter. She looked at Hilary and saw her sister watching with concern.

"Well, hello, my darling," Lady Helena said, in a controlled, pleasant tone of voice Emily recognized. She'd heard Lady Helena use that same tone socially when circumstances had forced her to greet someone she would have preferred to avoid. Emily's heart sank.

"Nanny," Lady Helena called, "will you take my sweet daughter back to the nursery? Emily, Hilary, please forgive me, but I'm feeling quite weak today. Perhaps another day we can have a longer visit."

She closed her eyes as Agnes took the baby from her arms.

"Have you decided on a name, my lady?" Emily asked. She was desperate to help strengthen the connection before Lady Helena dismissed the baby from her room and her mind. Lady Helena opened her eyes and looked at Emily. Her face softened when she saw the concern in Emily's eyes.

"She shall be called Sophia Elizabeth. After my Aunt Sophie."

Emily nodded and rose to leave. Lady Helena held out her thin hand, and Emily took it.

"Thank you for caring for her," she said, and Emily heard the past, the present and the future implied in her words.

***

Emily, Agnes and Mrs. Farnum, the nursemaid, quickly established a comfortable routine. Agnes was younger and less experienced than most nannies in other grand homes—Lady Anne's desire to avoid any gossip getting out about the infant's unique condition ruled out more seasoned, but better-connected nannies they might have otherwise chosen—but Agnes's youth served her well in the role. She was not arrogant about her position and got along well with Emily, whose help and presence in the nursery she appreciated rather than resented. Her brother was a well-liked member of the household staff and helped her make fast friends of the other servants. She had cared for young children in much humbler homes, and she was efficient, but gentle and jovial in her care of Sophia, who was thriving at eight months old.

Mrs. Farnum was mother to seven children, and she enjoyed the temporary escape and comfort of the quiet, elegant nursery. Emily remembered how quickly and competently Mrs. Farnum had stepped into action when Sophia's original nursemaid abandoned her, and she made a point of seeing to the nursemaid's comfort, providing her with a well-cushioned nursing chair and requesting special tea cakes from the kitchen for her.

Lady Helena never visited the nursery, so Sophia's caregivers had little contact with her. She summoned Emily to join her in her room or down in the drawing room far less often than before, and Emily sensed that she reminded her of Sophia and made her feel guilty.

Emily was surprised and delighted when one of the maids appeared at the nursery door to invite her to have tea and cake with Lady Helena. She hoped she had finally come around to accepting Sophia and wanted to discuss having the child brought to her again.

When she arrived, she found Lady Helena lounging on her settee and in excellent spirits. The first thing Emily noticed was the curve of her stomach. Lady Helena had remained alarmingly thin, even after her recovery. Her cheeks were sunken and her arms frail, but, despite the loose-fitting dresses currently in fashion, Emily could see at once that she was pregnant.

"So, you see, I have some news," she said to Emily with a twinkle in her eye. Emily rushed to her side and knelt beside her. Lady Helena took Emily's hands.

"I'm so happy for you," Emily said, trying to keep the worry from her voice as she wondered what this new child would mean for Sophia.

***

Emily entered the nursery one afternoon, several days after her visit to Lady Helena's rooms, and found Mrs. Farnum and Agnes engaged in a hushed, sober discussion while Sophia slept. They stopped speaking abruptly when they saw her, and she walked over to where they sat. The whole household knew by now about Lady Helena's pregnancy. Spotting the anxious looks on their faces, Emily was instantly afraid something bad had happened.

"What is it?" she asked. Agnes looked at Mrs. Farnum.

"Agnes heard something," Mrs. Farnum said. Agnes cut in, anxious to clarify that she hadn't been eavesdropping.

"It was many months ago, Miss, when Miss Sophia was a few weeks old. I was walking down the back hallway to fetch some linens, and, on the other side of the wall, I heard Lady Helena's doctor speaking to her—I only heard because he has such a loud voice— he told her she must not have another baby anytime soon, that she needed a few years to heal, because it would be very dangerous."

"Perhaps he's changed his opinion since," Emily suggested, to calm their fears, but her chest tightened with anxiety, and a deep sadness came over her.

Chapter 24

Emily realized Lady Helena was in labor when she saw Sir Charles in agitated conversation with the doctor on the staircase. She was walking down the stairs, on her way to visit Hilary. She continued, past the two men, with her head down. They took no notice of her, and she could hear them arguing.

"Tell me she will come through this," Sir Charles said.

"I wish I could, Sir Charles! But I warned her explicitly not to have another child so soon! I will do my best to care for her, but I cannot promise!"

Once outside, Emily ran down the long road that led to Hilary's cottage. Henry stood outside the cottage, dressed for a ride into town. He saw Emily racing toward him, her face blanched with worry, and he ran to meet her.

"Emily! What's wrong?"

"It's Lady Helena," she said, trying to catch her breath. "The doctor is here!"

Henry brought her into the cottage and asked the cook to bring her some tea, while he went upstairs to fetch Hilary.

Together, the three of them rode back up to the house in a small wagon. Once they arrived, Henry went to the parlor in search of his brother, while Hilary and Emily hurried upstairs to offer their help to the doctor.

Sir Charles knelt beside Lady Helena's bed. He held her hand and fought back tears. Her face was pallid, and she grimaced in pain. She was feeble from months of lying in bed for most of the day and enduring rounds of bloodletting at her doctor's orders. She was ill-prepared to rise to the physical challenge demanded of her body. The room was hot, but Lady Helena shivered with fever. Finley and two other maids were rushing around, in rapid response to the Doctor's demands. Emily started to move forward to help as well, but Hilary put a hand on her shoulder, holding her back.

"Go attend to Sophia, Emily," she said softly into her sister's ear. "I'll stay here and help. It may be a long while, and I will send for you if we need you."

Emily nodded, giving in to the wisdom and protectiveness behind Hilary's words. She slipped out of the room and retreated to the nursery with Agnes and Sophia. She held Sophia close and rocked her.

***

The doctor delivered the stillborn baby boy in the last hours of the night. Sir Charles held his grief at bay to focus on his wife, who slipped in and out of consciousness. He stood close to her but when her eyes fluttered open, she looked right through him. For a brief moment, he was relieved that she was too drowsy to inquire about the baby, but his relief turned to concern as she seemed to fade, rather than fall, into a deep sleep.

She took her last, shallow breath as the dawn broke.

***

Emily, her eyes aching from the long, sleepless night, watched from the nursery window as Sir Charles raced his horse across the lawn toward the horizon. She walked over to the crib and looked down at Sophia, who slept, peacefully unaware that she had lost her mother. Listening to the soft cadence of the child's breath, watching her tiny eyelids flutter as she dreamed, love and sorrow overwhelmed Emily.

Part 3

Chapter 1

Emily found Sophia sitting in the tall, wing-backed chair beside the nursery window, watching her father and uncle walk across the wide lawn outside. The little girl loved to curl up in that chair and watch the daily activities outside: grooms bringing horses around from the stables, her father and uncle walking the land, or her Aunt Hilary leading her small flock of sheep from the little barn to their meadow. When there were no people outside, she watched the birds crossing the sky in graceful, swooping arcs and the treetops swaying in the breeze. Emily knew that her little post made Sophia feel secure and connected to the world around her, and, in the afternoons, she had Agnes serve Sophia her tea on the small table beside the chair.

Sophia turned at the sound of the door opening and smiled when she saw Emily.

"Hello, Sophie." Emily smiled warmly and sat in the seat beside Sophia's chair.

"Good morning, Aunt Emily."

"What's the news out there today?"

"Papa and Uncle Henry have gone for a walk. Earlier, one of Aunt Hilary's dogs chased a goose, but then, the goose turned around and began to chase him! It was so funny! I wish you could have seen it!"

She giggled at the memory, and Emily laughed, too, delighted to see Sophia in good spirits.

"Do you feel well enough to manage a walk in the garden with me today?" Emily asked, noticing the bruise-like rings beneath the child's eyes.

"A walk would be so lovely. Can we go through the roses?"

"Certainly."

The little courtyard in the center of the garden, surrounded by tall rose bushes, had been Lady Helena's favorite area of the garden, and featured a special rose bush named for her there that seemed to flower more often than the others. Sophia liked to sit beside it. She'd started asking about her mother more often, curious as any seven-year-old child would be about a parent she had never known.

They walked arm in arm down the hallway, carefully navigating the long, wide central staircase, and passing through the rear doors of the house and into the garden.

***

Lady Anne watched them from the window of her salon. When Sir Charles returned moments later from his stroll with Henry, he stopped in to greet her. After accepting his kiss on her cheek, she turned her eyes back to the garden outside, where Emily and Sophia were strolling among the flowers.

Her eyes followed her granddaughter. "Charles, I'm afraid I must ask you again to consider sending Sophia to a place where she can be properly attended by a doctor. Emily does not have the training to see to her medical needs for much longer. Do you see how slowly they walk? Her legs are getting worse."

Sir Charles noted his mother's stony expression as he considered her words. He wasn't surprised by her suggestion. He knew Sophia's presence made her uncomfortable. He'd grown accustomed to the strange shape of his daughter's face and could almost see past all that was abnormal. He could even spot glimpses of his beloved Helena in her eyes when she smiled. He'd hoped that his mother would eventually become used to Sophia, too, and accept her. But Lady Anne had never made any attempt to know her grandchild.

His mother expected him to marry again. She'd begun to insinuate that six years as a grieving widower was enough. She wanted him to find another wife of Lady Helena's social stature so they could reclaim the place in society she had enjoyed as Helena's mother-in-law. She hoped he would have a son, who would become heir to the estate, preventing Henry and Hilary from gaining control in the event of his death. Though she and Hilary were always civil to one another, Lady Anne had confided in him that she dreaded what would become of the estate and family name if Hilary were to become lady of the house. He didn't share her concerns about Henry's wife, but he hated to see his mother anxious.

As he followed her gaze to the garden, he noticed sadly that Sophia seemed to be moving slowly and carefully. Her right leg was shorter than her left, and she had always walked with a limp, but she seemed more tentative than usual, and he worried that she was in pain.

He watched as Sophia and Emily made their way to a bench beside a rose bush. When she sat, Sophia seemed to land heavily on the bench, and Emily sat beside her and put an arm around her shoulders to help support her. They began talking animatedly, and Sophia laughed at something Emily said.

His mother might be right about Sophia needing a greater level of medical care, but he saw the soft, loving expression in Emily's eyes when she looked at his daughter.

Since Sophia's dramatic birth, Emily had always been her strongest advocate. She had embraced the child when nearly everyone else in the house, including himself, had shied away from the inconvenience of her condition. It occurred to him to ask Emily, the person who knew Sophia best, what she thought would be best for the little girl.

***

After tea, he invited Emily to accompany him on a walk. They stepped out under the early evening sky. Though it was early summer, the night air was chilly, and, as she pulled her wrap tight around her shoulders, he marveled at how much like the women of his class she had become in the years since he'd first met her.

She was so graceful now, with her pale hair swept up and set in curls beside her face, her fine dresses and her soft, pleasant manner of speech.

"I don't thank you often enough for taking such good care of Sophia," he said. "I saw the two of you out here earlier today—she was laughing, and it was so nice to see her so happy."

Emily smiled.

"It's my pleasure, Sir Charles."

"Do you think her health is improving?"

"Well, I don't think she's getting worse," she said, but concern wrinkled her brow.

"But something worries you? Please speak plainly."

"It isn't her health. I think she is becoming more aware of how other people react to her appearance."

"Has someone been unkind to her?" He bristled at the thought.

"No. It's just that she, herself, has noticed the difference in her appearance compared to others. Lately, she has taken to observing how the servants interact with one another, and with us. She mentioned to me that they seem cautious around her, and she thinks it's because of how she looks. Also, she's afraid of her grandmother—she thinks Lady Anne hates her. And, I haven't been able to convince her otherwise, though I always try."

Sir Charles sighed. Despite her physical deficiencies, his daughter's mind and powers of observation were as sharp as any adult's. He looked at Emily. She was watching the path ahead as they walked. He was grateful to her for trying to hide the truth about his mother's feelings from Sophia.

"You and Sophia are quite close, aren't you?" he asked.

"She says she can tell I like her best, even more than my own nieces, and I have to admit she's right." Emily smiled.

Her affection for Sophia touched him. He wondered what his daughter thought of him. Did her keen eyes and ears perceive the tension he felt, always caught between his own fondness and his mother's disdain for her? He chose not to ask Emily.

"My mother thinks I should send Sophia to an asylum. She thinks her health is declining and we aren't prepared to care for her. I don't know if I agree with her, and I'd like to hear your opinion, since you spend so much time with her."

Emily couldn't believe he was considering something so drastic, and she struggled to maintain the polite composure she had kept up for so long in this house.

"Sir Charles, it seems to me that being near her family very much agrees with her. Even on her worst days, she takes great comfort in her own room, her own things, and, perhaps most of all, the view from her window. I don't see how she would fare better in a strange place, away from those who love her."

She paused for a moment, unused to having his attention so closely focused on her, then went on.

"She does like to visit with your brother, my sister and their children in the cottage—and Hilary comes up to visit her once a week or so, which she enjoys very much."

Emily didn't mention that she had lately curbed Sophia's visits with Hilary's children. Hilary's eldest daughter, at three years old, was beginning to notice the strangeness of Sophia's appearance. She was old enough to comment on it and stare, but not yet able to understand how and why to be tactful. Emily couldn't bear the chance that her niece's innocent, outspoken curiosity might hurt Sophia.

She was also hesitant to admit to Sir Charles that Sophia could no longer make the trip as easily as she once had. She'd started to become exhausted by the long walk to and from Hilary's cottage, so they'd ridden a wagon the last few times. But even when they'd taken the wagon, the trip had tired Sophia so much by the time they returned that Emily had feared she might become ill.

As she walked beside Sir Charles, Emily felt guilty about hiding the full truth, but she couldn't bear to think of him sending Sophia to live in a strange, clinical place. She knew Lady Anne well enough to understand that, when she made a suggestion, she was determined to see it done, and, as much as Sir Charles seemed to value Emily's opinion, she feared her arguments would fail against the influence his mother held over him.

She might be able to convince him to put off the decision for now, for Sophie's good, but she knew she was buying a finite amount of time, not really securing Sophia's situation at the house. She felt desperate for a solution, for a line of reasoning she could offer, that would be powerful enough to persuade him not to send Sophie away. She needed time to think.

"May I speak with you again about this situation in a few days' time? I would like to observe Sophie with our discussion in mind—so I can give you a proper response."

"Yes, of course."

They were near the stone steps that led to the door of the great house. The sky was dark now, and Emily glanced over her shoulder and saw the firelight glowing in the windows of her sister's cottage. She wanted to run across the lawn to ask Hilary for her advice. Instead, she held Sir Charles's arm and allowed him to lead her into the house and across the shining marble floor.

Chapter 2

E mily turned the problem over in her mind for a few days. An answer finally came to her when she was looking out the window of the nursery one early evening. In the periphery of her gaze, she saw again the firelight in the window of her sister's cottage. She stared at the glowing light, and, suddenly, she had a solution.

***

The next morning, she dressed quickly and set out to intercept Sir Charles on his way to meet Henry. She needed a moment of his time, and she worried that waiting even a few hours might weaken her resolve.

He was leaving the house as she came down the stairs. She hurried after him. He heard the soft commotion of her rushing feet and looked back. He stopped to wait for her.

"Good morning, Emily. Is something the matter with Sophia?"

"Oh no, Sir Charles! Sophie is well. I've come to speak with you because I think I may have a solution to the matter we discussed a few days ago."

"Please tell me."

"If you are thinking of sending Sophie to live away from the manor, would you consider sending her instead to a place much homier, where she would be lovingly cared for and would have access to fresh air and peaceful meadows and paths for short strolls?"

"What place do you suggest?" he asked.

"I wondered if perhaps a small cottage could be constructed, out on the farthest end of the estate. Agnes and I could stay there with Sophia. We could ride to the house to fetch her meals. The ride would not be much farther for her doctor."

She considered mentioning, but did not, that Sophia would have no need to come back to the house, which should satisfy Lady Anne.

His expectant expression softened with regret and, as he smiled gently, her heart sank.

"Emily, I know you have Sophia's best interests at heart, and I appreciate your commitment to her, but I'm afraid it would be an impossible solution. While it is a lovely idea, you and Agnes are young girls, and Sophia will be harder to lift as she becomes frailer and can't stand on her own. She'll require more help and sending her to a cottage near the woods is hardly more practical than sending her to live in a place where people are trained to care for her."

Her composure crumbled.

"But she won't like it! She'll be so lonely! She needs—"

He put a hand up to stop her from speaking.

"Emily, I am grateful for your suggestion, but let's put this discussion to rest for now, shall we? It was unfair of me to put this on your shoulders."

He held her gaze, pressing for an end to the discussion. She saw the weariness in his eyes, and she nodded, feeling miserable. She let him pass, and she went back into the house and up to her room.

***

That night, Emily dreamt of Karen. Her dream began with a memory of Nathaniel's horrifying attack. She was in the water, and he was trying to force her back to shore, when the long dark shape brushed past them beneath the surface and he was torn away from her.

Instead of hurrying back to shore, as she had in reality, Emily dove beneath the waves. Nathaniel was gone, but Karen was there, waiting for her, long fair hair floating around her head in the water and a sweet, familiar smile on her face. She swam, and Emily followed. As they moved through the water together, Emily noticed that Karen wore a long gossamer gown that obscured her legs from view. Karen smiled at her as they swam, radiating affection, and being with her sister again filled Emily with joy. The dream moved them languidly through the blue green water until Emily realized they were heading in the direction of their childhood home. Warmed by peace and certainty, Emily relaxed more deeply, falling from the dream into a heavy sleep.

She woke with a smile on her face. She would take Sophia to her mother's cottage. She imagined helping Sophie cross the sturdy threshold, smelling the baking bread and hearing her mother's kindly voice greet them. The vision crystallized before her eyes, obscuring the petite oil paintings on her bedroom wall. Aila's cottage would be the right place for Sophie.

Sir Charles cared for his daughter, but his feelings would always be complicated by his responsibilities as head of the estate and as his mother's son. As it was, he couldn't spend much time with Sophie, and Emily knew he would have far less time for her if she was away in an asylum, especially if he remarried.

But if she went with Emily to live with her mother and Morgan, she would be cared for every day by people who were kind and accepting, and Emily was certain her mother and sister would love Sophia as much as she did.

She felt foolish for rushing to Sir Charles so soon with her earlier idea. She had sounded naive, and, now, he would likely dismiss her future suggestions out of hand. She had to convince him to let her take Sophie home with her. She would write to her mother at once, and, with Aila's permission secured, she'd make her case to Sir Charles as soon as she could see a way to convince him.

Chapter 3

The week after Emily's discussion with Sir Charles, Lady Anne announced to the family over dinner that they would soon be having guests at the house. Hilary and Emily exchanged surprised glances. The family hadn't entertained in years.

Lady Anne had removed herself from society after Lady Helena died. Even after the traditional mourning period was over, she'd felt uncertain of how to proceed in society without her daughter-in-law by her side and had declined all of her friends' invitations. She had grown so accustomed to her role in their social partnership—she had been the dignified matriarch, the elegant, circumspect foil to Helena's bright, engaging exuberance—that she feared people might find her dull on her own.

She'd also known that people would expect her to reciprocate if she accepted their invitations, and the thought of any of the ladies and gentlemen of her social circle encountering Sophia had given her chills of terror.

But once she planted the first seeds of suggestion in Charles's mind that Sophia might be better served in an institution and he should remarry, she found a purpose that eclipsed her worries, and she grew impatient to move her plans forward. To find her son a suitable second wife, she needed to reestablish Charles and herself as part of the society where Helena had once reigned. Since they had declined so many invitations after Helena's death, it now fell to her and Charles to host a gathering.

She wouldn't have to invite every member of their circle to dinner or throw a large and expensive ball. Rather, a few choice invitations issued to certain acquaintances would launch their return to society and guarantee some invitations as well.

Charles was wealthy and handsome, and Lady Anne recalled that many young ladies had been heartily disappointed when his engagement to Helena was announced. She was sure her son had lost none of his appeal, and she noted that he had an air of quiet dignity now that he was older and had masterfully guided the family through so much tragedy. Women would find this aspect of his character especially compelling.

She decided to invite her old friends, Lord and Lady Saliswain, along with Lady Saliswain's visiting sister, to her first dinner party. Agnes would be instructed to keep Sophia in her rooms. Henry and Hilary would have to attend to fill out the table. Their daughters, who, despite their mother's wildness, were quite lovely and polite, would be brought up to the house to greet the guests. Emily could help Agnes with Sophia, but it might do to have her at the table, to keep the numbers even.

She was often at a loss about what to do with Emily. That, too, had been much easier when Helena was alive. She had taken a keen interest in the girl and had entertained hopes of making a suitable marriage for her, perhaps the third brother of a good family. Lady Anne had borne this suggestion with silent irritation. Henry was a third son and she was reluctant to foist a wife with Hilary's lack of station and rebellious nature on another mother in her position, even though she would acknowledge that Emily and Hilary were quite different in temperament, and Emily had amiably allowed Helena to mold her into a proper young lady. She would be unlikely to embarrass Lady Anne, and, in fact, she might even be a credit to her, if a modest marriage were made.

She would have Emily attend the party, but she put any notions of helping the girl attain security through marriage to the back of her mind. She had to see to her own family first, Charles most urgently.

***

The dinner party was a rousing success. Henry's and Hilary's young daughters met the guests in the hall when they arrived and delighted them with their sweet voices and pretty manners. Lady Anne and Sir Charles enjoyed hosting guests, and Sir Charles was almost as gregarious as he'd been in the past, when Lady Helena had sat nearby delighting him with her warm smiles and sparkling eyes.

Lady Anne enjoyed her friends' reminiscences of past visits, other dinners and times spent with her and her late husband. Hilary found much to discuss with Lady Saliswain's spinster sister, Miss Elliot, a countrywoman with simple tastes who kept sheep and managed a small garden.

When dinner ended, the ladies went into the drawing room. Miss Elliott and Hilary sat beside the hearth and continued their conversation, while Lady Anne and Lady Saliswain sat together on the settee.

Emily stood and gazed out the large window, thinking about how lovely the evening had been. She had enjoyed herself at dinner and found her little nieces' brief appearance enchanting, but she realized Sophia, the first daughter of the house would never be welcomed to her own rightful place at such parties, not as a child, nor as a young lady.

Though Lady Anne's focus on reviving her social life seemed to provide a temporary distraction from her campaign to send Sophia away, the evening's events had strengthened Emily's resolve to take Sophia to a place where no one would exclude her or pretend she didn't exist.

Chapter 4

L ady Anne allowed herself the pleasure of a bite of cake. She was taking her tea alone in her sitting room, and she deserved a little reward.

Her plan was working. She and Charles had attended a dinner at Lady Saliswain's home four months earlier, officially signaling their return to society. They received many more invitations after that. Charles's old friends had welcomed him back into the social scene. They missed Lady Helena's effervescent presence but were glad to find him in good spirits.

And, as she'd predicted, his handsome face and distinguished manner excited many young ladies and their mothers, who knew of his fine house and holdings.

Lady Anne was particularly delighted to note his reciprocated interest in Lady Katherine Wainwright, whose family's standing was only slightly inferior to Lady Helena's. For months now, the pair seemed to find each other at every party, and her son clearly enjoyed the pretty young woman's company.

To move things along, Lady Anne decided to host a ball at their home, which would surely impress Lady Katherine and her parents and underscore the suitability of a match.

***

She told Henry of her plans during a walk in the garden a few days later. She'd already told Charles, who had agreed and surprised her with exciting news.

"Henry," she said, patting his arm. "I know your wife doesn't much care for big parties, but it's rather important to me that you both attend this one."

He sighed.

"And why is it so important to you that we both attend,

Mother?"

Lady Anne's face lit up with excitement.

"Because, my dear boy, I think your brother will be making an important announcement!"

"Has he proposed to Lady Katherine? Has she accepted him?"

"Not yet, not yet! But Lady Katherine's parents have invited Charles to dine with them. He told me he will ask her father then."

"Well! You must be delighted." He smiled. At his words, her smile faded.

"I will be—once it's done."

***

Why must it happen so soon?" Emily cried when Hilary told her the news. She had run all the way up to the house to find Emily after Henry told her.

"Perhaps they'll have a long engagement."

Emily shook her head.

"Not if Lady Anne has anything to say about it. I hope she'll leave Sophia alone until I can find the right time to talk to Sir Charles. I shouldn't have left it this long—it's just that he hadn't mentioned it again, and everything seemed so settled. I'm going to ask him if I can take her to live with me at Mother's house."

"Oh! But, that's the perfect place! Have you asked Mother?"

"I've written to her," Emily said. "And she's agreed. Now, I have to convince Sir Charles."

"Would you like me to ask Henry to speak to him about it?"

"I think it would be best for me to do it. Can you keep it a secret for now? Until I speak to him?"

"Of course. Though, I'll miss you so much."

"I'll miss you, too, and Henry and my sweet little nieces. I wish we could stay, that they'd allow her to stay. But I think going to Mother's may be the only way."

Hilary nodded and hugged her.

***

Lady Anne's sharp mind turned over the most miniscule details in her quest to make the ball a perfect success. She thought of the servants' liveries, the silver, the carpet at the entryway. She imagined greeting guests with Charles, Henry and Hilary beside her.

The thought of Hilary reminded her of Emily, and she considered whether to have the girl at the party. She was quite pretty, and pretty girls were entertaining at a ball. But something was making her hesitate...what was it? Then she remembered. Emily might want to stay with Sophia.

Sophia. She considered the implications of having her granddaughter in the house during the ball. The house was so large, and the child's nursery wing so remote, that she needn't fear a guest stumbling upon the girl. She knew this, but, once she had considered how unlikely the possibility, her mind began to dwell on the fact that a possibility did exist, and she could not relax. If someone saw Sophia, if word got out about her deformities, people might speculate about the Northam bloodline. Lady Katherine and her parents might decide not to risk the possibility that another child of Charles's would have the same defects.

She hurried to her son's study and entered behind a footman who was bringing him his coat. She was glad she'd caught him before he went out.

"Charles," she said. 'It's time we do something about your daughter."

***

Emily would never have known in time that Sir Charles had agreed to send Sophia to an asylum if Agnes's brother had not been the footman summoned to deliver his coat. He overheard the conversation between Lady Anne and Sir Charles and relayed it to Agnes, out of concern for her position in the household. Agnes, worried for Sophia, rushed to tell Emily.

***

In the middle of the night, Agnes gently lifted Sophia from her bed, murmuring reassurances as the child stirred, while Emily gathered a bag of belongings and medical supplies. They edged down the servants' hall to the back stairs.

"Agnes, are you sure you want to go with us?" Emily whispered.

Agnes replied over the shoulder of the sleeping child.

"Yes, Miss Emily. You don't want to do this alone. The ride is too far. Besides, I won't have a place here with Miss Sophia gone."

They stepped out of the back stairwell and slipped quickly down the unlit stone hallway on the bottom floor, moving past the vast kitchen and out through the servant's entrance, where they crossed a small service yard toward the carriage house and stables.

As they walked, Agnes pulled the blanket she'd wrapped around Sophia over the top of the girl's head to shield her from the chilly night wind. Emily reached in her pocket for the key Agnes had taken for her earlier, and she unlocked the door to the dark carriage house. They crept inside and found the smallest, lightest carriage. They bundled Sophia into it, laying her on the cushioned bench under her blanket, while they walked to the adjoining stables.

The horses shuffled and whinnied at their approach, waking the two young men who worked the stables and bunked in an attached room. The men rushed out to investigate the noise.

"Miss?" the older of the two stable hands called out when he spotted Emily. She and Agnes both jumped in surprise.

"I need a carriage," Emily said, mustering an authoritative tone. "Immediately. I am quite ill and must get to the doctor."

"Shall we fetch the driver for you, Miss?" the bewildered stable hand asked. The servants all knew the story of the two girls from the north. The elder one, Mrs. Northam, was an eccentric, tending animals like a farmer and riding often and for fun, like a man, but this sister had always seemed more like the other ladies of the house.

"No, no," she insisted. "I prefer to go myself."

"But who will drive you?" he asked.

"My maid."

Emily pointed to Agnes, who hid her face as she nodded.

The groom raised his eyebrows. He turned to the other groom and whispered an instruction. The younger man nodded and stepped back into the bunkroom.

"As you wish, Miss," the older groom said, and he moved toward the horses.

"We will want that carriage," Emily said, pointing to the carriage where Sophia slept. "And two horses."

Her heart was racing, but she saw that it would work out better and they could be on their way faster if the young man rigged the carriage for them. They had to prevent him from looking inside. She hoped Sophia wouldn't stir until they were on their way and out of his earshot.

He seemed to be taking an extraordinarily long time in preparing the horses, and Emily was beginning to grow anxious when she heard a commotion at the stable door.

Sir Charles burst in, followed by the young groom. He was wearing a nightshirt over breeches and boots, and his dark hair was wild.

"Emily! What's the matter? Come back to the house, and we'll summon a doctor!"

Emily stared at him. She was caught, and she had no idea what to do. As Charles waited for her answer, he noticed Agnes, who was cowering behind Emily now, and he registered the nanny's presence with confusion.

"Is it Sophia?" he asked, looking quickly back toward the house, his mind struggling to wakefulness with growing alarm.

Having suffered so many losses in recent years, he was sensitive to tragedy and reacted with haste to all illnesses and emergencies in the house. Emily felt suddenly defeated, unable to continue pretending in the face of his obvious worry.

"Sophia is with us, Sir Charles," she said. "She's not ill."

"Then, what the devil are you thinking taking her out in the middle of the night?"

"I cannot bear for her to be sent away! I was going to take her to my mother's cottage, where we will all care for her and keep her safe."

He stared at her, shocked.

"Where is she?" he demanded.

"In the carriage."

He ran for the carriage, and Emily followed.

He saw his daughter lying on the bench, and he climbed inside.

The air inside the carriage smelled sweetly of the warm child. The soft cadence of her deep, peaceful breathing filled the small space. Instead of lifting her up right away, he knelt on the floor and looked at her. She lay on her side, resting her head on her arm, her small, plump fingers curled in a gentle fist, her other arm dangling across her body. Her dark hair fanned out on the bench and over her shoulder. He reached down and gently brushed a wayward strand back from her face. Her long eye lashes fluttered. She looked so beautiful to him, the absence of her nose making her seem otherworldly, but lovely, nonetheless.

Curled up on the bench, she looked to him like any sleeping child, and his heart tightened with remorse for not having seen before how like any other child she really was, and for treating her like a problem to be solved. He put his face in his hands and wept quietly. Emily stepped back away from the carriage.

When he lifted his head from his hands and wiped his eyes, Sophia stirred, and her eyes fluttered open. She started in surprise to find herself in the small unfamiliar space across from her father.

"Papa?" she asked in confusion, her voice raspy with sleep.

"Yes, child."

"Where am I?" She sat up slowly.

"You're in a carriage, my dear."

He hesitated a moment, letting the possibilities race through his mind before continuing.

"We are taking you to visit for a while with Emily and her family in the north, near the seashore. The air up there will be good for you, and they will take fine care of you."

She nodded, undisturbed, and he realized Emily must have told her many stories of her own childhood and family. He thought of his mother's adamant rejection of Sophia, and he suddenly felt resolved.

"We shall take breakfast first," he said. "Let me help you out of there, and we'll start again at dawn."

He helped his daughter from the carriage and turned to the groomsmen who waited in the doorway.

"Ned, prepare the travelling coach, and send word to the coachman. We will leave at sunup for the north."

Emily's looked up at him in surprise, and his eyes met hers.

"Your mother is prepared for this?"

"She is, Sir. I've corresponded with her about it, in case..." She hesitated, ashamed of her secret machinations.

"I should be furious with you, but I understand why you did it," His gaze softened. "It was foolhardy to attempt it on your own, but I know why you felt so desperate. I love my daughter, but you have been like a mother to her, and I won't separate you. I will see you both safely to your mother's home. I want to be sure it will be an adequate place for Sophia and she will be comfortable, but I trust that you will take care of her. Like no one else could."

She nodded, fighting back tears of relief and gratitude.

Chapter 5

The small party of Sir Charles, Emily and Sophia left at dawn, fed and rested and driven by a proper coachman. Sir Charles had summoned Hilary and Henry, who had joined them at the house for breakfast, where they discussed the dramatic events and decided Agnes would not be punished for helping Emily.

They knew she had acted out of devotion to Sophia. Impressed by Agnes's fortitude and loyalty, Hilary insisted she remain employed by the family to help care for her daughters.

Lady Anne was asleep when the team of horses pulled the coach out of sight. She would be annoyed when she woke to learn that her son had left on a two-week journey without informing her—and before proposing to Lady Katherine. But she would also be relieved to learn of the departure of her inconvenient grandchild.

Inside the coach, Emily and Sophia sat facing forward. Sir Charles sat opposite them. He'd brought books and papers to review, and he read while the girls watched the moving countryside from the carriage windows and chatted pleasantly.

Sophia felt it would be impolite to say so in front of her father, but she was glad to be leaving the manor. She was excited to go to Emily's childhood home. Whenever Emily had described it, it had sounded charming to her, like a fairy house from her favorite books, small and easy to navigate, unlike the long reaching halls of the gigantic manor house, with its forbidden rooms and frowning faces.

At first, she'd sat quietly, too self-conscious around her father to carry on with Emily as she normally would have, but Emily's engaging conversation encouraged her, and soon they fell into an easy chat. Her father, a pair of spectacles she'd never seen him wear before perched on his nose, was so focused on his reading materials that he seemed not to notice their discussion.

***

After several hours on the road, they stopped beside a wide field, and Emily spread a blanket so they could sit on the grass and eat the lunch the cook had packed for them. It felt good to stretch their legs. Sophia could see small houses with thatched roofs across the pasture. Smoke billowed from stone chimneys, and she hoped Emily's home would be as charming.

"How are you managing, Sophia?" her father asked. "Has the ride been tolerable for you?"

"Yes, Papa. I'm quite enjoying it! Will we sleep in the coach tonight?"

"No, my dear. We'll stop at an inn in a village a few hours' ride from here."

This unnerved Sophia, and she looked to Emily for comfort.

"It will be alright." Emily patted her hand. "No one will bother you."

"May I wear my hood?" Sophia asked, her eyes wide with apprehension, despite Emily's assurances. She did not expect people to react with horror, but chance encounters with servants over her years in the manor had taught her to fear stares of shock and pity as much as those of disdain.

"Of course," Emily said, with gentle, natural authority, and Charles looked at her. He had been about to answer because he'd assumed Sophia's question was for him. He noticed the way his daughter and Emily looked at one another. Emily's warm gaze was protective and reassuring; Sophia's was grateful and admiring.

He realized Emily had grown up. He glanced at her over the tops of his glasses. He contemplated all she had sacrificed for the sake of his child, the difficult decisions she had made, including forfeiting any match his mother might have made for her, which would have guaranteed her a modest place in society and a comfortable life, something he'd assumed all women wanted most. He tended to think of her as his little sister-in-law, a much softer, more graceful version of Hilary, whom he admired for her dauntless, out-sized spirit, but of whom, he would admit only to himself, he was also a little bit afraid. After her attempt to rescue Sophia, he could see that Emily possessed a similar spirit, beneath her soft composure. She was careful, quiet and thoughtful, but she was also surprisingly strong.

***

Arriving at the inn in the dark of night helped them preserve Sophia's privacy. Sophia wore her hood and looked down at the floor, trailing behind Emily, who held her hand. They followed the young maid, who was too busy to be curious about them, up a staircase and down a narrow but well-appointed hallway to their room.

Sophia retreated shyly behind a dressing screen while the maid brought dinner to their room and set a table for them. After they ate, they went to sleep.

In the morning, a soft knock on the door woke them, when the maid brought them toast and tea. They met Sir Charles and the groomsman at sunrise to embark on the next leg of their journey.

***

During the next two days of their ride, they covered much ground. They spent the nights in a series of comfortable inns, and an amiable companionship blossomed between the three of them. Sir Charles soon put aside his papers and joined their conversations, which he found much more amusing.

He was delighted to learn how well his daughter knew her sums and that she was an accomplished reader. Basking in the novelty of his focused attention, Sophia said she wished they could have managed to bring a piano forte in the coach so she might play for them. They all laughed at the idea. Emily and Sir Charles joked about where they might put it in the small interior and who would have to sit on top of the thing so all could fit. Sophia teasingly suggested her father might have to do it, and he laughingly protested.

"Me? Oh no! I'm far too tall! I'd be hanging over you like a parasol while you played!"

They all roared with laughter at the mental image.

***

For the last night of their journey, Sir Charles arranged for them to stay with good friends of his, who lived in the northern countryside. When he told Emily and Sophia of this plan, the warm, happy feeling Sophia had been enjoying faded into worry, and she glanced at Emily, who looked to Sir Charles to reassure them both.

"Don't worry, my dear," he said gently. "These people are my good friends, and they will not shun you or hurt your feelings in any way. I am quite sure of them."

As the horses turned onto a long road lined with trees and leading to a stately brick square of a home, Emily suddenly recognized the place.

"Is this the home of Lord and Lady Bertram?" she asked Sir Charles who looked at her in surprise.

"Yes, it is! But how do you know that?"

"We stopped here on our first night after leaving my mother's cottage," Emily reminded him, smiling.

"So, we did! I'd completely forgotten!"

He laughed, and Emily turned to Sophia.

"They were very kind to us," she told Sophia. "Especially Lady Bertram. I was about as nervous as you are – I'd never left my home before then."

Emily's assurance comforted Sophia.

***

Lord and Lady Bertram met them in the courtyard in front of their home. Servants lined up behind them, ready to attend to the visitors.

Sophia lifted her hood and carefully followed Emily out of the carriage. Her father patted her shoulder reassuringly.

"Welcome, my dear Miss Emily!" Lady Bertram said, taking Emily's cool hands in her warm ones. Emily smiled and curtsied.

225

Lord Bertram greeted Sir Charles enthusiastically, and then the two men walked over to join the ladies. Sophie stood close behind Emily. Lord Bertram marched up to her.

"Hello there, my young friend," he said, and Sophia lifted her face to him in answer. His kind, welcoming expression didn't waver in the slightest when her hood fell back, revealing her face.

"There you are, my dear!" Lady Bertram exclaimed as if she had been waiting for weeks to behold her long-lost friend. She linked her arm with Sophia's.

"Let's get you something to eat, Miss Northam! You must be so hungry after your long ride!"

She led the party into the house. Emily followed behind Lady Bertram and Sophia. Sir Charles and Lord Bertram walked a few paces behind Emily.

***

Out of Emily's earshot, Lord Bertram leaned close to Sir Charles.

"That young lady is a diamond of the first water, Northam! I daresay you will miss having a beauty like that under your roof!"

His comment was wistful and jolly, and he spoke of Emily with a kind of amazement. Charles had never heard him exclaim so, and he looked at his friend.

"Forgive me, dear boy," Lord Bertram said, embarrassed at his own outburst. "I cannot believe that is the same little girl who visited us years ago."

Charles followed his gaze and watched Emily, who was smiling and answering the many friendly, chatty questions Lady Bertram was asking her. He had seen her nearly every day and had seen her grow from a child to a young woman. Her loveliness had been a sweet constant that, along with her delightful demeanor, had enchanted his late wife, but he had never seen her through another man's eyes until now, and he was startled and discomfited to realize he agreed with his friend. She glanced back then and caught his eye for a moment, her smile friendly and conspiratorial. Sophia was happy, her smile told him, and she was grateful he had brought them here. He smiled broadly in answer. Then, she turned her attention back to Lady Bertram as they all entered the drawing room and he followed, feeling stunned and confused by his own emotions.

***

That evening, Sir Charles found himself watching Emily and Sophia during dinner. It touched and surprised him to see how Sophia comported herself like a tiny lady, gracious and demure, but clearly thrilled to be included as they dined in their hosts' opulent dining room. His friends' kindness to Sophia filled his heart with gratitude and appreciation for them. He knew they were not simply patronizing the child but were looking easily past her unusual appearance and seeing her for her sweet self.

Their easy acceptance painted a picture of what might have been in his own house, which filled him with a deep regret that seemed to collect in his chest and flood his throat. Seeing Emily, poised and comfortable, smile radiantly at his daughter, and watching her charm their hosts, he found himself wondering what it would be like to enter a room with her on his arm.

Chapter 6

hey said good-bye to Lord and Lady Bertram and left for Aila's house in the morning, and Sophia slept during the early ride, leaning against Emily, who placed an arm around her small shoulders. Emily gazed sleepily out the window.

Charles, now warmly content to be in such proximity to Emily and Sophia, relaxed against the seat back and found himself daydreaming. He imagined they were a family of three, heading home after a visit to friends. In this daydream, Emily was his wife and, upon returning home, Sophia would enjoy the welcome and privileges any normal child might expect in her house. He envisioned an eccentric lifestyle, such as Lord and Lady Bertram had modeled the prior evening, in which Sophia dined with the adults every night and played the piano for them in the drawing room before dinner. The three of them would ride together in the afternoons sometimes, Sophia on the gentlest pony, to enjoy tea in the meadow with Henry, Hilary and their children.

He met Emily's gaze and smiled. Her smile in return was warm and shy, and his heart leapt at the sight and implication of it. He wondered if she shared a similar vision. Sophia stirred then and woke, and asked questions about the town they were passing by, an old village with worn, decrepit buildings and wild brush ringing its boundaries.

After their conversation faded into a relaxed silence, Charles returned to his reverie, imagining himself marrying Emily in the small chapel where Hilary and Henry were married. Their sweet, simple wedding had touched and impressed him, the devotion of the young couple charging the atmosphere of the intimate space. He envisioned Emily, beautiful in a simple gown with flowers adorning her hair, gazing up at him as they exchanged vows. The vision felt so real and fulfilling, tears pressed the corners of his eyes.

Then, unbidden and disruptive, he saw his mother's dour, disapproving face among the small gathering of guests, clouding the dream. He tried to disregard it and reengage in his wonderful imaginings but found now that she haunted his mind like a desperate, persistent wraith, reminding him of his duty to the family and his title. He sighed heavily, as the scene in his mind faded away.

They turned onto a road close to the ocean, its glimmering blue infinity visible in the distance. He felt sadly resigned, as Emily and Sophia chattered excitedly about the sea view, to accepting the way his life and theirs would have to be. They were close now to Emily's home, an hour or so away. He steeled himself to bid them farewell, and to endure the long, lonely ride back home without them.

***

The joy Aila felt when she saw Emily step down from the carriage overwhelmed her, and she lost her composure for a moment. She brushed the tears from her eyes and hurried forward to embrace her youngest daughter, with Morgan hurrying behind her. Aila and Emily held onto one another for a moment, a sensation of relief and comfort washing over both of them. Then, Emily turned to kiss Morgan's cheek in affectionate greeting.

"Oh! Mother, Morgan it is so wonderful to see you!"

She turned back to the carriage where the driver was now helping Sophia down onto the dusty ground.

Emily put an arm around Sophia's shoulders and guided her gently forward. Well-prepared for the child's unusual appearance, both Morgan and Aila greeted her kindly in their efficient manner, as they would have greeted any new and welcome visitor. Morgan offered to show Sophia the chickens.

"May I go?" Sophia asked Emily.

"Yes," Emily said. She watched as Morgan and Sophia walked toward the barn.

Sir Charles stepped forward.

"Thank you for extending your hospitality to my daughter," he said to Aila. "If you do find it to be more than you all can handle, please write and let me know and I shall return for her. I don't wish to burden you."

Aila waved her hand, dismissing the suggestion.

"I'm certain we will manage well, Sir Charles. Emily will write to you regularly to report on your daughter's condition. Will you join us for tea?"

***

When they entered the house, the scent of wood that had always permeated the main rooms was as strong and rich as ever, mingled with the delicious aroma of baking bread. The shining stone floor and scrubbed walls, free of smoke or smudge, impressed Emily. She realized that, when she had lived there as a child, she had never noticed how fastidious her mother had been. They sat at the plain, thick wooden table while Aila poured tea and served bread on porcelain dishes.

"Are these new?" she asked her mother.

"They are, a bit. I bought them at a shop in the new village."

"They are quite nice," Sir Charles said.

"What new village?" Emily asked. On the drive over, she had noticed a small number of houses where none had been before, spread out along the road leading to her mother's cottage.

"It's been recently built and is much closer than the others, which has been good for us. We don't have to travel as far to buy supplies. The buildings are modern, and the streets are well-kept."

"I noticed on the ride that you have new neighbors as well," Emily said.

"Yes, some of the surrounding land has been sold, and there are new tenant farmers. Morgan has become friends with some of them, who are young like she is."

Emily looked at her in amazement. Aila laughed and nodded.

"It's true! They've even convinced her to go with them to dances in the village hall."

"She never said so in her letters!" Emily exclaimed.

"I don't think she considers it to be news worth writing about," Aila said. "Don't tease her about it."

"I never would!" Emily said.

Sir Charles watched the exchange with amusement. Aila inquired politely after Lady Anne.

"Mother is well, thank you. Henry and Hilary are doing wonderfully. Their girls are a delight!"

Aila smiled at the mention of her young granddaughters.

"You are welcome to visit anytime you like," he said. "I will gladly send my coach for you all, so you may ride in comfort."

"Thank you. Perhaps, someday, we shall."

For now, she knew she would stay where she was and help Emily tend to the shy little girl who had come to live with them.

Laughter drifted in from the open door off the kitchen, and Sophia and Morgan soon appeared at the door. A large shaggy dog followed them closely. Emily smiled in surprise, recalling Morgan's affection for her long-ago lost Wooly. Morgan smiled back at her.

"I've a little business now," she told Emily with a grin. "I raise these wonderful creatures and supply the local farmers with protectors for their flocks. We're between litters now, and my Maisie is resting up, or I'd show Sophia the puppies, but she'll get to see some soon enough."

Sophia beamed at the prospect. The dog took the little girl's excitement as an invitation to enter the house and began sauntering across the threshold.

"No, Shadow," Morgan said to the dog. "You may not come in."

This made Sophia burst into giggles.

Morgan laughed, too, and the dog regarded them with a pathetic frown and reluctantly lay down outside the door.

"It would seem Miss Northam has a new friend, whether she wants him or not," Morgan said, gesturing to the dog. They all

231

laughed, and Sophia said, "I think he's wonderful!"

***

After tea, Charles knew he had to leave them and start his journey back home. He had to get on with the business of his life without them, and they had to start getting Sophia settled, but he felt reluctant to part with his daughter and Emily.

They all walked outside. Aila and Morgan said farewell to him and went back in the house to clear the table, while Emily and Sophia walked with him to the coach. He turned and embraced his daughter tightly for a long moment. Then he bent to look into her eyes.

"I love you, my child. Please write to me, and do let me know if you need anything," he said.

"I will, Papa. I love you, too," she said, and he quickly embraced her again.

"Off you go," he said when he released her, and, with a small curtsy, she turned and walked toward the house.

"I will write to you regularly with reports on her health," Emily promised. He found the formal tone she used jarring, and he wondered if he'd imagined the dreamy link between them. But, when he met her eyes, he saw regret and longing that matched his own.

"Thank you, Emily," he said, sadly, wanting nothing more than to lean forward and kiss her soft lips. He looked at the ground for a moment before summoning the composure he needed to meet her eyes again.

"Good-bye, Emily."

"Good-bye, Sir Charles."

He climbed into the coach, and, when he looked out the window, he saw her running toward the door of her mother's house.

232

Chapter 7

S ophia settled into her new life with ease. Despite her disabilities, she was keen to help, which impressed Morgan and Aila. Emily had to insist on several occasions that Sophia stop and rest. She became deeply engrossed in weeding the small garden or spinning the wool. For a while, she grew stronger with her efforts and learned to enjoy the feeling of falling into the deep, satisfying sleep that followed a day spent moving and working.

They all soon came to see her as a natural part of the household. Emily made sure she rested, ate, read and found time to play. She enjoyed revisiting her own childhood by playing with Sophia.

The warm days of late summer brought an enchanting warm breeze and the rich scent of blooming meadow flowers. Emily considered taking Sophia down to the little beach, but she worried the walk down the hill would be too taxing for the little girl.

***

One morning, while Sophia was sleeping, Emily found Aila in the barn, preparing to let the sheep out to pasture.

"Good morning, Mother!" Emily stepped onto the fence rail to gently prod a sheep who was lagging behind the others. Aila smiled at her.

"Thank you, Emily. She's lazy today."

They watched the reluctant sheep shuffle past, as one of Morgan's dogs jogged back to investigate the delay.

"Mother, do you think it would be dangerous for Sophia to walk down to the beach?"

Aila looked thoughtful.

"Perhaps not if two of us were to help her. The path is steep in some places but has been worn pretty smooth."

"Have you and Morgan been going down to sing?"

"We have," Aila smiled radiantly. "And we've seen Karen!"

Emily felt a ripple of excitement run through her.

"Oh! That's marvelous! Does she seem well? Is she happy?"

"Yes, she's quite happy. She looked different, but we were able to recognize her."

"Do you see her often?" Emily asked, thinking of her own encounter with Karen years earlier when Nathaniel had threatened her.

"We see her about once a year or so. I don't know that she always stays near here."

"I hope I'll get the chance to see her!" Emily said. She considered telling Aila about her own experience but decided not to mention it. She didn't want her mother to fret over the danger she'd been in.

"May I tell Sophie about her?" she asked.

"Oh, Emily, I don't know." Aila looked concerned. "She's a young child—if she returns to her home, she might feel compelled to tell others."

"Mother, I am certain she will keep our secret," Emily said.

Aila had grown to care deeply for Sophia, but until now, had seen her as the child of another family. She realized Emily saw Sophia as her own, not in a proprietary sense, but by the measure of how much and how unconditionally she loved her.

"Then, yes," she said. "I suppose you may tell her."

***

Once Emily told her the story of her sister who lived in the sea, Sophia was desperate to go down to the water in hopes of seeing Karen. She regarded with fresh awe the little miniature portrait Hilary had painted of Karen when they were young, which hung by a ribbon outside the bedrooms.

***

One afternoon, Emily, Morgan and Sophia took a walk to the beach, the two ladies carrying the little girl over any difficult terrain. They allowed her to remove her shoes and stockings, which thrilled Sophia, and the soft, warm sand felt glorious against her feet.

Emily showed her the jetty where she had spent so many days as a child singing to their undersea friends. Sophia wanted to climb out on the rocks and peer into the sea, to sing and see if they might summon Karen. But the rocks weren't safe for her, so she entertained herself by dipping her feet in the frothy tide and inhaling the salty air.

When they reached home later that day, after a long, careful climb back up the hill, Sophia thanked them enthusiastically, declaring that it had been the best day of her life. Emily and Morgan grinned at each other, and they knew they would hear many requests to go to the beach again.

***

Emily wrote to Sir Charles regularly, as she'd promised. They'd corresponded almost monthly at first, and he'd commended her in his letters for taking such fine care of Sophia, who wrote him letters of her own.

His letters to Emily were kind, but formal, almost perfunctory, and she wondered if she'd misread the wistful tension she'd felt between them on the last days of their ride to the cottage. She'd felt embarrassed and was certain she'd imagined it when he started to mention his new wife in his letters.

After the summer, he grew busier with his marriage and responsibilities on the estate and he wrote to them less frequently. Emily worried that his daughter was slipping farther from his thoughts, as she'd feared would happen if he'd sent Sophia to an asylum. She was especially glad the little girl was here, happily attended by people who loved her, when they received a letter from Hilary.

Dear Mother, Emily and Morgan,

I hope you are all well, and that Miss Sophia is still enjoying the sea air! Emily, I miss you terribly, but I'm certain that you'll be much happier there than if you'd stayed. The new Mrs. Northam, Lady

Katherine, who was as sweet and meek as could be before the wedding, has revealed herself to be quite a tyrant! She can barely stand to be in the same room with me, my lack of status is an affront to her. She has all but banished Henry and I to our cottage (much to my preference).

Also, without even bothering to consult Lady Anne, she's set about making renovations to the manor house. For all her haughtiness, Lady Anne has lost her footing as mistress of the house and is frequently snapped at or dismissed outright by her new daughter-in-law! Sir Charles doesn't see her as we do because he is often out managing the estate, and she is much softer to everyone when he is at home.

I suppose I should be happy to see Lady A. served some of the treatment she once gave me, but I am surprised to say I feel quite sorry for her. Not sorry enough to invite her to live with us, of course, but hopeful that she'll find some peace with Lady K. I know she'd imagined that she'd have another bosom companion, like Lady Helena, but this new wife is a very different sort of woman!

Don't worry about Henry, the girls and me – we'll keep to ourselves and are happy on our little farm! Perhaps we'll finally be prompted to make the journey up to visit you sooner than we planned (I would now if the girls weren't still a little young for the ride) I miss you all very much.
With love, Hilary

Emily clenched the letter in her hand, nearly tearing it at the thought of Lady Katherine insulting Hilary. And when she thought of Sir Charles, the soft way he'd gazed at her on their journey and how much he and Lady Helena had adored one another, her anger turned to worry —she couldn't imagine him married to a woman who could be so harsh to his family.

***

Sophia enjoyed several more trips down to the beach before cold winds began to gust over the fields. By mid-Autumn, she had yet to see Karen and was disappointed when Emily told her they did not plan to go again until the next spring.

Emily, Morgan and Aila believed the cold air presented a special danger to Sophia, who had seemed to gain strength in her first several months with them, but now seemed to them to be growing thinner and more fragile. Her appetite seemed to ebb, and she tired easily.

Chapter 8

A little more than a year after they'd arrived at the cottage, Emily found Sophia wincing beside the fire one evening. She had to persevere through Sophia's multiple protests that she felt fine before the girl finally admitted she was suffering from a headache, a new and worrying symptom to add to the number she seemed to be collecting.

On the advice of the local doctor, who rode out monthly to check on Sophia, they hadn't been able to take her to beach that summer. Emily's letters to Sir Charles about his daughter's persistent exhaustion had yielded only superficial well wishes in response.

***

By late autumn, Sophia was spending most of her time in bed, and Aila summoned the doctor, who confirmed Emily's fear that it was time to write urgently to Sir Charles about her worsening condition.

After the doctor left and Sophia had gone to sleep, Emily confessed to her mother that she worried she had over-estimated her ability to care for the child.

"What if she would have been healthier in an asylum, Mother? Was I foolish to bring her here?"

"Emily, from your letters, it seemed to me that Sophia's health was declining well before you came here. If they had taken her to a place where she didn't know anyone, she would have been so lonely, and she would have gotten worse much sooner. In your heart, you know this." Aila touched her hand.

Emily nodded. She knew she was looking for someone to blame for the agony she felt, and she found herself to be the easiest target.

But, even in the midst of thinking she was the one who had made the critical error, she realized that by blaming herself, she was also opening the door for the hope that her mistake could be fixed by someone else if they acted quickly enough. Admitting to herself, as Aila was asking her to do, that she had truly done the best thing for Sophia, forced her to accept that nothing more could be done. Even the best solution led to an awful, inevitable outcome, and it terrified her beyond anything she'd ever faced or imagined.

***

A week after she'd written to Sir Charles, Sophia was getting worse and Emily received a letter from him that had apparently crossed her own. In his letter, he wrote that he and his wife would be taking a trip abroad and he planned to visit Sophia sometime in the following year bringing presents from the trip. There was no address to reach him, so Emily could only write to Hilary, hoping she and Henry had a better location for him.

Over the next few days, the doctor stopped in daily and the three women worked to keep Sophia as comfortable as possible. The doctor warned Aila and Emily gently that the little girl wouldn't survive much longer. Aila and Morgan fussed over her, which touched Emily, who had never heard them speak so sweetly, and their attentions gave her a sense of hope in the face of the doctor's devastating prediction. Sophia loved to have them sit beside her, telling her stories. Her favorites were stories of the sea woman, and they repeated those stories for her as often as she wanted, their words and memories filling the air with an exhilarating sense of the mystic.

***

One morning, after Aila rode off to the village to check for a letter from Hilary or Sir Charles, Emily entered Sophia's room with a tray of breakfast. She was prepared to tell the romantic story of how her Aunt Hilary found her Uncle Henry on the beach. She noticed that Sophia's complexion was pale and waxy, and she was struggling to breathe. Emily threw the tray on the floor and ran to Sophia's side. She stroked her forehead, and she could see that the child was dazed and in pain. With tears in her eyes, Emily wrapped her arms around Sophia, cradling her.

"Oh, Sophie," she cried.

"Tell me again about the sea woman?" Sophia's voice was weak and raspy. Emily opened her mouth to obey, and then suddenly stopped, as an idea came to her in a furious flash.

"Morgan!" she shouted. "Morgan!"

Morgan ran in from the kitchen and saw Sophie lying limply in her Emily's arms. Her face clouded with sorrow, and she hurried over, confused by her sister's hopeful expression.

"I'll ride out for the doctor," Morgan said.

"Wait—What if we took her to the sea woman?" Emily said suddenly, halting Morgan as she walked toward the door. "Karen once told Hilary that they save drowning sailors and they live much longer than we can. Maybe they can save her!"

Morgan stared at Emily, her mind racing as she considered the idea. Her ever-practical instinct was to reject it, and hurry to get the doctor, whose office was two hours away at a breakneck speed, but she saw that they were losing Sophie, and she knew Emily's heart was breaking. It would be no worse for the child to go out into the cold now as it would be for her to stay in the warm house. Their only enemy now was time.

"We can try," she said. "At least we can try."

"Would you like to meet Karen?" Emily asked Sophia.

Sophia smiled and nodded feebly.

They bundled her up and carried her together through the frigid wind, down the dirt path to the cliff, and carefully down the hill. White frost dotted the beach. They carried her onto the rocks and held her close as they began to sing. Gazing at the face of the little girl she loved, Emily began to cry as she sang, at once hopeful and desperate.

Sophia drifted in and out of consciousness as they sang. The chill seemed to bite through all the layers of clothing they wore, and with each pang of cold she felt, Morgan sang defiantly louder. She had grown to love Sophia, too, and she felt determined to save her. It felt much too soon to lose her.

They were singing their third song when they saw Karen. Sophia spotted her first.

"Karen," she said softly, and Emily took her word, at first, to be part of a dream, but then she saw that Sophia was looking toward the water. Emily looked, too, and, indeed, saw Karen. Her face was different, yet so familiar, and Emily felt new tears of hope springing to her eyes.

"Can you help us?" Emily said, as Morgan said, "Can you save the child?"

Karen didn't speak with a voice like theirs, but they could hear, as she agreed to help them and explained what would have to be done. Two others appeared beside her in the water, and Emily felt a strange elation as she realized they were finally seeing the sea woman.

The sea woman's green eyes regarded them calmly, and, beneath the water, she reached her arms out toward them. Emily hesitated, suddenly afraid. But Sophia was no longer conscious. Emily knew she had this one hope. She slipped into the icy water, her feet finding a ledge of rock to stand on beneath the water's surface, and she slid Sophia into the mermaid's arms. Beneath the water, Karen held Emily's hand as they watched the sea woman embrace the child. For several moments, they disappeared from view and Emily felt panic rise in her heart. Karen sensed her anxiety and soothed her. Then, guided gently by the sea woman, Sophia reappeared beneath the surface. Her expression was blissful, and she moved slowly, but with a strength and surety she had never known on land. Karen explained to Emily that Sophia would soon become used to moving in the water and that she and Manae would protect her.

Morgan watched in awe, suddenly realizing they had succeeded.

"Thank you," she whispered, her voice breaking with tears. Karen's response was pure love, which overwhelmed Morgan. Then, Karen told Emily and Morgan that they must leave soon; she was afraid they would freeze, especially since Emily was wet. Morgan obediently moved to leave, reaching a hand to help Emily up onto the rocks. Emily was gazing down through the water at Sophia, who was now holding her other hand.

"Karen, may I come with you? I belong with Sophia. Please?" she asked.

Karen paused, uncertain, but she felt her sister's determination. She looked to Nai questioningly, and Nai agreed to change Emily if that was what she truly wanted.

Morgan gasped.

"Emily, no! It isn't the right time! You're so young!"

Emily looked up at her sister and smiled with the serenity of certainty.

"She's my child," she said, stroking Sophie's hand. "I don't want to live without her."

She leaned up to kiss Morgan's cheek, and then she slipped beneath the surface.

Morgan watched as the sea woman embraced Emily and they drifted down, out of sight. Karen and Sophia followed, and, soon, she could sense that they had all gone deeper into the sea and were no longer near. Stunned, she stood and walked back to the house.

***

When she returned that evening, Aila found Morgan sitting close to the fire with a blanket over her shoulders. Morgan looked up at her with sadness in her eyes.

"Morgan, what's happened?" Aila asked. Aside from the crackle of the fire, the house was silent. "Did Emily ride with Sophia to the village?"

She could imagine Emily becoming so concerned for Sophia that she'd go off in search of a doctor, but she was surprised Emily wouldn't have waited the few hours for her return, since Aila knew the way. She stepped toward the door, ready to ride out after them.

"No, Mother. There wasn't time for that. Sophia was dying. She would never have made it to the village. So, we took her down to the sea."

Aila's eyes widened in confusion.

"To Karen," Morgan said, and then Aila understood.

"Did she come to you?"

"Yes, with the sea woman and her daughter."

She watched tears spring to her mother's eyes

"They transformed Sophia, and she was healed," Morgan said.

"Oh! That's wonderful! But where is Emily? She's not still down there?"

Aila imagined her daughter standing in the icy wind for hours, reluctant to part with the child, ignoring the danger to her own health. Morgan shook her head and swallowed back her own tears, dreading what she had to tell her mother.

"She wanted to be with Sophia."

She got the words out, but her voice broke.

Aila understood, and she gasped and wrapped her arms around Morgan. She cradled her daughter and rocked her as they both wept.

Once the shock passed, Aila realized, in her heart, she was not completely surprised by the turn of events. She had feared what would happen to Emily without Sophia. She knew, when she got past the fresh pain of losing her youngest daughter to the sea, she would be consoled by the knowledge that Emily was where she could be happiest and that she and Karen were together. And, it comforted her to know she could go to the rocks and sing for them, and she might see them all again in the spring.

Chapter 9

T he sea, so flat in aspect from their previous points of view, opened up for Emily and Sophia in endless thrilling sensations. Massive rock and coral formations seemed to rise before their eyes, shimmering with sea life. The songs of distant whales rolled past them on the currents, like the melody of a thousand violins. The salty, satisfying taste of the sea stayed in their mouths. They never felt the discomfort of hunger, and only ate when instinct commanded.

Sophia felt wonderfully alive, elated to be able to move without pain or fear of falling. She flourished in the joy of gliding through a vast, open atmosphere.

Emily stayed by Sophia's side, her happiness and awe hindered only slightly by a protective wariness. Her new senses and her natural instinct to take care of Sophia, alerted her to the dangers of the deep. Nai taught them the scream she used to ward off sharks. She welcomed them to join her large shoal of mermaids, but Emily and Sophia chose to stay with Karen and Manae, creating their own little shoal of four.

Watching Sophia thrive in their strange new home assured Emily that she'd made the right decision. Shortly after their transformation, once she had become accustomed to the new features of her body, Emily noticed with amazement that Sophia's face had changed very little. Her narrow face, with its wide set eyes and absent nose, which had set her so far apart from people on land, was remarkably like Manae's and Nai's. Their faces had small nostrils, but not a human-like nose. Karen's nose was still present but much less pronounced, and Emily had touched her own to find that it had become smaller as well.

Here, Emily and Karen were the most peculiar ones, but the adult mermaids had serenely accepted them as part of the undersea community. Emily and Sophia were delighted by the mermaid children, who liked to laugh and play. They'd immediately welcomed Sophia enthusiastically and invited her to play with them.

Emily knew she would never fully understand the miracle of their wonderful new life, but, with Sophia safe and healthy by her side, she would always be grateful for it.

Chapter 10

The morning was quiet and cool, and a haze of soft green shimmered over the fields, signaling the gentle shift from winter to spring. Morgan had been awake for several hours. She'd fed the chickens, let out the sheep, and prepared breakfast. She ate at the table and placed a bowl on a tray to carry to Aila, who was in her room. Aila was awake and dressed, sitting in a chair beside her bed, when Morgan entered her room.

"Mother!" Morgan was surprised and cheered by this sign of recovery.

The winter had been long and cruel, and Aila had been ill throughout it. Morgan had feared she wouldn't survive. When her mother had good days, Morgan read her Hilary's letters, full of stories of her granddaughters, who were becoming spirited young ladies, and of the progress of their little farm on the estate.

Now, as she stood in her mother's room, watching Aila sitting quietly in her chair, Morgan realized suddenly how much time had passed since her sisters had each left to begin new lives. It had been nearly ten years since Emily and Sophia had slipped into the sea and almost two years since Aila had been well enough to go down to the beach. Aila had encouraged Morgan several times to go without her, but she'd always felt too busy or tired, and the years had slipped past quickly.

Aila looked small and frail. Her eyes had lost their intense, shining determination. Her expression was much softer, relaxed and serene.

"Are you feeling better?" Morgan said.

"I do feel better, but I know it won't be long now."

Aila watched her daughter's face fall with sadness.

"Morgan, thank you for caring for me, but I want you to know I have no expectations of you. You must feel free to decide your own fate. If you wish to stay here, of course, the house is yours, but if you wish to leave, to join Hilary or to go live in the village, do so. You are a woman of means now and can live comfortably wherever you decide, which gives me great peace of mind. But please don't feel bound to this house, my dear. You may leave it, and you may sell it, if you wish."

"Mother, you are not dying yet," Morgan said, her voice shaking slightly. She did not want to consider her life without her mother. In the darkest hours during the winter, she had tried to imagine what she would do if Aila were to die. But she had been unable to complete these thoughts. She'd remained stubbornly undecided and had been able to push the question aside because, each time, her mother had recovered.

"I worry that you have lived your life to please me and have never felt free to choose your own path."

"But I have, Mother, this *is* my path. I love this house and this land. I have my dogs here and I have friends nearby. I'm happy here—I always have been."

"You don't seek your friends out much. You wait for them to invite you. You are so like me in that way. Will you try to engage them more when I'm gone? I worry that they will forget you, and you will be all alone here. I was never alone because I had you, but I don't want to leave you by yourself."

"Mother, I will try to see my friends a bit more, if it will make you feel better, but please don't worry. I don't mind being alone. I prefer it. I'm happiest when it's quiet. I love my sisters, but I have enjoyed these peaceful years with you the most."

Aila took Morgan's hand and smiled at her.

"I am always surprised at the difference between what I assumed about you girls and who you really are. You are all so much more than I ever could have imagined," she said.

They sat in silence for several minutes, enjoying each other's company. Aila patted Morgan's hand.

"Will you take me down to the beach?" Aila asked. Morgan was surprised.

"Do you feel well enough for the walk?"

"Yes."

Morgan helped Aila stand, and they stepped out into the cool spring morning. They walked to the cliff side and carefully down the hill to the beach.

Once they reached the sand, Aila began walking into the water.

"Mother, no! The water is too cold!"

Aila looked over her shoulder and smiled at Morgan, who had started to follow her.

"No, it feels nice," she said. Morgan heard the certainty in her voice and stopped walking.

"Morgan, I'm not ready to die. I'd like to live on for a while longer, here in the sea, with Karen and Emily and Sophia...and my old friend."

When the water was almost up to her shoulders, Aila began to sing, her voice floating above the crash of the waves. Morgan's eyes widened moments later, when she saw a shimmering golden tailfin rise from the water in the distance. She rushed forward and wrapped her arms around her mother, feeling the cold of the water and the heat of the tears streaming down her cheeks. Aila held her close and stroked her hair.

"My darling girl. Thank you for all you've done for me."

She pulled back gently and looked into Morgan's eyes, "My beloved child."

Morgan saw the tailfin again, much closer now. She looked into the water and saw the sea woman and her daughter. Beside them were Sophia, Karen and Emily, their faces, alien and beautiful, adapted for the sea. She reached into the water and felt her sisters each take one of her hands in greeting. She squeezed their smooth hands and released them. Aila was smiling with joy and anticipation.

Morgan considered for a moment that she, too, could join them. She could settle her dogs with new owners and come down to the sea herself. She would not have to lose her mother. She could live with Aila, Karen, Emily, Sophia and the sea women beneath the waves.

But she was not ready. She glanced back toward the cliff and her house, where her beloved dogs waited for her in the barn, and she felt great comfort at the thought of returning to them. She thought of her friends, who she'd ride out to visit more often now on her way to the village, the ones who had convinced her, at the first barn party she'd braved years before, to dance with them, despite her many protests. The thought made her smile. She had much left to do on land.

She embraced Aila tightly, kissed her soft, beautifully lined cheek, and walked out of the water. From the beach, she watched her mother move forward until she disappeared beneath the waves.

Morgan stood on the shore a while longer, watching the tide roll in and out, until she saw six tailfins rise from the sea. Smiling, she turned and made her way back up the hill to her home.

The End

Made in the USA
Middletown, DE
24 August 2021